A Marc LeB

JEREMY A

BEST
SERVED
COLD

Best Served Cold
© 2024 Jeremy Akerman

Cover art by the author
Cover design: Rebekah Wetmore
Editor: Andrew Wetmore

ISBN: 978-1-998149-56-8
First edition October, 2024

Moose House Publications
2475 Perotte Road
Annapolis County, NS B0S 1A0
moosehousepress.com
info@moosehousepress.com

Moose House Publications recognizes the support of the Province of Nova Scotia. We are pleased to work in partnership with the Department of Communities, Culture and Heritage to develop and promote our cultural resources for all Nova Scotians.

We live and work in Mi'kma'ki, the ancestral and unceded territory of the Mi'kmaw people. This territory is covered by the "Treaties of Peace and Friendship" which Mi'kmaw and Wolastoqiyik (Maliseet) people first signed with the British Crown in 1725. The treaties did not deal with surrender of lands and resources but in fact recognized Mi'kmaq and Wolastoqiyik (Maliseet) title and established the rules for what was to be an ongoing relationship between nations. We are all Treaty people.

Also by Jeremy Akerman

and available from Moose House Publications

Memoir
Outsider

Politics
What Have You Done for Me Lately? - revised edition

The Marc LeBlanc Mysteries
Holy Grail, Sacred Gold
Unspeakable Evil
The Plot against the Premier

Fiction
Black Around the Eyes – revised edition
The Affair at Lime Hill
The Premier's Daughter
In Search of Dr. Dee
Explosion

I gratefully acknowledge the unstinting assistance and encouragement from my wife, Caroll Anne, in writing this book.

I also wish to offer hearty thanks to Andrew Paul Shakespeare of Abertridwr, for doing on-the-ground research for Chapters 9 and 10, since I was unable to afford to take a trip to Wales to conduct it myself.

Best Served Cold

Jeremy Akerman

1

My name is Marc LeBlanc and I am a private investigator. Having written that, I see how pompous it seems.

The truth is that I am an amateur investigator who happens to have a license to practice in the profession. That license was given to me by the Premier of our province, Wendell Proctor, as thanks for helping him fend off a serious threat.

I have only worked on two other cases to date, one a search for the Holy Grail and the other an attempt to establish the murky antecedents of my friend Ray Bland. I have written about these cases, or adventures, in *Holy Grail, Sacred Gold*, *Unspeakable Evil* and *The Plot to Kill the Premier*.

I live in Grand Pre, Nova Scotia, in a large, luxurious, modern house, with my wife, Rosalie, whom I met and fell in love with on my first case. She has been an essential partner in all my ventures, as she is an associate professor of history and an expert in conducting research.

We live a very comfortable life, largely due to the proceeds of my speculation during the 2008 recession, when I bought large quantities of Royal Bank stock at the rock-bottom price of just over $15 a share and subsequently sold them at close to $50.

Since I had sold my car and my house in London, used all my savings and borrowed as much as I could, I was able to purchase over 60,000 shares, so eventually cleared a profit of close to $2 million. In addition to that, I had inherited well over $1.5 million from my father after he was murdered.

This wealth had enabled me to travel freely, to keep an extraordinarily good wine cellar containing many old and rare bottles, and to buy my 2015 Bugatti Veyron Sports Vitesse from an

Arab sheik.

The Bugatti is an enormous conceit which, I confess, is my pride and joy. Had I been able to purchase it new, it would have cost me $2 million, annual service costing $20,000, and tires requiring $30,000 and a trip back to the factory to be fitted. Getting it second-hand from Sheik Mohammed Aziz saved me a great deal of money, although the annual insurance premiums are astronomical.

It has a 258 mph (415 km/h) top speed and a 1,001 horsepower engine, initially making it the world's fastest production car. Although he asked me to keep it to myself, Sheik Mohammed Aziz, who lives in Switzerland, moved on to the one-off Bugatti La Voiture Noire, for which he paid a cool $18.7 million.

Rosalie works part-time at Acadia University, which is located in Wolfville, only minutes away from our house in Grand Pre. This enables her to maintain her academic standing while occasionally being free to join me on my investigations, in which her insight and encouragement are invaluable.

When we are together we read, talk endlessly, enjoy food and wine, and entertain our friends. When she is teaching, I am usually preparing meals, patrolling my fields, or attending to my wine store in town, which is proficiently managed by my business partner Louise.

This seemingly-idyllic existence, however, often appears boring when no adventure is on the horizon or if nothing out of the ordinary looms in our social life. As is often the case in life, long deserts of inactivity are suddenly inundated by floods of opportunities.

And so it was this May, when a quiet, almost tedious winter abruptly changed into bright, noisy spring.

"Let's go away," my wife said.

"Where to? Caribbean? Hawaii? Bora Bora?"

"Wales and Scotland."

"It's a bit cold there right now. And it's rainy."

"We could go in a few weeks. It would take time to plan, anyway."

"Why there?"

"To search for my roots."

"Your roots? Aren't your roots firmly in Nova Scotia?"

The reason I was surprised was that Rosalie had told me she was one of seven children—two girls, five boys—and came from Digby in southwestern Nova Scotia, where her father had been a fisherman. He had died at age 42, having been lost in a storm at sea. Her mother died a year later, and the children were divided between various aunts and uncles.

Rosalie spent her formative years with a much-loved aunt whom she still visited in Bear River. She had worked hard, won scholarships, done well at university and now looked forward to a life in academia. Beyond that, I knew little about her background and had no idea she had any relatively-recent antecedents in Britain.

"Not really," she said. "My grandparents on both sides came from across the pond."

"You never told me."

"You never asked." She put down her magazine and walked to the huge window overlooking our hill.

"I'm asking now. Who were they? Where did they come from?"

"My mother's people were Welsh and my father's were Scottish."

"Really?"

"Yes. Mum's mother was a Frost."

"That doesn't sound like a Welsh name. Not like Jones or Thomas or Williams."

"Well, he was Welsh. Her father was descended from some revolutionary."

"A revolutionary?"

"Apparently, he was hung, drawn and quartered, the last person to be sentenced to the punishment in Britain."

"Indeed, a famous man! What was his crime?"

"Treason."

"Wow! When was this?"

"I should have looked it up before. I think it was in the early 1800s."

"Sounds like it could have something to do with the Chartists. They were stirring up trouble about that time."

"Yes! That's it. He was a Chartist leader. I can just remember Mum mentioning it several times before she died. I was quite little then."

"Do you know any more about this Jack Frost?"

"He wasn't called Jack, idiot, but it was something similar. Maybe James or John. I'll Google it after dinner."

"That'll be interesting. What about the other side of your family?"

"That's a little murkier. As you know, I am a Fletcher. Dad, who died shortly before Mum, came from down the shore where, like him, his father was a fisherman. His father came from Scotland, but I know nothing about him, although Aunt Bronwen's husband used to say he was descended from a 'Pupaid de na Caimbeulaich', which I gather meant he was somehow associated with the Campbells."

"What does it mean?"

"Something like 'a puppet of the Campbells'."

"Strong stuff. What was his problem with your dad?"

"He was a MacDonald."

"Am I supposed to know the significance of that? I'm an Acadian."

"It's all about a place called Glencoe and how the Campbells butchered the MacDonalds. It's a long story and I don't know all the details, but apparently the Campbells violated the ancient laws of hospitality and killed the MacDonalds after they had been wining and dining with them."

"Sounds like you have a lot of Googling to do. Will you make the travel and accommodations bookings and occasionally consult me?"

"I should be happy to do that, O Lord and Master."

"Approximately when shall we aim to leave?"

"Depends on what flights I can get, but I thought in about two weeks. That alright?"

"Yes. Let's do Wales first. That will give Scotland time to warm up a bit."

"I'll get on it right away."

At that moment the phone rang and Rosalie went into the kitchen to answer it. I heard her talking to the caller.

"It's for you," she finally said. "A Mrs. Withers."

"I don't know anybody called Withers."

"I think it might be an investigation."

"Aha! Then in that case, Watson, I'll speak to her."

I went in and sat at the big deal table. "Hello, Marc LeBlanc speaking."

"Mr. LeBlanc, my name is Valerie Withers."

"Yes, Mrs. Withers. What can I do for you?"

"I've heard that you do investigations free of charge. Is that true? I mean, the free of charge part, because I am a widow and quite poor. I couldn't possibly afford to pay."

"Yes, that's true if I decide to take the case. What is the problem you want investigated?"

"My husband, William, recently died."

"I'm very sorry to hear that."

"He drowned in the bathtub."

"And why would you come to me?"

"The police say there was no foul play, just that he accidentally drowned."

"That's possible isn't it? What makes you think he wasn't?"

"In fourteen inches of water?"

"It's still possible."

"Mr. LeBlanc, Bill was six foot three and weighed almost 250 pounds. He was a huge man. When he was in the tub there wasn't much room for anything else."

"Ah I see. Were there any marks on his body?"

"The police said nothing significant."

"Did you see any marks?"

"There was a kind of mark on his head. But the police said that wouldn't be enough to indicate that a struggle had taken place."

"This mark, was it as if he had received a blow?"

"No, I couldn't say that."

"Well then, what could it have been?"

"The mark where someone had pushed him under."

"But you said he was a very big man. How would it have been

possible for someone to have done that?"

"He could have been drugged."

"But wouldn't the substance remain in his system, at least for a while? Did the post mortem find anything?"

"There wasn't one. The police said it wasn't necessary."

I paused because it occurred to me that, while it would be costly, we could have an autopsy done privately. That might reveal something, although many toxic substances dissipated after a few hours. Is there still time? I wondered.

"When did your husband die?"

"A week ago. The cremation is tomorrow."

"Ah. Mrs. Withers, I am going to be honest with you. There doesn't seem at first blush to be anything I could do. However, if you could come to see me and bring photographs of the bathtub together with some pictures of your husband, I will talk some more with you."

"Oh, thank you, Mr. LeBlanc."

"Where are you?"

"I live in Dartmouth."

"Do you have a car?"

"No, but I could get my son to drive me. Where are you?"

"I am in Grand Pre, just outside of Wolfville. Could you come the day after tomorrow?"

"Yes, certainly."

"I should also warn you that I am due to leave the country in two weeks' time and will be gone for some time."

"Please do what you can, Mr. LeBlanc. I'll see you the day after tomorrow. What time?"

"Shall we say one o'clock?"

"That will be alright. Thank you."

When I returned to the lounge, Rosalie was sorting through the day's mail. She handed me one of the envelopes. It had a distinguished-looking crest on the back involving a stag's head and some kind of tartan.

I was about to open it when the phone rang again. It was our old friend Patrick Kennedy.

"Patrick! How are you?"

I had known Patrick for some years, since my father's murder, in fact. Patrick had been a detective sergeant with the Halifax police and was the CIO in charge of the investigation. Later he switched to the RCMP, rising first to become an inspector, then to a superintendent. Although our early relations had been somewhat frosty, over time we had become fast friends, and we had worked cheek by jowl on the adventure with Premier Proctor.

"Fine, Marc," said Patrick in that breezy style of his. "I know it's a bit cheeky of me, but could we invite ourselves to stay with you tomorrow night?"

"Not at all cheeky! We would love to see you."

"Ruth will be with me. Her sister in Yarmouth is not well, so we're going down to see how we can help. It occurred to me it would be a great opportunity to drop in on you and Rosalie on the way."

"Of course. Come in time for dinner. I'll cook something special."

"That sounds wonderful"

"Okay. See you at about five?"

"Sure, that'd be great."

Rosalie was thrilled at the news. She had always liked Patrick and more recently had gotten to know and like his wife, Ruth.

"What fun!" she said, "We'll push the boat out for them."

"Indeed we will. I think we still have a brace of partridge in the freezer. I'll do something nice with them. And if we can get some fresh salmon in the morning, I'll make a mousse for starters. Will you make dessert?"

"Of course. Maybe a strawberry shortcake."

"Oh, yes, please!"

"Then it shall be done. What's that letter you got?"

"Oh, I forgot about that. Let me have a look."

The letter, again with an impressive crest, was headed 'The Single-malt Scotch Whisky Society of Nova Scotia,' and was from a Donald Alistair Chisholm, who signed himself president. The letter explained that he had been informed—he didn't say by whom—that I was a devotee of the ineffable substance and that they would like me to join their society. They met once a month at different locations around the province to taste a series of malts, to be followed by dinner.

I passed the letter to Rosalie, who said, "Ugh!" because she hates whisky.

"You join, you go, but count me out. Horrible stuff!"

"Okay, I will. By the way, we may have a case. That Mrs. Withers is coming the day after tomorrow for a talk. I want you to sit in and see what you think."

"Okay."

"And in case we decided to follow it up, I think you'd better book our trip in two separate parts. Wales for two weeks first, then home for a few weeks, then Scotland for another few weeks."

"Sound sensible. I'll do it right away."

2

When I got up the next morning I went to take the partridges out of the freezer to allow them to thaw, but on finding the birds I discovered they were in fact guinea fowl. I was annoyed that I had been confused, but it did not matter because guinea fowl can be delicious if cooked properly.

I laid them on a slab in the larder and went out onto the deck.

It was a beautiful day, with dew sparkling on the grass of the field and the sun just coming up over the top of the vines in the most easterly of John Dempster's vineyards. I was a major shareholder in the winery, but I took no direct part in its operational decisions due to my falling out with John a few years ago.

The woods at the top of my hill were showing a light green dusting of leaves, and a number of crows were having an aeronautical competition, diving, wheeling and cawing loudly. I shivered because it was cold and I had forgotten to put on a sweater, so I retreated to the kitchen.

The sounds of Rosalie starting to move about upstairs meant I could begin to make breakfast. Apart from our favourite Blue Mountain coffee and croissants with locally-made jam, I wondered what else I could serve, so I rummaged in the fridge and found some lovely cold ham and a number of leftover boiled potatoes.

I thinly sliced the ham and put it on a platter with some cocktail tomatoes. Then I also sliced the potatoes and put them into a huge, cast-iron pan of sizzling olive oil and butter to fry until golden. Then I would add some cremini mushrooms and chopped parsley just before serving.

"Some nice smells coming from the kitchen," called Rosalie as she came down the stairs. "I hope you're making lots, because I'm starving."

"Lot's for me," I called back, "but you'll have to go to McDonalds to get your breakfast."

"If I do," she said coming into the room, "afterwards I'll go straight to Walter Bryden's office and have the divorce papers drawn up."

"Well, under those circumstances, I guess I'll find a crust for you."

"Better be more than a crust!"

The combination of hot and cold food proved most enjoyable and we resolved to do it more often.

Over breakfast, I explained to Rosalie everything Mrs. Withers had told me, and said I didn't think there was much we could do for her.

"Poor woman. If the body's being cremated this week, is there any chance we could find out if he was drugged and pushed?"

"I can't see how. I suppose that if we had a suspect and a motive, we could guess at foul play, but we could never prove it."

"Will you run it past Patrick tonight?"

"Only if he starts talking about police work first."

"And if he does?"

"I'll ask him if he's familiar with the case—he may not be—and, if so, if he was satisfied with the police's decision."

"The death took place in Dartmouth, so the investigators would have been the Regional Police, not the RCMP."

"Damn! Of course. So it's not likely Patrick would have even heard of the case."

While Rosalie was clearing the breakfast things away, I took another look at the letter from the Single Malt Whisky Society. I thought the prospect of tasting a row of single malts every month rather excessive, but I might be able to attend two or three such events a year. I decided to call the president, Donald Alistair Chisholm, in Antigonish and say I would join, and find out when the next meeting would take place.

"That's grand!" Mr. Chisholm pronounced loudly when I told him I would be glad to join his group. "We'll be glad to have you, even though your antecedents are not from the banks and braes."

"There's nothing I can do about my ancestry, I'm afraid, and I realize the Acadians are not known for their love of malt."

"No they are not." Chisholm said, a little savagely, "but if you're willing, we might make you an honorary highlander."

"So long as I don't have to wear a kilt."

"Some of us do, some of us don't. It is not a requirement."

"Good. When is the next meeting, Mr. Chisholm?"

"Donald, please, call me Donald." He paused, "But never, never Don."

"Okay, Donald: I'll remember that."

"Please do. We are having a meeting on Friday in Halifax. Can you make that?"

"Yes, I can."

"It will be at the Muir Hotel. If you wish, I'll arrange a room for you."

"That's very kind of you. What time is the meeting and what should I bring?"

"We will gather at six, and dine at eight. You should bring a bottle of single malt. Keep it well covered. We taste blind."

Rosalie and I then took her Fiat into New Minas to get supplies for the evening meal. I had an idea in mind to roast the fowl with a white wine sauce, so for that I needed to get shallots, fresh tarragon, fat bacon and some whole grain mustard. For the first course, I needed Paris toast, fresh and smoked salmon, fresh dill, and heavy cream. For dessert, Rosalie needed strawberries, if we could find them at this time of year, and if we could not, she would look for rhubarb to make a crumble.

Fortunately, we were able to get everything we wanted at the supermarket, although the berries did not look as ripe and red as we would have liked.

We then drove into Wolfville to the wine store to see if Louise had recently acquired any specialty Champagne we could serve before the meal and with the dessert. She told us she had just yesterday taken delivery of a single case of De Venoge Louis XV Rosé Brut 2012, which was all her supplier would allow, as the Champagne was quite rare and difficult to find. Louise said she had promised six bottles to the President of the university, but would let us have the other six.

When we got home, I gently poached the salmon then blended it in a food processor with the smoked salmon chopped dill, a few tablespoons of mayonnaise, cream and a little gelatin dissolved in water. Once I had poured it into a terrine container, I put it in the fridge to set.

I seasoned and oiled the two now-thawed guinea fowl and browned them until they were golden, whereupon I took them out and added the whole shallots and chopped bacon to the pot.

When the lardons were crisp, I poured in a bottle of Alsace Riesling, a cup of chicken stock and several spoons of whole grain mustard. Having taken the pot off the heat, I put the guinea fowl on top, ready for the oven about half an hour after the Kennedys arrived.

I watched Rosalie slaving away over her shortcake, but it was all a mystery to me because I cannot bake cakes if my life depended upon it.

Then I went down to the cellar to choose the wines for dinner. Pre-dinner drinks and dessert were already taken care of, my having put two bottles of the *De Venoge Rosé* into the fridge, so now I needed a white for the salmon mousse and a red for the guinea fowl.

To accommodate the strong flavours of the former I chose a 2008 *Joseph Drouhin Corton-Charlemagne*, and to go with the latter a 1999 *Domaine Dujac Clos Saint Denis*, both from Burgundy. I gently carried the bottles upstairs and set them upright in the larder to be decanted about an hour before drinking. About fifteen minutes before serving the white I would put it in the fridge just to cool, because really good Chardonnay should never be served at lower than slightly below room temperature.

The Kennedys arrived just after five o'clock and, after some cheerful exchanges, I showed them up to their room to shower or freshen up.

They came back down in about an hour and we gathered in the

lounge, a large room with glass on three surfaces, giving views of the changing sky. Almost immediately, Patrick started talking about the plot to kill Premier Proctor, the case on which we had worked closely together.

"Patrick says it was the most exciting case he ever worked on" said Ruth, an attractive, middle-aged brunette with hazel eyes and a ready smile.

"Well, the closing events were exciting and no mistake," said Patrick, "but, to be fair, there were a lot of boring times leading up to the end."

"Yes," I said, "A lot of plodding and getting nowhere."

"I often wonder who shot the woman," said Patrick.

Rosalie and I exchanged furtive glances. We knew but did not dare say what we knew. We were momentarily embarrassed, until Ruth spoke.

"How can you be sure it wasn't a police officer, Patrick?"

"Their weapons were carefully checked. None had been fired and no ammunition was missing."

"Oh."

"Are you working any interesting cases now, Patrick?" I asked hurriedly, anxious to change the subject.

"Yes, as a matter of fact. Some very puzzling ones."

"Do tell."

"All this is in confidence, you understand, not a word to anyone else."

We all nodded our assent.

"I have a series of murders under my general supervision, all weird and not connected, as far as I know."

"What makes them weird?" Rosalie asked.

"The first, from Cape Breton, is a guy who was found naked in the middle of nowhere and died of exposure. It looks as if he had his hands bound at some point."

"Ugh!"

"Then, in Antigonish County, a man was found who the medical experts said had starved to death."

"Starved?"

"Yeah. Really weird."

"Could he have starved himself?"

"Again we found signs of restraints. Both hands and feet."

"Ah."

"And in Guysborough County, a man burned to death when his house was set on fire."

"How was that murder?" I asked.

"The body was found strapped to a steel chair."

"How horrible!" Ruth exclaimed. "Patrick, I don't think you should be talking about such things. We are about to eat."

"When we move to the table, I promise no more shop talk, darling. Besides I was through. There are only these three murders on my plate at the moment. By the way, Marc, this Champagne is delicious."

"Yes, wonderful!" said Ruth.

"Before we go into the dining room," I said, "can I ask you about a case I may be involved in?"

"Aha! You have another case! Tell me about it, Sherlock."

"Name of Withers. Drowned in the bath. No sign of restraints, but a mark on the head where he might or might not have been pushed if he was drugged."

"What did the post mortem say?"

"There wasn't one."

"Why not?"

"Halifax Regional Police didn't think it necessary. They said it was an accidental death."

"Then it probably was. Most likely they were right."

"But not certain?"

"We can rarely be certain, Marc, and neither you nor I have the evidence they had, so we can't make an informed judgment."

"Point taken."

"You might be able to get a private autopsy, but it wouldn't be cheap."

"The fellow's going to be cremated the day after tomorrow."

"Well, there you are. Case closed," said Patrick firmly. Clearly he did not want to discuss it further.

Dinner went off without a hitch, all dishes and wines being pronounced excellent.

When we had finished, Ruth and Rosalie expressed themselves tired and went up to bed. Patrick and I took the dregs of the Champagne into the lounge.

"Is there something you're not telling me?" I said..

"About what?"

"About the Withers case. You seemed anxious to end the discussion."

"I don't know what you're talking about."

"Patrick, if you're leery about another force's case, I understand. But if there is something not quite right, you can tell me."

"Marc, I have no reason to believe that anything was wrong with the way the Halifax police handled the case. None at all."

"Then what?"

"It's just that it occurred to me that the Withers case is somewhat like my other cases in some respects, and it crossed my mind..."

"That they're connected?"

"Yes."

3

Before the Kennedys left for Yarmouth the next day, we had a very pleasant breakfast together, with much laughter and conversation, which lasted until late morning. Rosalie must have made at least five pots of coffee, while I kept up a steady supply of bacon, ham, sausages, croissants, toast and scrambled eggs.

Everybody had hearty appetites, and Patrick in particular was in fine form, putting away several helpings. He was in a good mood, although he did take me aside for a few minutes before we sat down at the table.

"Marc, forget what I said last night. I had a little too much to drink."

"You mean about your cases and my case being connected?"

"*Possibly* being connected, yes. But it's a non-starter."

"I don't see why. They are all unexplained, with no obvious suspects or motives."

"Your case isn't even a crime, so far as we know. My cases definitely *are* crimes. Anyway, there's nothing either of us can or should do about it. Now let's eat. I'm famished."

After we had finally finished eating and talking, we saw them to their car and waved them goodbye.

As we were going back to the house, Rosalie told me she had made travel arrangements for the first half of our trip to Britain.

"That was quick work," I said. "When do we leave?"

"A week from Saturday."

"That early? Can you get time off from the university?"

"All arranged."

"Did you have to suck up to the department head very much?"

"Old Jefferies is putty in my hands."

"Okay, I won't pursue that line of questioning. Give me the itinerary"

"We go to Heathrow on Saturday—"

"Direct?"

"Yes."

"That means no business class?"

"Yes, but it's reasonably comfortable in Premium Economy."

"I guess, but sleeping will be difficult in those seats."

"It's a daytime flight, Marc. We leave at eleven in the morning and get in at nine, London time."

"I see, but we couldn't pick up a car and get on the road at that time of night, and if we went into town we couldn't check into a hotel until after eleven."

"Problem solved. I've booked a room at the Hilton Garden for the night."

"How far is that from the terminal?"

"Under 200 metres, lazy bones."

"Good. Okay. And we get the car on Sunday morning?"

"Quite so."

"What did you get? Some cramped economy job like your Fiat?"

"No, I did not get some cramped economy job. I got a Jaguar F-Pace."

"Not too bad. Isn't that an SUV?"

"Yes. Lots of room for baggage and hanging clothes."

"Well, Madame LeBlanc, you seem to have managed things quite well. What happens after we get the car?"

"Let me consult my notes. We head west on the M4 to Wales, over the Severn Bridge—"

"Which one?"

"The southerly one. Don't keep interrupting. Then we leave the M4 and go on to the A449 to Raglan."

"That junction with the A449 is a nightmare. The traffic circle is a confusing jumble of lanes, like spaghetti thrown at the wall. You could drive round and round there forever. Is there an alternative?"

"Let me see. Um, not unless you want to leave the M4 at a place called Magor and follow the back roads to connect with the A449 halfway to Raglan."

"Let's do that. I like the back roads. There's a good castle at Raglan. We can take a look at it."

"That'd be nice. From Raglan we head up to Abergavenny—am I saying that right?—where we take the road along the south side of the River Usk to Tal y Bont."

"What's in Tal y Bont?"

"Among other things, The Traveler's Rest."

"What's that?"

"Small restaurant with rooms. Comes highly recommended. We're booked in for four nights."

"Why?"

"Lovely countryside around there, lakes and mountains. It is also near some places associated with the Chartists."

"Ah! John Frost again."

"I've been doing some research on the net, Marc, and I think John Frost may be something of a disappointment."

"How so?"

"For one thing, he's buried in Bristol, not in Wales. And we don't want to go to Bristol. For another, as far as I can discover, he only had a daughter. Which means I can't be descended from him at all."

"Oh, that's too bad. Any chance you can follow up the Frosts who were on your mother's side?"

"Maybe. My mom's dad was William from the Welsh coal valleys before he moved here and eventually became a fisherman. His father was Rhys Frost from a place called Tredegar, where he got into some kind of trouble, I don't know what kind."

"Maybe fighting for the people's rights, like John."

"Somehow, I get the impression not. But that's something we might be able to find out when we get there."

"Checking local records and such?"

"Yes."

"It works for me. You know I'm just excess baggage on this trip."

"Humph."

"So the John Frost—the one you're apparently not related to. Was he from Tal y Bont?"

"No, John Frost was from Newport, which we may want to visit because he was mayor of the town for a while, and it was the site of the final showdown between the Chartist rebels and the army."

"Exiting stuff. Was it a pitched battle? Any killed?"

"About 20 Chartists out of four thousand, and fifty injured. Sixty of them were tried and found guilty. John Frost and his co-leaders, Williams and Jones, were sentenced to be hanged, drawn and quartered."

"That spectacle must have drawn a large crowd. The public was very bloodthirsty in those times."

"The sentence was commuted by the British cabinet to transportation to Australia."

"Wow. So that was the end of them."

"For Williams and Jones, yes, but in 1856 Frost was pardoned and came back to Britain."

"Good for him. So remind me. If Frost wasn't from Tal y Bont, why are we going to be staying there?"

"Because it's supposed to be a nice beauty spot from which we can reach all the places associated with the Chartists within a two-hour drive. I figure if I can't make family connections the excuse for a visit, we can pretend we're following in the footsteps of the Chartists."

"Sound reasonable. But we don't really need an excuse to visit Wales. You'll love it. What then?"

"We follow our noses wherever the evidence leads."

"You lead, I shall follow!"

"I'll remember that. What time is Mrs. Withers coming?"

"In about ten minutes."

"I'll put on some more coffee."

The Withers were about half an hour late, apparently having had some difficulty finding the place. I found that hard to believe, as our house is unmistakable, being the only one of its kind in the area and highly prominent from the road.

When I met Mrs. Withers' son, Norman, I thought I understood. He was a great lump of a man in his mid-twenties, red-faced and goggle-eyed, who proved to be annoyingly insensitive and slow to understand. His mother, on the other hand, was a tiny, grey woman, plain and pale, but neatly dressed.

I had placed one chair at the desk and another behind it, against the wall. When I invited her to sit, Norman pushed her aside, taking the chair at the desk. As politely as I could, I asked him to move to the other chair.

"Wha?" he bawled.

"That chair is for your mother. Please move to the other."

"Huh?"

"Please move. Let your mother sit here!"

"Yes, Norman, please do as Mr. LeBlanc says," Mrs. Withers pleaded.

With an ugly snarl he got up and slumped himself against the wall.

"Now, Mrs. Withers—"

"Please call me Valerie," she said, to an accompanying snort from Norman.

"Fine. Now, Valerie, did you bring the photographs I asked for?"

"Yes, Mr. LeBlanc. Here they are." She handed me a bundle of paper.

My first surprise was that one of the photographs was of her dead husband, showing the mark on the top of his head. The mark was not very pronounced, but if one used one's imagination it could have been the imprint of a hand.

The second surprise was that Mrs. Withers had possessed the presence of mind to put a tape measure in each of the photos so that I could judge the sizes of everything. The tub was smaller than most, being only 106 centimetres long by 50 cm wide and 26 cm deep. A photograph of Mr. Withers, from when he was alive, showed a heavy-set man standing with his head almost touching the door lintel.

These pictures strongly suggested to me that for William Withers to have accidentally drowned in his bath would have been almost impossible. Previously, I had been fairly certain the Halifax police were right in not proceeding with an investigation, but now I was not so sure.

But the only avenues which I could pursue were suspects and motives, the latter presumably not being obtainable until the former had been established. It crossed my mind more than once that the obvious prime suspect was Norman, but I feared that my personal dislike for him was clouding my judgment, so I struggled to keep an open mind.

"Valerie, did your husband have any enemies?"

"Not that I know of."

"Had he argued with anyone recently?"

"No, I don't think so."

"Was there any dispute in the past which could have led to somebody doing this?"

"I can't think of anything."

"He did get into an argument with that bastard at the shopping centre," Norman interjected.

"That was ages ago," said Valerie.

"It might be significant," I said. "Do you have the man's name and address?"

"No, sorry."

"Anything by which he might be identified?"

"The bastard was black!" Norman snarled.

I winced, but chose to ignore him. To his mother, I said, "What line of business was your husband in?"

"He was a butcher, at the Superstore."

"Hmm. Not an occupation which would make many enemies."

"No, I guess not." Mrs. Withers seemed very apologetic.

"Did he have any surviving brothers or sisters?"

"He had a brother somewhere out west. I don't know where. And a sister living in Halifax. She's quite a bit older than Bill was."

"Fucking bitch!" Norman muttered, which made me lose my temper.

"Look Norman, if you have anything constructive to contribute, please do so. If not, please shut up and keep your thoughts to yourself."

"Yes, Norm, do like Mr. LeBlanc says." Valerie's voice developed an edge for the first time. "Norman and Iris don't get along," she said to me.

I felt like saying, 'I'm not surprised' but held my tongue.

"Iris is old school, very prim and proper, while Norman is..." She trailed off. She did not need to say more.

"Well, Valerie," I said, rising from the desk, "unless we can find a strong motive for someone killing Bill, and identify a viable suspect, there's not much more we can do."

"Oh, Mr. LeBlanc!"

"But I'm not closing the file and will do some more thinking. If you give me her address, I'll visit Iris. Is she a Withers, or—?"

"Yes, she never married."

"Who'd have her?" Norma sneered.

"You just shut your filthy mouth, you great heap of shit!" shouted Mrs. Withers.

I was shocked by the sudden transformation of this tiny, quiet woman. I was quite disconcerted and did not know where to look.

Norman got up and stormed out.

"I'll go and talk to Iris soon," I said finally, "I shall be in Halifax on Friday, so I'll go to see her then. Do you know if she is usually at home on Fridays?"

"Oh yes. She doesn't go out very often. Yes, I'm sure she'll be there. Here's her phone number. You can check before you go."

The tiny, subdued, quiet woman had returned, and gently found her way to the front door.

After she left and had walked to the car, I looked out of the window and saw her pounding a cowering Norman with her handbag.

I turned back from the window and went over to Rosalie, who had been quietly sitting in the next room, with the door slightly ajar.

"Did you get all that?"

"Oh, yes."

"And what do you think?"

"If you ask me, I think they're both suspects."

"I could see Norman, the great brute, but surely not Mrs. Withers herself?"

"I wouldn't rule it out."

"But how would she do it? How *could* she do it?"

"I'm not sure, Marc, but I don't buy that sweet, little old lady routine. You heard how vicious she got when she erupted at Norman."

"Hmm. Of course, I suppose it's possible they were in it together but, if so, there is another big question to answer."

"What's that?"

"Why on earth would she want me, or anyone else, to investigate the death?"

"Good point. When are you going to see the sister-in-law?"

"Friday."

"Ah, yes, before your gathering of the clans to get drunk on malodorous whisky!"

"I shall not get drunk, and it is an exquisite distillation of barley combined with the skilful application of time, oak and, in some cases, peat and heather."

"Ugh!"

4

On Friday morning I called Iris Withers. She sounded like a very nice old lady, well-spoken, and obviously with all her faculties intact.

"If you think I can help you in any way, I would be glad to see you," she said. "But I think I should tell you that I haven't been in touch with my brother as much as I should."

"I understand Ms. Withers—"

"It's Miss Withers, Mr. LeBlanc. I'm old school and proud of it. None of that Miz nonsense!"

"Very well. Would you be available this afternoon?"

"Yes. Come about one o'clock. It's 2681 Isleville Street, in the North End."

"I'll be there. Thank you."

Recently, I had my mechanic, Liam Candow, do a complete overhaul of the Bugatti, so it ran like a dream. On a short, straight stretch between Ellershouse and Sackville I took it up to 170 kph, and it was a smooth as silk and steady as a rock.

Of course, the car was capable of more than twice that speed, and I could feel the reserves of power remaining within the amazing engine designed by Hartmut Warkuß and Wolfgang Schreiber. I wondered what kind of road, and under what weather conditions, this model had broken the world record in 2013 when it had reached 408.84 kph.

In the event, I reached downtown Halifax in forty-three minutes.

I could not park on Isleville, but managed to find a space on Bloomfield Street, and walked back. Even had I not had the address I would have been able to pick out Miss Wither's house immediately. It was not that the others were dilapidated in any way, but that hers stood out like a new pin. What some might consider twee, I thought appealing in a Bijou way, with neat lace curtains and well-attended window boxes in which some plants were starting to poke their heads above the earth. The door was somewhere between a powder blue and a dove gray, with maroon trim. There was a ceramic knocker above a quaint, hand-painted welcome sign.

When she opened the door, she was not at all the tiny old maid I expected. Before me stood a very tall, upright woman of, I guessed, about seventy-five, wearing a tweed suit, woollen stockings and horn-rimmed glasses.

"Come in and put the board in the hole," she said in a sergeant-major tone. "Don't hang about out there or you'll give the place a bad name."

I carefully wiped my feet on the stiff-bristled mat by the front door and followed her into an immaculately-kept living room, where she invited me to sit. It was clear that this woman lived alone and had always done so. It was not just that there was no sign of any other human being, but I was impressed by the certainty that every item in the room—from furniture to the smallest ornament—was exactly in its place. I was sure that if I moved anything by even half an inch, she would immediately move it back.

"What a lovely house you have," I said, not knowing quite how to start out conversation.

"Yes. I bought it in 1960 for $32,000."

"Good heavens!"

"You're surprised I'm that old? I'm now 86. I was one of Mr. Stanfield's secretaries when he became premier in 1956. I was well-paid, so I could afford the mortgage. But I didn't have the down payment, so Mr. Stanfield had a quiet word with the bank."

"Remarkable."

"Wasn't it? And lucky. He was a very kind man. I've been content here for 64 years."

"How old was your brother?"

"Ah, you're wondering about the age gap. Bill was only 64 when he drowned."

"Yes, I did wonder."

"He was my half-brother by a different mother. My mother died a long time ago and father remarried."

"I see. That explains it."

"So. What do you want to know about Bill?"

"Basically, I need to know if he had any enemies."

"You're making the assumption that his death was not accidental?"

"I'm not making any assumptions, Miss Withers. I'm making inquiries because your sister-in-law asked me to look into the matter."

"Hmm. I can't see her being able to afford a private investigator, but that's none of my business."

"I don't charge."

"Really? How extraordinary. I must remember that in case I ever need your services." She laughed the most peculiar, strangled, dry laugh I had ever heard. For a moment I thought she might be choking.

"May I ask if your half-brother did have any enemies?"

"Almost certainly."

"Are you sure?"

"We all do, Mr. LeBlanc. It is integral to the human condition."

"I mean, anyone specific."

"Alas, I couldn't speculate on that. There were none of whom I was aware."

"And you can't think of anybody who would want to kill him for any reason?"

"Not off-hand."

Something outside in the street caught her attention and she gazed out of the window for a few seconds before turning back to me. "Of course, he didn't lead a blameless life, so it is conceivable he might have rubbed somebody the wrong way."

"In what ways did he not lead a blameless life?"

"Oh, you know: drinking, gambling. The usual."

"Was it serious?"

"I don't think so. Valerie and"—here she took a quick breath, and blew it out again—"Norman never wanted for much, as far as I know. There was always food on the table. That sort of thing."

"So it was just that he liked a good time?"

"Yes. The men in our family have always liked a good time. It goes all the way back to the Spoons."

"I'm sorry. The Spoons?"

"Yes, I think it was my great, great, great—I can't keep track of exactly how many greats—grandfather who got rid of the Spoons when he immigrated to Canada."

"I still don't understand."

"Originally our name was Witherspoon, but he changed it to Withers."

"Ah, I see. Where did he come from?"

"Scotland."

"Why did he change his name?"

"I don't know.

"Well, thank you."

"Goodness me!" She suddenly exclaimed. "I clearly forgot to offer you a cup of tea. Please forgive me. Would you like a cup now, Mr. LeBlanc?"

"You know, Miss Withers, I rather think I would."

Iris Withers and I drank several cups of tea and had a wonderful gossip about the people she had known during the Stanfield-Smith government, and later when she went to City Hall to work for various mayors. We talked so much I almost ran out of the time I needed to check into the hotel and get ready for my first meeting of the Single Malt Association.

I said a hurried goodbye to Miss Withers and drove downtown to the Muir Hotel.

Except for the desk personnel, the lobby was empty and I had no problem checking in, so, leaving the concierge to park the Bugatti, I went straight up to my large, comfortable, but somewhat sterile room to have a quick shower and change. When I had dressed I grabbed the bottle of malt from my travel bag and hurried downstairs.

The gathering was being held in a private meeting room, which was intimate without being crowded. When I put my head round the door, Donald Chisholm hailed me like a long lost brother.

"Mr. LeBlanc. *Ceud mìle fàilte! Tha e na urram dhuinn le do làthaireachd!*"

"*Je suis heureux d'être içi pour accepter votre aimable invitation,*" I replied, hastily looking around the room.

There were four other men standing around, three of them, including Donald, wearing some degree of what is generally accepted as Highland dress: kilts with shirts, ties and tweed jackets. Like me, one was in an ordinary business suit.

The other, a dark, intense young man about thirty, was outfitted in the entire regalia, complete with buckled shoes, knee-length socks—the right one containing a *sgian-dubh*—sporran, vest, a blazer with silver buttons and a white shirt, frothing with lace at the neck and wrists.

Donald was in his early sixties, stout and hearty, with an abundance of wavy gray hair. The man in the suit, a slight, willowy man in his forties, he introduced as Harold Westwood. The two in what I would call the semi-official attire, were Murdoch Mackay and Lachlan MacLeod, both tall, but the former being about fifty and the latter in his seventies.

I shook hands with each of them and exchanged pleasantries. I particularly liked old MacLeod, who struck me as a jolly man who might have a hundreds stories to tell.

Then Donald took me to the young, dressed-to-kill fellow, who was lurking malignantly in the corner.

"Marc, this is my son and heir, Duncan."

"Pleased to meet you, Duncan," I said, although I did not mean it.

He said nothing, but merely clicked his heels and scowled.

"Duncan is not a regular, full member of the group, so to speak. He substitutes for Sandy MacNeil who, sadly, is under the weather these days. I suggested that a good dose of Uisge Beatha would likely cure what ails him, but apparently his doctor disagreed. You will probably see him at our next gathering."

As Donald was delivering this little speech I was unable to take my eyes off his most disagreeable son. I don't think I had ever loathed anyone at first sight the way I loathed Duncan Chisholm.

His breathing the same air put my teeth on edge, and what I considered his preposterous over- dressing infuriated me. When he looked at me I imagined I saw arrogance, insolence and malevolence in equal measures, and it was as much as I could manage not to strike him.

This, I realized, was totally irrational, but I could not help it. So I tore myself away and moved back into the room, determined to get a seat at the table which was as far away from him as possible.

In the event, I was lucky, as Donald had allocated our places with small signs, I being at the foot of the table, and Duncan being next to his father, who was presiding at the head. On one side were Harold and Murdoch, on the other were Lachlan and Duncan.

On the table were myriad small glasses, six bottles in brown paper bags, jugs of water and, much to my surprise, containers of ice and soda.

"Sit ye down, sit ye down." Donald boomed, and with much wriggling of his ample posterior, he ensconced himself as presiding officer. He instructed Duncan to serve the first malt, which came from a bottle marked A.

With unnecessary fastidiousness, I thought, Duncan very slowly poured about an inch and a half of whisky into each of the glasses. As we were settling in our places, and watching Duncan, I noticed that all but Harold and I had each, unobtrusively, pulled a carafe of water from the line in the centre of table, and had put it in front of him.

Then Donald rose. "Gentleman, The King!"

"The King!" they all echoed, raising their glasses.

I quickly glanced around the table and noticed that Harold and I were the only ones who did not hold our glass over a carafe before taking a sip. This puzzled me, so I leaned over and whispered, "Whats that all about?"

"They're Catholics," he muttered.

"So am I. I don't understand."

"They're not toasting our King Charles III, they're toasting *their* King Charles."

"Their King Charles?"

"Yes," whispered Harold, "the King Over the Water."

Then it dawned on me that these men were still living the 18th-century battles and dreams of the Jacobite rebellions which ended in tragedy and bloodshed at Culloden in 1746. I had no idea how seriously they took this and suspected it was just a bit of fun, but told myself to tread very carefully.

"Marc, while we are all devoted to the whisky of our homeland, we are not pedants and do not force rules on others." Donald announced. "Purists such as Murdock here insist that a dram of malt must be tasted untainted by any other substance."

Murdock inclined his head and murmured his assent.

"Others, like my son and myself, prefer our dram adulterated by a drop of pure water."

"It's the only way," Duncan said defiantly.

"Well, no, we mustn't say that. Lachie likes a piece of ice in his dram. God help me if I did that, but each to his own. Harold says that the bubbles in soda bring out the flavour of the barley. Where did you stand on this mighty question, Marc?"

"I'm afraid, I have to stand with Harold." I said.

Duncan snorted.

"Ach. No matter. It would be a boring world if we were all the same. Now let's taste Malt A and get our opinions, and then we'll take a stab at identifying it. Who brought A?"

"I did," said Lachie.

"Then you're out of the guessing!" Donald said, to universal laughter.

Malt A was a very smoky, peaty drink which was not to my liking at all. Years ago I had favoured these distinct whiskies, which came mostly from the Isles, but I had grown out of them and now preferred the Speyside and some of the Highland malts. This one was stronger than most and tasted as if it had been rescued from a building which had just been burned down.

The table offered comments with all but me guessing the malt came from Islay. Three said it was Ardbeg and one said they thought it was Laphroig.

"Marc, do you have any views on this?" Donald asked in a kindly, somewhat condescending, way.

"I have to disagree with everybody," I said, at which they all laughed. "I have an idea this is from Orkney."

"Oho!" Donald cried.

"And, because I thought it more alcoholic than the usual dram would be, I am guessing this is a Barrel Strength malt, which means it would be around 60% alcohol rather than 43%."

I looked across at Lachie who was beaming from ear to ear. He gave me a wink.

"So, my guess would be Barrel Strength Highland Park."

"Well done!" Lachie said as he removed the bottle from its bag. "A remarkable effort!"

With the exception of Duncan, who frowned, the whole table erupted in applause. Even if I did miserably with all the other malts, this success was assured of assisting me in becoming 'one of the gang.'

I was not, however, quite as successful with three of the remaining four malts. Harold had brought a lovely 18-year-old Abelour which I did identify, having had it only recently at home. Donald had brought a 15-year-old GlenFarcalas and Murdoch one of the many curious, sweetish whiskies from Glen Morangie, on neither of which I had a clue.

My own 21-year-old Caperdonick stumped them all because the distillery closed down in 2002 and consequently had made no new whisky since.

The best malt of the night, much to my chagrin, was the one which Duncan brought. It was a rare, 30-year-old Macallan which had been matured in Oloroso sherry cases and was a dark, rich, luscious drink. I wondered how he could have afforded this malt, and since he appeared far too young to have succeeded in business, I thought the family must be wealthy.

In any event, he gave us a condescending smile when his was proclaimed the best, as if he himself had made it.

Then Donald called in the hotel staff, who cleared the table and set it for the dinner which he had ordered prior to our arrival. We retook our places, whereupon he turned to Lachlan.

"Lachie, please may we have The Selkirk? Gentlemen, please rise."

"Certainly, Donald," Lachie responded gravely. "'Some hae meat and canna eat, And some wad eat that want it: But we hae meat and we can eat, And sae the Lord be thankit'."

As we sat down I again turned to Harold for an explanation. "The Selkirk?"

"The Selkirk Grace. Most people think it was written by Burns, but it goes back to at least the 17th century. It's sometimes called the 'Covenanters' Grace' or 'Galloway Grace'."

"Thanks, Harold. You learn something every day."

Donald had made a good effort ordering the dinner, as it more or less seemed to please everybody. We started with a Beef Marrow Rarebit, a concoction of black winter truffle, Knoydart farm cheddar, leek piccalilli, and matchstick frites. Then we had a Seafood Hodge Podge of butter-braised halibut cheeks, mussels, matane shrimp, scallops, littleneck clams, salt cod brandade croquette, and green beans, which was an agreeable mix of flavours.

We finished the meal with a Blueberry Buckle, with crème anglaise, brown butter crumble, and sour cream Chantilly. This latter was less to my liking, because I always find blueberries to have a glue-like texture.

Worst of all for me was that there was no wine served, all participants continuing to drink malt. I confess this was too much for me and I left early with a splitting headache.

"Sleep well, Marc." Donald said. "Shall we see you next month?"

"Likely not," I replied. "I shall probably been in Britain."

"Scotland?" Lachie asked.

"No, Wales this time. We shall be in Scotland later on in the summer."

"Well, away to your bed. *Codladh sámh!*"

"*Fais de beaux rêves à toi aussi*," I said and took my leave of this very unusual group of men.

5

When I awoke the next morning, I thought I would see if Patrick Kennedy was back from visiting Ruth's sister in Yarmouth. I wanted to tell him what I had discovered in the Withers case, but, truth to tell, I was more anxious to pry out of him additional information about his unsolved murders. I had a feeling about them without actually knowing what that feeling was. I could not put it into thoughts, let alone words, but I knew I needed to know more.

Of course, Patrick would be well within his rights to refuse to supply me with further facts, as I was not a policeman and, in theory, I could jeopardize his investigation if I was privy to evidence known only to the investigators.

It was a Saturday and I hoped he might be more relaxed and forthcoming than he had been on the last occasion when we had seen each other.

Ruth answered the telephone. "Why Marc! What a nice surprise hearing from you so soon."

"How is your sister, Ruth?"

"Much better. To be honest, Helen's a bit of a hypochondriac and she was in a terrible fluster about some medical test results."

"I'm sorry to hear that."

"Oh, you need not be. She got herself so worked up she thought that 'negative' actually meant 'positive'."

"A lot of people make that mistake. I did once myself."

"Yes it can be confusing. I guess you're looking for Patrick."

"Yes, is he home?"

"No, he just left for a breakfast meeting with his Chief Super, who has to go Ottawa later today. Then he's going to take the dog for a walk in Point Pleasant Park."

"Did he take the dog with him?"

"Oh yes. Stalker is very well behaved."

"Stalker?"

"The dog. He's a bloodhound."

"Oh, I see."

"Pat will go straight from his meeting to the park. So if you go there in about an hour and a half you should be able to find them."

"Thanks, Ruth, I'll do that."

If it proved as productive as I hoped, my time with Patrick could take up most of the day, so it would mean my staying in Halifax for another night. After I called Rosalie to let her know my plans, I went down to reception to arrange a further night's stay.

As I was leaving the desk, old Lachlan MacLeod came out of the elevator. "*Madainn mhath, Marc! Ciamar a tha thu an-diugh*?"

"Good morning, Lachie. If that means what I think it means, then I am fine. I'm not used to drinking so much Scotch, so I have a bit of a headache."

"You'll soon get rid of that after you've had a bite to eat. Will you take breakfast with me?"

"That's very kind of you. Where are the others?"

"Harold lives here in Halifax, but the rest flew the coop early this morning."

"Did they have far to go?"

"The Chisholms live near Antigonish, and Murdock MacKay is from Hopewell."

"Hopewell? Where's that?"

"Just outside Stellarton."

"Ah. Where do you live, Lachie?"

"I'm from Skye Glen, in the county of Inverness."

"Nice country. Been there long?"

"A little while. About 250 years."

"Haha! Not quite as long as my people."

"The Acadians?"

"Yes, we came in the 1600s."

"Then I bow to your superior standing. You may lead the way to breakfast."

When we had settled at our table and received our coffee, I asked him to tell me how the group had been formed.

"Donald put it together about ten years ago. Membership is strictly by invitation." He winked at me. "Which means only those Donald likes or wishes to impress."

"He hardly knows me. Why on earth would he want to impress me?"

"Ah." Lachie's eyes twinkled. "Maybe that will be revealed to you in the fullness of time."

"I'm not sure if that sounds mysterious or ominous."

"Maybe both," said Lachie, beaming with mischief.

The waiter arrived, and Lachie ordered two poached eggs, salt cod, potatoes, onion, baked beans, and chow chow, which struck me as a very strange combination. I chose two fried eggs, peameal bacon, black pudding, sausage, griddled potatoes, devilled tomato and roasted mushrooms. My choice came with baked beans, but I asked the waiter to omit them from my plate.

"Murdoch seems like a decent guy," I said.

"He is a decent guy. I don't know him awfully well, but I gather he's widowed and has one of the largest farms in Pictou County."

"And Harold?"

"I know almost nothing about Harold other than meeting him at group functions. I think he's an accountant. He seems innocuous to me."

"That's a strange way of putting it."

"Maybe."

"What about Donald, himself?"

"Ah, I've known him for at least thirty years. We are members of several other groups and committees. He has a trucking company in Arisaig. And he has his fingers in a number of other businesses. He's a fine fellow and no mistake."

"What's your story, Lachie?"

"Mine? I have some woodlots and a bit of farmland. My wife died some years ago, leaving me with three sons, Angus, Cullum and Archie. But, Marc..."

"Yes?"

"Why don't you get to the point," he said, grinning from ear to ear. "It's not any of us you really want to ask about, is it."

I was embarrassed. Lachie had seen right through what I thought was rather subtle subterfuge. I grinned back. "You're right."

"It's that conceited little popinjay you want to know about, isn't it?"

"Yes, it is." I laughed.

"Duncan's been spoiled. He never wanted for anything, never had to work for anything, and he's the apple of his father's eye."

"I see. He seems to be—"

"A proper little prick?"

"Well, yes." I was both surprised and amused by his frankness. "Is he employed?"

"He does some work for the family business, but, as far as I can tell, most of his time is spent on his studies."

"What kind of studies."

"Studies of Scotland, of course."

"Ah. Of course."

"Yes, he knows everything there is to know about Scotland's history and traditions. Traditions which he rigorously maintains. He is very committed to all things Scottish and has very strong opinions."

"About?"

"Everything, but especially the infamous Act of Union in 1706, and the grievances springing from that act."

"Do the Scottish have many grievances?"

"Indeed, the Scottish people—by which I mean the Highland people—have many grievances, bitter and brutal." A look came over his face which slightly disconcerted me. "Duncan has looked into all of these, making them a study of a lifetime, and, as Burns says, he nurtures his wrath to keep it warm."

"I see. A fanatic?"

"Not a term I would use myself, but I guess you could say that. He loves to dress up—as you have seen—as sometimes boast that his father is the *Ceann Cinnid*."

"The what?"

"It means the clan chieftain. In his case, *An Siosalach*."

"What does *that* mean?"

"The Chisholm."

"So is Donald The Chisholm? Chieftain of Clan Chisholm?"

"I shouldn't think so. I haven't looked into it, but it seems very unlikely. I doubt there is one nowadays. I guess you might be able to trace some ancestors, but I think the last of the direct line passed away in the 1850s."

"Does Duncan still dream of Bonnie Prince Charlie?"

"Probably." Lachie laughed out loud. "Useless little coward, he was. He recklessly led his people to certain destruction at Culloden and then fled, ending up in France, drinking himself to death."

"Sounds like Duncan's not the only one with strong opinions."

"The Scottish people—"

"By which you mean the Highlanders?"

"Yes. The Highlanders were loyal and devoted to their leaders but nearly all of those leaders were unworthy of that loyalty. Especially James Stuart and his son, Charles."

"Well, Lachie, this has been both a pleasure and an education," I said, rising. "I shan't see you at the next group meeting, but likely I will at the one after that."

"I'll look forward to that, Marc. *Biodh do bheannachdan lìonm-*

hor, agus do thrioblaidean tearc."

"Goodbye Lachie. *Bonne chance à toi et à ton entourage."*

I drove the Bugatti down to Point Pleasant Park, left it in the lot, and wandered into the tree-lined trails. It had been years since I was last here, and I had forgotten how large the park was and how many lanes and tracks traversed it. I quickly realized that my chances of finding Patrick were slight.

Several times I tried calling Stalker's name, but to no avail. The animal did not know me, and even had it heard me calling, there was no reason why it would come to me.

Then I started stopped everyone I met, asking them if they had seen a man with a bloodhound. At length two young women told me that had, and pointed in the direction of the sea.

When I finally found them, Patrick was sprawled on a bench overlooking the ocean, with Stalker happily snoozing by his feet.

Patrick smiled up at me and patted the bench beside him. "Sit. Didn't expect to see you so soon, Marc."

"I was in town for a meeting of the Single Malt Society last night and thought I would look you up today."

"There's a Single Malt Society?"

"Oh yes, and they take themselves very seriously. I've only joined recently. This was my first meeting."

"Try many single malts?"

"Six."

"Any good ones?"

"A couple were superb."

"No doubt incompatible with the budget of an RCMP officer."

"I should think so. One of the malts, brought by an arrogant little toad, would cost all of $10,000 a bottle."

"Wow! Obviously not the place for me!"

We sat in silence for several minutes, watching a large tanker creeping along the horizon. On the beach and rocks below us a congregation of gulls was noisily arguing over what looked like a wet cardboard box. Stalker made a spluttering sound, then rolled over and went back to sleep.

Patrick sighed deeply and hoisted himself up on the bench. "What is it, Mark? Mrs. Withers again?"

"Since you ask, yes. I have spent some time with her. Also with the deceased's half-sister. Charming old lady of 86."

"And what did you learn from them?"

"First, the man was 250 pounds and 6'3" tall."

"So?"

"His tub was minuscule. He could not possibly have drowned without either being drugged or being pushed, and likely both."

"But since the man has now been cremated, there is nothing further you can do, even assuming you are correct that foul play has taken place."

"True. Unless...."

"Unless what?"

"Unless I could find a motive."

"No motive, no suspect, eh?"

"Precisely."

"Enemies?"

"None that anyone knows of."

"You can't manufacture a motive out of thin air, Marc."

"I know. Shall we walk?"

"Sure." Patrick stood up and stretched. As he did so, Stalker jumped up and started panting. "Say hello to Stalker, Marc."

"Hello, Stalker," I said, stroking him. He was huge, about waist high, about 110 lbs and with a multi-wrinkled, lugubrious face.

"Patrick," I said interrupting of the crunch of our feet on the gravel path. We were almost back to the parking lot.

Slightly irritated, he turned to me. "I can read you like a book, Marc LeBlanc. You want to know more about my unsolved murders."

"Well, yes—"

"And if I don't tell you now, you'll pester me incessantly until I do."

"Patrick, what a thing to say!"

"Oh, alright. I don't have the files at home, so let's go to the office. I suppose you'll come to dinner tonight."

"Oh, well, I—"

"That means yes. I'll call Ruth and let her know."

"Thanks, Patrick."

"Need a bed, too?"

"No. I'm booked into the Muir."

"The Muir! Alright for some, living the life of Riley. Just don't expect Ruth to have smoked ortolans on Melba toast with a Madeira sauce tonight. It'll probably be sausages and mashed turnips."

"Suits me fine. Any wine?"

"Maybe Hungarian plonk. If you're lucky."

~

We drove to my hotel, where I dropped off the Bugatti, then we went over to Dartmouth in Patrick's car.

At H Division headquarters, after Patrick had signed me in at the security gate, we went upstairs and walked the length of the building to his corner office. It being a Saturday, I expected the offices to be deserted, but the place was a hive of activity.

On the way to his office, Patrick stopped by one room, opened the door with his photo ID and took three files out of a large cabinet. I was surprised at how slim they appeared. Holding all three in his right hand, Patrick slapped them against his thigh as he walked.

Once we got to his office, he turned to me. "Sit down, Marc.

Again I must impress upon you that what I tell you is in the utmost confidence."

"Sure. I understand."

"I hope you do. If this thing goes tits-up as a result of your reck-lessness, I shall find myself back on the beat."

"Understood."

"In no particular order, first, Leonard Lake. Fifty-six years of age; single. Lived in Ogden. Well, actually between Ogden and West Roachvale, south-west of the town of Guysborough on the Salmon River Lake Road. He had been a long-standing member of the com-munity ever since he came there when he was a young man—"

"Where did he come from?"

"Um…it doesn't say. Respected citizen and neighbour. Had a gen-eral store until he became disabled two years ago."

"How?"

"How what?"

"How did he become disabled?"

"Doesn't say. Oh, wait a minute. Yes, it does. Car accident when he was driving in icy road conditions. Hurt his hip and leg, so had difficulty walking. Sold his store but continued to reside in the community."

"Okay. Go on."

"Fire Brigade called out to a fierce house blaze on the night of May 2 at 11.32. It was thought to be a regular fire until they found him tied to a chair. Body was in an advanced state of damage, but there was just sufficient uncombusted material to identify the vic-tim. Chair was metal, likely steel, and had buckled under intense heat. Victim was confined to the chair by means of plastic rope, which had largely melted and combined with burned flesh. Rope of a similar type, yellow in colour, was discovered in a nearby shed. Subsequent investigations discovered a common accelerant had been used."

"Motive?"

"None."

"Suspects."

"None."

"None? No enemies, no arguments with neighbours, no run-ins with young punks?"

"Nary a one. Victim was very well liked. In recent years had kept himself to himself."

"Huh!"

"Look, Marc, there's so little in these files, I'll just make copies of the other two and we'll take them with us."

"Are you allowed to do that?"

"Not strictly speaking, but today I'm in charge while the Chief Super's away, so I'm ruling that exigent circumstances require me to study them at home."

"Okay."

Stalker roused himself and followed us to the car. He hopped into the back and we drove to the Kennedy's house on Beech Street in the city's west end. It was the kind of dwelling which is both modest and substantial at the same time, in that it was a fair size, but was not in least showy.

As we walked up the driveway, I realized that, although I had known Patrick for almost four years, I had no idea if he and Ruth had any children. They were both in their fifties now, so if they had offspring, I imagined they would either be at college or out in the world earning their living.

Ruth greeted me warmly at the front door. She was a cheery, well upholstered woman, wearing "sensible" clothes. She had particles of flour on her hands and cheeks, and in her hair.

"When Pat told me you were coming to dinner, I knew I had do something special," she said. "So, I abandoned the left-overs Pat and I were going to have. I'll give them to Stalker instead."

"You're teasing me, Ruth. Patrick has already done the routine about my being a food snob, so you don't have to keep it up. I am able to take nourishment without having foie gras and Champagne, you know."

"I'm glad to hear that," she said with a laugh. "Where do you stand on steak and kidney pie?"

"I love it!" I said truthfully.

"And I'll search the basement to see if I can find a bottle of wine," Patrick said.

"Pat, when you've found a bottle, you guys can retire to your den. Dinner will be about an hour."

"Okay, sweetheart. Marc, come downstairs with me. You can help me choose."

In the basement, I was surprised to see row upon row of shelves bearing twinkling bottles. I hadn't known Patrick was that much of a wine lover, nor such a specialized one. All the wine was Italian, some of it quite old and of high quality.

"I fell in love with Italy and its wine shortly after I fell in love with Ruth," he said. "We went there on our honeymoon, and the rest is history."

"I think that's marvellous."

"Now, Marc, what do you think will go with steak and kidney pie?"

"Hmm. I'd say an old Barolo, an even older Brunello, or—" I broke off because at that moment I saw several bottles of Sassicaia 1998. "Or this. This would be perfect."

"I agree. Now, please select another, slightly gentler bottle, to go with the appetizer. Ruth is making *melanzane*. She just grills the eggplant and sprinkles a little cheese on top."

"Sound wonderful."

I walked along the shelves until I noticed a bottle of 1997 Castello di Fonterutoli, Chianti Classico. "This would be my choice.

Maybe my first pick if we could only have one bottle."

"Then this is your lucky day, because we can have both."

We took the wines upstairs to the dining room, where Patrick decanted both bottles over a candle flame to make sure no sediment remained in the wine. Then he poured two glasses of the *Fonterutoli*, grabbed the files he had copied, then led me to his den.

"Right," he said, sitting in a big arm chair. "Case Number Two. Struan Robertson, aged 60, Lakevale, on the Sunrise Trail in Antigonish County. Victim was reported missing by his wife on April 3rd of this year. Twelve days later, Robertson was discovered in a barn some five miles from home. Victim was tied to a supporting beam and was severely dehydrated. Post mortem revealed that Robertson had ingested neither food nor water for well in excess of a week. Cause of death inanition."

"Inanition?"

"Starvation, to you and me."

"Suspects?"

"None."

"So, no motive?"

"Not that we can determine."

"Nobody had any disagreements with him?"

"Not that we find. Door-to-door canvassing took place over a twenty-mile area."

"What did Mrs. Robertson have to say?"

"Nothing of any use. She was completely bewildered."

"Hmm."

We paused to try the wine which was now opening up in the glasses. The aroma was superb, and it tasted delicious, of black cherries with a hint of raisins.

"Next," I said.

"Okay. April 17th. Alex Gillespie, aged 45, of South Harbour, Victoria County, Cape Breton. Single. Victim worked at a store in Dingwall, a few miles from his home, part of a house which he rented from a Douglas Rankin. When Gillespie didn't turn up for work several days in a row and couldn't be reached by telephone, the store owner called the landlord. Rankin let himself into Gillespie's unit, but there was no sign of him or that he had recently been there. After searching the area for over a week, officers from the Ingonish detachment discovered the victim naked and tied to a tree just off the Cabot Trail, southwest of Cape North. Medical opinion was that he had expired as a result of hypothermia—or exposure. Given the weather at the time, around or below zero with snowstorms, the victim was judged to have been at the mercy of the elements for about three days."

"Motive?"

"Who knows? What motive could anyone have for leaving a man out in the woods for several days?"

"Suspects?"

"None."

"Enemies?"

"Not that can be discerned. Apparently he was well liked and customers at the store said he was always friendly and polite."

"Patrick, be honest with me. These murders are connected, aren't they?"

"How are they? There's nothing to connect them."

"Except that there was no motive and no suspects in each case."

"That is an absence of evidence. An absence of evidence is not evidence that there is no evidence. It just means we haven't found it yet."

"And you won't concede any similarity between your cases and Bill Withers'?"

"I can't. I have to go by facts, not feelings. I'm not saying that they cannot be connected or that subsequent investigation may not find they are connected. I'm saying that as of now, there is nothing on which any firm conclusions can be based."

"I guess you're right." I took a sip of the Chianti. "My God, this is spectacular."

"It is rather good isn't it? And my guess is that the *Sassicaia* will be even better. Let's go down. Ruth will likely be ready to serve soon."

6

When I got back to Wolfville the next day, I related to Rosalie everything I had learned while I was in Halifax. She insisted on hearing every detail, even about the Single Malt event, and it took me almost an hour to cover that, the interview with Valerie Withers and the information I had received from Patrick.

She sat back, just looking at me for several minutes.

"What are you thinking?" I asked.

"I'm thinking that you're correct. Without a suspect or motive you can't go any further with the Withers case."

"No. I really don't see any way forward."

"But Marc..."

"What?"

"If it's your considered judgment that foul play took place, then I think you have a duty to tell Mrs. Withers."

"You think? Won't that raise expectations—if you can call them that—which can't be fulfilled?"

"Maybe, but you have to tell her something. You just can't take off for Wales in two days' time and leave her hanging."

"Two days' time? I thought we were going later in the month."

"I brought everything forward. I've rearranged flights, bookings, the lot."

"Wow. Thanks for telling me."

"You've nothing on. You said you wanted to get away."

"I guess. Yes, okay. Why not? So, you think I should call Valerie Withers before I go?"

"Yes, I do. Today."

"Right. I may as well do it right away."

The wretched Norman answered the phone, and when I told

him who was calling, he grunted and slammed down the receiver. Soon Valerie picked it up.

"Hello, Mr. LeBlanc. Did you see Iris?"

"Yes, I did. I spent quite a bit of time with her."

"Oh good. Did you learn anything from her which was any good?"

"I'm afraid not. Mrs. Withers—"

"Valerie, please."

"Valerie, there's something I must tell you."

"Yes?"

"I believe your husband was murdered—"

"So! I knew it!"

"But wait. You must understand that I have no proof, no evidence whatever to support my belief. It's just that—a conviction....a hunch, if you like."

"What would you need to be sure?"

"As I said, we would need a motive, and a suspect, in order to investigate any further. You haven't remembered anything, like a fight or an argument, anything like that?"

"No, I'm afraid not."

"Did you overhear any phone conversations he might have had which were in any way heated?"

"No, none."

"Did he get any letters which upset him?"

"No, nothing like that. Oh..."

"Yes?"

"Well there was some religious flyer that came in the mail. Bill did curse a bit over that. He is...he was...an atheist, you know."

"Do you still have the flyer and the envelope?"

"Not the envelope. That would have gone straight into the garbage. I might have stuffed the flyer into the old vase to tease Bill with sometime."

"Will you go and look, please?"

"Yes, right away. Shall I call you back?"

"No, that's alright. I'll wait."

I heard her footsteps move away from the phone, then her muttering to herself, and then returning and shuffling papers.

"Yes, here it is."

"Please read it to me. Very slowly, so I can take it down."

"Alright. At the top it says: 'Bible Thought of the Day', then underneath it says: 'It is mine to avenge; I will repay. In due time their foot will slip; their day of disaster is near and their doom rushes upon them. Deuteronomy 32:35'."

"Is that all it says?"

"Yes, that's all."

"No handwritten notes on the back. No marks of any kind?"

"No, not a thing Mr. LeBlanc."

"Read it to me again, please, to make sure I have it down right."

She re-read the flyer. With the exception of her mispronouncing 'Deuteronomy' differently each time, it was identical with the first reading.

"Do you think it means something?" she asked.

"I don't know, but I would guess it does."

"What do you think it means?"

"I have no idea, Valerie. I have no idea."

It was true, I did not. I was forming some very vague notions in my head, but was not ready to verbalize them.

"Look, I am leaving for Europe the day after tomorrow. I shall give this a great deal of thought. If I come up with anything—which is very unlikely—I'll call you."

~

I went back to the kitchen, where Rosalie was brewing coffee, and described the conversation I had with Valerie. She took the notebook from me and earnestly read what I had written.

"Hmm," she said, "Clearly, the day of doom rushed upon poor Bill Withers, but why?"

"Search me."

"It is mine to avenge. I will repay. Presumably, Bill's death was the payment, but what was it avenging?"

"I have no idea, darling. But I know I must call Patrick and alert him of this."

"Good idea."

Patrick seemed surprised when I told him about the flyer.

"You've had nothing like this in any of your cases?"

"No, but then our people may not have asked if the victims received any strange mail in the weeks leading up to their murders."

"But you'll make inquiries? You'll get the facts?"

"Oh, you amateurs! I've been a policeman for over thirty years and here you are asking me if I'm going to do my job properly. Of course I'll find out if the victims got strange mail!"

"Sorry."

"So you should be. I'll let you know what I find out."

"Thanks, Patrick. We're going to Wales in two days."

"How long for?"

"Not certain. It depends on events. Maybe three weeks, maybe a month. We're going to try to trace Rosalie's ancestors."

"Well, have a nice time. Oh, and Marc..."

"Yes?"

"Make sure you get the facts."

We had a quiet dinner of Potage St. Germain, bright-green pea soup with mint and a swirl of cream, then baked salmon with asparagus and Hollandaise sauce. We sipped some 2005 white Chateau Haut Brion with the soup, and had a lovely 2002 Domaine Leroy Corton Charlemagne with the fish.

We had an early night, but I did not actually sleep until well after midnight. I felt I had answers close to my fingertips, but not close enough to know what they were.

Finally, I drifted off, hoping that my doom would not come rushing to me in the night.

7

The flight to the United Kingdom was uneventful and we arrived on time at Heathrow Airport at 9 pm. We disembarked, cleared immigration and customs, and got to our hotel a little before 10. There was a line-up at the desk so it was 10:20 before we were shown to our room. Although it was only 6:20 Halifax time, we did not feel like eating, so we went straight to bed.

The next day presented a typical British morning: grey and raining. We had a very standard breakfast and, after a while, checked out and dragged our baggage to a location which a sign told us was the waiting place for Hertz customers. Soon the distinctive bright-yellow mini bus came and took us to the company's depot on the North Perimeter Road.

As a Gold Card client, I had no paperwork to do, so I picked up my key and went out into the lot.

It was not difficult to spot the black Jaguar F-Pace among the other vehicles, so we loaded our suitcases and climbed in. Initially I was unpleasantly surprised to find that the car was an automatic, much preferring a standard gear shift which, of course, I have in the Bugatti. However, I had no doubt I would get used to the lazy way of driving after I had been on the road for an hour or two.

We edged out onto the M4 motorway and headed west for the 456-metre-long Prince of Wales Bridge over the River Severn. On the other side we branched off the motorway onto the 449 towards Raglan.

About half way along that road we took a detour into the charming old town of Usk, (Brynbuga in Welsh), and walked about in a fine blowing drizzle. Rosalie loved the quaint old clock tower in the town square, the picturesque narrow streets, and the ancient bridge over the River Usk (Wysg).

Since it was now midday, we went into the Castle Inn, more for shelter than from hunger. There we shared some fish and chips, and Rosalie had a glass of Pinot Grigio while I had a very welcome pint of bitter ale.

After lunch, the weather cleared up and the sun started to peep over the blanket of clouds. Ten minutes' driving brought us to Raglan, a rather nondescript little town, but with a spectacular castle.

We paid nine pounds each for our tickets, went in and wandered around. Rosalie was in seventh heaven, nosing and poking into every corner. Apparently, this castle had been the seat of the earls of Worcester, and in later years became a fashionable house with magnificent gardens and a famous long gallery. In spite of a very large garrison of troops, the castle fell to Cromwell after one of the longest sieges of the Civil War, after which it was wrecked and plundered. Rosalie was still singing its praises after we were on the road to Tal y Bont (which means 'high bridge' in Welsh).

At first we had a fast stretch of very good road as far as Abergavenny (Y Fenni) when we came unstuck at a roundabout just outside the town. We found the road signs so confusing we circled three times before finally picking the right turning onto the Heads of The Valleys road.

At a place called Gilwern there was another tortuous roundabout which disgorged us onto a town street, and then a sharp right by the Beaufort Arms pub. Once we were through the town there were 13 miles of a narrow, twisting road alongside the River Ywsg ahead of us.

A few miles along this road, when we came to a small village called Llangynidr, Rosalie cried out, "This is where the Chartists hid their weapons in 1839."

"No kidding?"

"Up on the mountain there is a huge, deep cave where the rebels stockpiled their guns and pikes and stuff, in advance of their march on Newport. Can we go and see it?"

"Not now. We'd better check it out with someone who knows

the area. I've heard that the tops of the mountains hereabouts have a lot of dangerous sinkholes."

"What're they?"

"It happens when the ground surface collapses. Rainfall seeping through the ground absorbs carbon dioxide and reacts with decaying vegetation, creating an acidic water which dissolves limestone and creates a network of holes."

"I don't like the sound of them."

"You certainly wouldn't if you fell into one."

"How come you know so much about them?"

"I didn't until our first case a few years ago. Remember when I had to tramp through the barrens near Baddeck?"

"Oh yes," she said. "Those were sinkholes?"

"Lots of them. I nearly died that day."

"We'd best not take chances then."

As we wound our way along this road we noticed that for much of the distance we not only had the river on our right, but a canal parallel with the road on our left. I knew from a previous visit to the area that this canal ran from Brecon (Honddu), the old county town, to Gilwern and beyond.

Finally we reached Tal y Bont. The Travellers (formerly The Travelers' Rest) was a smallish, low inn on the left-hand side just before the main village. Here we introduced ourselves to two of the nicest people we have ever met, Joy and Doug Browning, the owners.

Joy, a friendly, outgoing woman, managed the front of house, while Doug, the more reserved, spent most of his time in the kitchen, where he did the cooking. We were given the Blue Room, situated in the front of the inn with windows overlooking the Usk valley towards Llangorse Mountain.

We unpacked and, since it was late afternoon, decided to stroll around the village before dinner. Towards the village there was a narrow road to the left which took us to a bridge over the canal. The waterway was a lot busier than we anticipated, there being five or six barges, or narrow boats, as they are known, some moored, others chugging in both directions.

After my previous visit, I learned that the canal opened in 1800 to transport lime, coal and iron to Newport and agricultural products to Brecon. Just over the bridge to our right were about a dozen lime kilns built into a great wall. Raw materials for the kilns came from limestone quarries high in the mountains, some eight miles away, and were transported to this spot via a horse-drawn tramway.

I explained to Rosalie that this tramway was built in 1815 and served the Bryn Oer collieries and the limestone quarries, dropping 330 metres, or 1,080 feet, along its route to the canal, running down a steep set of mountains and through forest for much of the way. Years before, I had walked several miles of the track and because of the steepness and because stone sleepers remained in place, it was one of the roughest and most uncomfortable walks I have ever had.

The finished product of lime was loaded from the kilns onto barges and shipped to factories in the South Wales Valleys, where it was used to convert iron into 'pig iron' which was later processed into steel. Lime was also used to extend the life of the furnaces.

We strolled for a while along the footpath by the canal. In days when the narrow boats were pulled by horses, this would have been the towpath. Except for some gentle chugging of engines, it was quite peaceful, and Rosalie particularly liked the way the trees hung over on either side to form a tunnel of leaves.

We followed the footpath until we came to another bridge, one which lifted to allow boats to pass. We crossed the bridge and walked for about a mile until we came to a little village called Aber, which consisted of a narrow main street with small houses and cottages on either side.

Rosalie proclaimed herself to be in love with Aber, so we agreed we would come back the next day and continue from there to the reservoir, another mile further on.

Apparently, the lake, or reservoir was originally a narrow valley of some 318 acres until it was flooded to provide water for the city of Newport, 40 miles away to the southeast. The work started in

1926 and was in full operation by 1939. The flooding consigned 17 farms and houses to a watery grave and I teased Rosalie, saying that if we looked very carefully, we might be able to see their roofs under the surface.

We said a temporary farewell to Aber (which means 'estuary' in English) and strolled back along the main street, passing two pubs, The Star and The White Hart. We arrived back at The Travellers tired and hungry.

After a quick wash and change we went down to a spacious, well-lit dining room, where an always-smiling Joy waited on us. Doug gave us a little wave from the back of the room and disappeared to the kitchen.

We started with massive prawns sautéed in garlic and lemon, then had the roast lamb with three vegetables and gravy. With our meal we decided to try Welsh wines, made locally, so to start we had a bottle of Gwin Gwyn ('Wine from the River Wye') white made with the Phoenix grape, one previously unknown to me. From the same vineyard, White Castle, we had their Pinot Noir with our main course. The food was spectacular, and the wines interesting but underwhelming.

As we were preparing to leave, Joy came hurrying to the table. "There's a phone call for you," she said. "From Canada."

"I wonder who it could be," said Rosalie. "I hope it's not bad news."

"We'll soon find out," I said, following Joy to a quiet spot where I could take the call.

"Hello."

"Marc?"

"Yes, who's that? This is a terrible line."

"It's Patrick."

"Good God. How did you track me down here?"

"I'm a detective, remember?"

"How could I forget? What's up?"

"Alex Gillespie."

"He's the case in northern Cape Breton, right?"

"Yes."

"What about him?"

"When they were clearing out his place, they found a bunch of unopened mail, flyers and the like."

"So?"

"In one of the envelopes was an unsigned Biblical message."

"Really? Just like Bill Withers. What did it say?"

"I'll read it to you. 'Doom has come upon you—you who dwell in the land. The time has come, the day is near; there is panic, not joy, upon the mountains. I am about to pour out my wrath on you and spend my anger against you; I will judge you according to your conduct and repay you for all your detestable practices. Ezekiel 7.'"

"Wow! So now are you convinced the cases are all linked?" I must confess I was gloating a little.

"I think that two cases—Withers and Gillespie—may well be linked. Can't say about the others. We'll go back and take another look at the Robertson case. His widow may have forgotten him receiving a message, or he may have concealed it from her."

"Good. What about the guy in Guysborough County? What was his name?"

"Leonard Lake?"

"Yes, what about him?"

"He was killed in a massive fire, remember? We'd hardly find a piece of mail in that burned out place."

"I guess not. Well, thanks for bringing me up to date, Patrick. I appreciate it."

"Don't mention it, Buddy. Have a good vacation."

When I got up to the room Rosalie was changing into her nightie.

"Who was that?"

"Patrick."

"What did he want?"

"To tell me that one of his victims also received a warning from the Bible. Just like Withers."

"That's interesting. It can't be a coincidence, can it?"

"I don't see how."

"Well, just don't get any ideas about cutting our trip short, Marc.

We're here to relax and have a lovely time. The murdered men will still be dead when we get home."

Jeremy Akerman

8

The next day we set out very early, because we knew we had a lot of territory to cover. We had no time for breakfast, but Joy had kindly prepared some ham and cheese sandwiches which she had wrapped and left for us. We planned to get water from one of the many mountain streams in the area.

The sun was barely up, and was very pale, as we passed through Aber village and made our way along the reservoir until we came to the huge dam, which we walked across in order to take photographs of the looming mountains on the western side. Nearby there was a spectacular spread of wild rhododendrons in a variety of colours, which contrasted delightfully with the deep green of the forests behind.

Standing at the foot of Tor y Foel (Bald Mountain) at the eastern end of the damn, Rosalie took pictures of Craig y Fan (Rocky Place), the first of six mountains in a range, of which Pen y Fan (Top Place) was the most famous and dramatic, at 2,900 feet high.

At length we came to a few houses and a stream, which a sign told us was Abercynafon ('estuary before the river'), where we greedily ate our sandwiches and filled our flasks from the Caerfanell River, which had its source high in the mountains and ran into the reservoir.

I tried to translate the name of the river, using my Welsh dictionary, but the best I could come up with was "panelled fort" which didn't sound at all right.

After a brief rest, we soldiered on as the road became progressively steeper until it felt as if we were scaling an almost-vertical hill. I needed to rest every hundred yards but, being fitter than I, Rosalie plodded on, unhelpfully calling, "Come on, slowpoke. We haven't got all day!"

When I got to the top, Rosalie was sitting smugly on a rocky bank, basking in the now-hot sun.

Nearby, next to an idyllic stream, we found a pathway to the top of a curious conical mountain called Craig y Fan Ddu, which, as far as I could discover, roughly translated into English as "The place of the black rock." We sat for a few moments listening to the sounds of birds and insects, then bent our backs and began the ascent.

It was very hard going because we did not have the correct footwear for climbing, and it took us the best part of an hour to reach the summit, but when we got there the views were breathtaking.

We could now see that our mountain did not stand alone, as we had thought, but was part of a range, the peaks of which were all connected. From here we could see the great Pen y Fan and its partner Corn Du, which means 'Black Horn'.

When we got closer to it some hours later, it looked nothing like a horn and a lot like a black crown (which would be Coron Ddu), so I speculated that English mapmakers had misheard or misreported what the local Welsh had told them were the names of topographical features.

The hours we spent walking on the roof of the Brecon Beacons, as these mountains were collectively called, were among the most blissful either of us has ever experienced, and if we had had a tent, we would have happily stayed up there for several days. But while the weather had been perfect, with little wind, I knew that in Wales, meteorological conditions rarely stayed the same for long, that cloud and rain could come quickly, and that it would be miserable up here in a storm.

I had forgotten to bring my compass, but we followed the lay of the land, were sure we knew where we were going, and set off along the mountain tops in roughly an easterly direction. We knew Tal y Bont was somewhere to our east, so we resolved to travel away from the gradually-setting sun.

The vistas were absolutely spectacular, our being able to see as far as fifty miles in every direction.

People generally think that it is in the thick of forests where they get lost, and that to become disoriented on top of a mountain range is difficult. They are wrong. So enamoured of the scenery were we, that Rosalie and I wandered blindly onward, and got completely lost.

While we were admiring LLangorse Lake, away to our right, it occurred to me that we were too far to the north of where we should have been. So, seeing what looked like an old farm track, we followed it downhill for a mile and a half until we came out in a quaint little village, which a road sign announced as being Llan-frynach. I figured out from my dictionary that this meant the Hill Church, but when we came to the gray stone building and its spa-cious graveyard, it was on flat ground.

We walked tiredly on, and rejoiced when we saw a sign for a pub, the White Swan, ahead. We quickened our pace, visions of cooling pints and snacks driving us on, but were devastated to find that the place was permanently closed.

We crossed the street and wearily sat on the churchyard wall, wondering where we were and if we would get back to Tal y Bont before nightfall. Just then a man, who had been washing the win-dows of one of the cottages next to the pub, threw his chamois into his bucket and came over to us.

"London, are you from?" he asked.

"No, Canada," said Rosalie.

"Canada is it? *Dew.* That's a long way."

"Yes."

"Come off the mountain, have you?"

"Yes, I'm afraid we're lost."

"Lost is it? Where you going?"

"Tal y Bont."

"Tal y Bont. *Da grasol!* That's only ten minutes away."

"Really?"

"Aye, down this road by yere," he said pointing past the pub.

"Thank you very much," said Rosalie." We wouldn't have known which way to go."

"Listen," he said. "Lemme put my bucket away or some bugger'll pinch it. Then I'll give you a drive in my van."

"Thank you."

"Don't mention it. You just wait by there."

In a few minutes he had moved his van from where it was parked a little way up the street, and pulled it alongside us.

"'Op in. I got some rubbish on the back seat, but just you push it to one side, like. You'll only be in there a couple of minutes."

We squeezed in and did our best to dislodge a pile of what looked like wallpaper pattern books.

He roared off down the narrow lanes at what seemed like a breakneck speed.

"Where you 'eading?"

"Traveler's Rest."

"Oh aye. With Doug and Joy?"

"Yes."

"There's tidy. Good people, they are."

"Indeed," I said.

He screeched to a halt outside the hotel and disgorged us with a grin. "If you're ever in Llanfrynach again, look me up. Elijah Ellis is the name."

We stumbled inside just in time to have a wash and get down again for dinner. We were ravenous, and had no problem putting away Doug's luscious soup and the roast beef with Yorkshire pudding.

We had no idea how many miles we had walked that day, but it seemed like a hundred. We were so sore and tired that, after dinner, we climbed the stairs and went straight to bed.

9

After our initial foray on the mountains of Wales, Rosalie was anxious to try to pursue her family connections. Since I was still sore from our exertions, I voiced no opposition as most of the travel involved in her research would be done by car.

As it turned out, her efforts were largely disappointing, because many hours spent in musty libraries and town halls, and an equal number of hours in wet churchyards, revealed very little of what she hoped for, and none of what she expected.

Her previous, reluctant conclusion that she was not related to the Chartist leader, John Frost, was confirmed. However, the most likely leads pointed to a Rhys Frost who did not seem to have been at all the kind of person Rosalie wanted in her family! We found him cropping up in reports of the miners' strike of 1910-11 in the small town of Tonypandy, which is some twenty miles northwest of Wales' capital, Cardiff. This little place is a typical, rather dismal, former mining community which had seen a more prosperous, but also a more violent, past.

The town is infamous for one of Wales's greatest and most often perpetuated myths, namely that the-then Home Secretary, Winston Churchill, had personally been responsible for the death of a miner, Samuel Rees. The strike was bitter, and hand-to-hand fighting had broken out, involving widespread destruction of commercial property. The local authorities asked London to intervene with armed troops, but Churchill felt that the local authorities were overreacting and instead dispatched London police, but also sent some cavalry troops to stand by in Cardiff.

Later, when events had escalated even further, the local magistrates asked for military support and the troops were mobilized.

From that day to this the miners' unions and the other political parties have endlessly repeated, with considerable success, the calumny against Churchill as proof that the Conservatives were the enemy of the people. The real irony was that Churchill was actually a Liberal at the time he is alleged to have committed the heinous deed!

I think Rosalie was hoping that her ancestor would have been a working-class hero who had led the strikers, but search though she might, she could find nothing along those lines. What she did turn up was a newspaper report to the effect that Rhys Frost had been attacked by a group of miners who accused him of assisting the troops!

Subsequent research was even less encouraging. She found that Rhys had only moved to Tonypandy a few months previously, from Tredegar, another mining town four valleys over to the east. There, Rhys had been involved as one of the leaders of anti-Semitic riots when the miners attacked and pillaged twenty local shops owned by Jews. After several days, the chief constable of Monmouthshire called on the Home Office for help, and again Winston Churchill obliged, describing it as an anti-Jewish pogrom, and the riots came to an end.

Clearly, Rosalie was unhappy with her discoveries. "Well!" She said disgustedly. "This genealogy is for the birds!"

"Yes, it is a bit like political polls."

"What on earth do you mean?"

"People love them when they tell them what they want to hear, but hate them when they don't."

"Yes, I guess you have a point. If I'm being honest, I would rather Rhys had been a more attractive character."

"You are attractive enough to make up for the entire family's failings, my darling."

"Thanks," said Rosalie, blowing me a kiss. "What do we do now?"

"There are lots of beautiful places to see in Wales, but before we do that, why don't we retrace the movements of John Frost in 1839?"

"You mean follow the Chartists to Newport, where the riot occurred?"

"Yes."

"Okay, I'm game. Where first?"

"There won't likely be much to see which connects with the Chartists in these old mining towns, but we should go to each place from which the three main forces left. Or were supposed to leave from."

"Remind me what they are."

"The first is Blackwood," I said looking at the map. "That's where Frost's crowd left from. That's in the Sirhowy Valley. Then two valleys over is Nantyglo, in the Ebbw Fach valley."

"That where Zephaniah Williams was?"

"Correct. Then, in another valley to the east is Pontypool, which is in the Afon Lwyd Valley. That means 'the gray river.' I can't remember who the Chartist leader was there."

"Let me see...."—Rosalie had her laptop open and was checking her notes—"That would be William Jones."

"That's him. Wasn't he the guy who didn't show up for the pre-riot rendezvous?"

"Yes. I'm not sure why he let the others down, but his non-appearance delayed their march on Newport."

"Where were the three wings of this citizen's army supposed to meet?"

"At Rogerstone. Just outside Newport. We should go there, too."

"Sure. So, that makes five visits in all, including Newport itself."

"Yes...no."

"Yes, no?"

"Rogerstone is out."

"Why?"

"I've just seen on the net that the Welsh Oak Inn where Chartists met was burned in a fire in 2017 and has since been demolished."

"Damn, I was hoping to get a pint there."

"You can get a pint in any one of three thousand and ten pubs in Wales."

"Thanks: you're all heart. This means we can probably do it in two days. One day for the valley mining towns and another for

Newport."

"And then?"

"We'll check out of The Travellers and go into central, west and north Wales."

"Sounds good. Will you help me draw up an itinerary tonight?"

"Certainly. Let's head back now."

~

When we got back to the Inn, we had another lovely dinner cooked by Doug. I chose a simple, but excellent, trout dish to start, while Rosalie ordered a creamy scallop concoction which she said was superb. Then we both had roast pork with wonderful crackling and lots of vegetables. Our choice of Chablis to drink went surprisingly well with the food. Neither of us felt like dessert, so we went out to watch the sunset, then headed upstairs.

Once in the room, I decided to call my answering machine to see if there was anything from Louise about a shipment of wine which was very late being delivered. There was nothing from Louise, but, to my surprise, there was a message from Iris Withers.

"Oh Mr. LeBlanc, it's Iris Withers here," she said. "After you left here I was searching my mind about the old times and racking my brains about possible enemies Bill might have had. Then I re-membered the Wind in the Willows camp. That was a summer camp for children—non-denominational—in Guysborough County, I think. I recalled there had been a bit of a ruckus when Bill was a camp counsellor there. I can't remember the date, I'm sorry, but apparently there was a young lad who accused another person—I can't remember whether he was a counsellor or another juvenile—of..." At this point Miss Withers coughed several times, apparently to indicate that she could not bring herself to actually mention the alleged offence. "Er...interfering with him. As you can imagine, this caused quite a bit of bad blood and Bill and another counsellor were accused of not protecting the boy properly. Well, that's it. Oh yes, I don't recall it coming to very much. You know, like going to court or anything. I think the police were involved, but it was dismissed as one person's word against that of another. I thought you should know. Well, goodbye."

When I told Rosalie what Iris had said, she said I should call Patrick and let him know.

"I can't. It's well after midnight in Halifax."

"No, it isn't, silly! It's four hours behind us, not ahead."

"Oh, yes, of course, you're right. What time is it now?"

"Nine seventeen."

"So he would likely be somewhere between the office and home. I'll wait until tomorrow. There wouldn't be anything he could do tonight, anyway."

"Will he be able to do anything tomorrow, either?"

"Well, I guess he could check to see if Robertson, Lake, or Gillespie also went to the Wind in the Willows camp."

"Good luck with that. Gillespie was single, wasn't he?"

"Yes; so was Lake. Robertson left a widow behind."

"So, apart from him we can't hope to find out if the other two were at the Wind in the Willows unless the camp kept records and those records still exist."

"I wouldn't bet on that, but you never know."

10

Next morning we enjoyed a full Welsh breakfast of bacon, eggs, sausage, fried bread, black pudding and laverbread. The last is something of an acquired taste, being a rather slimy, dark-green substance made from boiled seaweed. I believe it is known only in Wales, although the weed is found all around the British and Irish coasts.

Rosalie absolutely refused to have it or the black pudding on her plate, and I ate only a little. It is said that the high iodine content gives the laverbread a distinctive flavour in common with olives and oysters, but I could detect neither, only salt.

After we had eaten, I called Patrick and told him of the message Miss Withers had left me.

"That's interesting," he said quietly. "Marc, how old was Bill Withers when he drowned in the bathtub?"

"I'm not sure. I don't think I ever knew, but judging by Valerie's appearance, I would guess he was around 60. Maybe a bit more."

"I see. And how old are camp counsellors, usually?"

"I have no idea. I'll ask Rosalie." She was in the bathroom so I repeated Patrick's question, then relayed her answer to him. "She says 18 to 22 or thereabouts."

"So that would have him born around 1963 and be at the camp somewhere between 1980 and 1985."

"That sounds about right."

"What was this place?"

"The Wind in the Willows."

"Lovely book."

"I beg your pardon?"

"I was just thinking about the book. I read it when I was a kid.

'Messing about in boats' and all that stuff about Mr. Toad. 'Poop, poop!'"

"Patrick, what on earth are you talking about?"

"You don't know the book? *The Wind in the Willows,* by Kenneth Grahame."

"Oh, vaguely. I never read it."

"You should."

"I'm a bit old for it now. It's a children's book."

"Nobody is too old for *The Wind in the Willows.* So tell me, where was this camp?"

"She wasn't sure, but thought it was in Guysborough County."

"I wonder if it's still there."

"I don't know."

"Okay, Marc, leave it with me. If I find out anything, I'll get in touch."

"We're going to be leaving here soon and will be on the move for at least another week."

"Don't worry. I'll track you down."

"So are we ready to go to Blackwood?" Rosalie was impatient to follow in the steps of the heroic Chartists.

"Yes. Let's go."

I headed the Jaguar back down the road by which had arrived several days ago, passing over the Heads of the Valleys highway to Garnlydan, and then down the Sirhowy Valley to Blackwood. It took us the best part of an hour, not least because I was not used to the roads.

"Remind me what it was the Chartists were asking for," I asked Rosalie as I drove.

"Their Charter called for universal suffrage—"

"Women and men?"

"No, just men."

"Ah, so not so progressive."

"It was for its time. Then they wanted voting by ballot—"

"As opposed to what?"

"They had to cast their vote vocally. So everyone, including their employers and landlords, would know how they voted."

"So, intimidation would have been widespread."

"Sure. They also called for annual parliaments."

"To be elected every year? That wouldn't be very practical."

"It never happened, anyway. They wanted electoral districts to be equal in population size."

"That did happen."

"More or less, yes."

"What else?"

"An important section of the Charter was that MPs should be paid. That was so ordinary people could be MPs. At the time only those with private means could afford to be in parliament."

"That came about."

"Yes, but not for another 72 years. The final demand was that there be no property qualification to vote. At the time if you didn't own land or property, you couldn't vote."

"We still have something like that in Canada. You can't be a Senator if you don't own land."

"You're joking?"

"No you have to own $4,000 worth of property in the province you'll represent in Senate, and another $4,000 in total property."

"That's ridiculous."

"Maybe, but it's the law. Oh Rosalie, look!"

We were just coming into Blackwood, and away to our right stood a tall metal statue of a man carrying what looked like a staff.

"That's the Chartist monument!" Rosalie said, "Let's go and see it."

After some lane changing and manoeuvring, we were able to get to the statue, which was being admired by an old man. When Rosalie introduced herself, he said his name was Ifor Evans, and told her the sculpture was by a Sebastien Boyesen. He said the Chartist Man was 26 feet tall and cost the taxpayers 33,000 pounds. Ifor said it was made from thousands of steel rings creating a mesh-like figure which symbolized the Chartist principle of strength in unity.

We asked him if there were any other tributes to the Chartists in Blackwood, but he said he did not know of any, so we returned to the car and headed off to Nant y Glo.

That next port of call was located two valleys over to the east, and to get to it we had to drive through Blackwood and heavily built-up areas of Pontllanfraith, Newbridge, Crumlin (where there used to be a spectacular viaduct towering some 200 feet above the town), Hafodyrynys, Llanhilleth, Six Bells, Abertillery and Blaina. Blaina runs into Nanyglo and, search though we might, we could find nothing to commemorate this as the place from which Zephaniah Williams led hundreds of miners to the Newport rising.

We later learned that, in the moorland above Blaina, there is a commemorative plaque marking the caves where some of the Chartists stockpiled weapons during the summer months of 1839.

We now had to retrace our route to Crumlin, and from there headed east across country to Pontypool, which is where William Jones held his men, but we could discover nothing there about the Chartists. So we went back to Crumlin and from there down the Ebbw Valley to Rogerstone, where we admired a colourful mural depicting the Chartists' procession through that community.

We also found what had been The Welsh Oak public house. Rosalie had been right that the pub had been badly damaged in a fire some years ago, but it was now being restored as a private house.

Frost and Williams met at the pub to shelter from the rain and to plan their strategy. Even though they had far less distance to travel than Frost and Williams, Jones' forces were dismally late, and the assault on Newport was consequently greatly delayed.

In view of the hour, Rosalie and I now had to make a decision as to whether we should press on to Newport, have dinner there, and return to The Travelers late that night, or check out the next morning and visit Newport as the first stop on our tour of the rest of Wales. After a brief discussion, we determined on the latter course, mainly because we did not want to miss Doug's cooking.

11

We got up late the next morning and almost missed breakfast. We had a simple meal consisting of masses of scrambled eggs and toast, and then settled our bill with Joy, telling her there was a chance we might look in on them on our way back to Heathrow in a few weeks.

It was almost lunchtime by the time we had packed and loaded the car. We were ready to leave when Joy came to the door and called me back.

"Marc, a phone call for you from Canada."

"Patrick?" I knew it had to be him.

"Yes. Good morning."

"What time is it there? Must be early."

"Past seven. Look, I wanted you to know that at least one of the others was at the Wind in the Willows camp at the approximate time."

"Really. Which one?"

"Robertson. His widow says she remembers his mentioning it when they were first married."

"Did she elaborate?"

"She wasn't able to. She recalled that he'd said there was some trouble at the camp, but that he didn't go into details."

"Did she say if he sounded like he was the accuser or the accused?"

"No. Like I said, no details."

"What about Lake and Gillespie?"

"Give me a chance. They were single men. I'll have to find out what relatives they have, where they are, if they'll talk, and if they remember anything."

"Yes, of course. Still, two out of three is pretty conclusive, isn't it?"

"No Marc, it's highly suggestive. If we find out that either Gillespie or Lake were at the camp then that would be convincing. If we had all four there, that would be conclusive."

"Yes, you're right. We mustn't get carried away."

"Indeed we must not. What do you have planned for the next week or so?"

"We're travelling to Newport today."

"I don't know where that is."

"It's in eastern South Wales. Then we are heading off into central and northern Wales."

"Well, have a good time. Did Rosalie have any luck tracking down her family?"

"Not really. The ancestors we did find turned out to be a rough lot. Not at all what she expected."

"That's risk you take when you go digging up the past."

We crossed over the River Usk in Tal y Bont village and turned right on the A40, a busy highway, which took us through the charming little town of Crucywel to Abergavenny (Y Fenni in Welsh). There we took the A4042 all the way into Newport (Casnewydd). With some difficulty we found our way to Westgate Square, the scene of the riot in 1839.

Apparently there had been talk of some kind of gathering or uprising for some days, because one of the Chartist leaders had been arrested and jailed, so the authorities were prepared for trouble. The mayor had sworn in 500 special constables and asked for more troops to be sent. About 100 soldiers were already in Newport at the Westgate Hotel and, presumably, had their guns at the ready.

Though it is no longer a hotel, we could see that, in its day, the Westgate would have been a fairly imposing structure. In front of what had been the hotel, and occupying most of the square, were a number of strange-looking sculptures depicting aspects of the historic event.

Rosalie, who was on her laptop, told me that around 10,000

Chartist sympathizers marched into the square and, believing that some of their comrades were imprisoned in the Westgate Hotel, surrounded the place and demanded their release. It must have been loud and chaotic, and amid the ruckus shots were fired.

A violent battle took place and the Chartists fired an estimated 100 shots into the hotel, which they entered, but were then forced to abandon.

When the smoke cleared, about twenty had been killed and a great many more wounded. The Mayor was wounded in the arm and groin when he went forward to implore the Chartists to lay down their arms, and one soldier was found dead with six bullets in his head.

It was difficult for us to imagine such rowdy and dramatic events as we sat, quietly sharing the square with these statues and a small flock of pigeons. Rosalie said that more than 200 Chartists were arrested for being involved and twenty-one were charged with high treason, including John Frost, Zephaniah Williams, and William Jones.

They were to be the last people in Britain to be sentenced to be hanged, drawn and quartered; but after a national petition and the intervention of the Lord Chief Justice, the government eventually commuted the sentences of each to transportation to Australia.

We wandered around the square for about half an hour before Rosalie engaged an old woman in conversation. She told us her name was Blodwyn Davies, and we asked her if there were other antiquities in Newport connected with the 1839 uprising. At first she seemed uncertain, then told us there had been "the wall".

"What was that?"

"You know, a wall with drawins and paintins on it, like."

"Oh, a mural," said Rosalie, "like the one up in Rogerstone?"

"Aye, aye, only this was much bigger. Longer, like."

"Where is it now?"

"Gone! They tore it down. The Council wanted the site for development, they said. Didn't ask nobody. Just went and did it. 'Elluva a fuss there was. All sorts of protests and that fellow Michael Sheen —"

"The actor?"

"Aye, thass 'im. 'E played Tony Blair in that picture about the Queen. 'E wrote to the papers and everythin'. Didn't do no good, though. They still tore it down."

On that rather despondent note, Rosalie and I drifted away to find our car. Truth to tell, we were glad to be getting away from Newport. Neither of us cared for its cramped, dirty streets nor its depressing atmosphere.

We had booked a room at the Priority Hotel in Caerleon, a small town a few miles to the east famous for its siting on the bank of the Usk, and for its being the location of a Roman legionary fortress. When we arrived, we were pleased to see that The Priory was a lovely old building surrounded by lawns and gardens and, we noted, bluebells still growing in the shade of some large trees.

Our bedroom was large, wonderfully light and airy, and over-looked the Priory gardens. Curiously, there was an old-fashioned bath tub at one end of the room, in addition to a large walk-in shower in the en-suite bathroom, which lent a certain risqué quality. After washing and changing we went down to dinner.

We were surprised to find that the dining at The Priory was a combination of Welsh and Spanish, with cooking done over open fires, but none the worse for that unusual characteristic. We were in no hurry, so we ordered a bottle of 2014 Piper-Heidsieck Vintage Champagne to sip while we studied the menu.

Rosalie decided to start with scallops knapped in a beurre blanc, which she pronounced "lovely", while I ordered an Iberian Scotch egg with saffron aioli. I hardly knew what to expect from such a weirdly-named dish, but it was delicious. Then she had whole sea bass baked in rock salt which, she said, tasted as good as it looked. Since lemon sole is one of my favourite fish, I had that with capers and nice new potatoes.

With the main course we drank a spectacular 2004 Louis Latour Chevalier Montrachet and did not regret our decision. We lingered long over our meal, finally going to bed when the dining room was empty.

12

The next morning we were up very early, so we went out to see what remains of the Roman town.

We were happily surprised to find considerable existing evidence of this once-magnificent fortress town of Isca, built in 75 AD as the base for the Second Augustan Legion. The fort, which was occupied for over 200 years, once must have housed around 5,000 legionnaires in barracks and as many as 100,000 people in the surrounding areas.

We saw remains of the baths, various ramparts and barracks, and the amphitheatre where the Romans would have been harangued by their commanders and entertained by various spectacles. It was built around 90 AD, and was the scene of some gruesome forms of fun, being the ancient form of a rather brutal fairground. The place could seat up to 6,000 spectators, who would gather to watch bloodthirsty displays featuring fighting gladiators and wild animals.

Much later, in the 12th century, the historical fantasist Geoffrey of Monmouth wrote in his *History of the Kings of Britain* that Arthur was crowned in Caerleon and that the amphitheatre was the remains of King Arthur's Round Table. This, of course, was nonsense as decades of excavation have shown, and is now believed only by a few New Age cranks.

Mightily impressed, we returned to The Priory for breakfast.

We both had worked up a hearty appetite. Rosalie ordered poached eggs, sobrasada with hash browns, sourdough and honey. Sobrasada, it turned out, was a Catalan cured sausage from the Balearic Islands, made with ground pork, paprika, salt and other spices. I did not feel as adventurous, so decided on the pork sausage, morcilla blood sausage, bacon, hash browns, tomato and eggs.

We made short work of this feast and, finishing our coffee, went to our room to plan the rest of our trip. We took out our maps and laid them on the bed. Rosalie asked me questions about places I had visited in the past and, based on those descriptions, she decided whether or not to include them in our itinerary.

From Caerleon we decided to get on the M4 and go to Wales' capital, Cardiff (Caerdydd). It would take us less than an hour to get there and I thought we could spend the day wandering around the city, seeing the ancient castle and the remarkable redevelopment of once grimy docklands into smart residential areas. We booked two nights at The Angel, an old hotel across from the castle that I used to visit.

Then we determined we would go to the Gower (Gwyr) Peninsula and stay at the Oxwich Bay hotel for several days, mainly because of its proximity to the Beach House, a Michelin star restaurant where Hwyl Griffith was the chef. If the weather remained fine, I knew Rosalie would love Oxwhich, as it has extensive, flower-covered sand dunes with a multitude of butterflies, and a beautiful, sandy beach which stretches for miles.

From there we would move on to St. Davids in Pembrokeshire, which I knew was a quaint, quiet little town with a spectacular cathedral, a Bishop's Palace and fine walking along the coast.

After that we would stay at Aberaeron for a few days so Rosalie could see a typical seaside place with fishing boats, wharves and tourists. Then, I proposed we go inland via a small, rustic town called Tregaron, and then take a precipitous route over a narrow, winding mountain road to the beautiful but little-known Irfon Valley. That would take us to the hamlet of Abergwesyn and thence to Llanwrtyd Wells, where we would stay for some days.

Rosalie was impressed that, when staying there some years ago, I had once walked thirty miles in one day, although she added, with some truth, "I bet you couldn't do it today!"

Following our stay in Central Wales, we decided to head north to Caernarfon, stay there for a week, and use it as a base to see the ancient Druidic Island of Anglesey (Mon) and the dramatic mountain country around Snowdon (Yr Wyddfa). This latter is the highest peak in Britain south of the Scottish Highlands, an area which we hoped to visit in some weeks' time.

Finally, we planned to drive to Shrewsbury, leave the car and get the train to London, where we would stay a few days before returning to Nova Scotia.

13

It was good to be back. I was very happy that Rosalie had enjoyed herself and that she had fallen in love with Wales. I was not surprised, because most visitors to that small country—half the size of Nova Scotia—are captivated by its natural beauty.

It has a 2,700-kilometre coastline on the Irish Sea, providing innumerable beaches, cliffs and coves; and inland there are thousands of streams, rivers, lakes, waterfalls and mountains. The most remarkable feature of Wales for the North American traveller is that the topography changes every few kilometres. You could be driving through a steep-sided valley with a raging river alongside, then amongst rolling farmlands, then on a coastland plain with dramatic views of the sea, then in dense forests all within the space of half an hour.

An additional blessing in most of Wales (although not in the southeast, where the coal industry used to thrive) is that the roads are not usually busy and, depending upon the time of day, often the driver will not encounter another vehicle for many miles. However, those roads are twisting and sometimes narrow, with few places to pass, so it would not be an ideal place for my Bugatti.

The people are very friendly and chatty ("talk the hind leg off a donkey," as the locals say) and, generally, the prices in hotels and restaurants are quite a bit lower than in North America.

Above all else, Wales is a wonderfully green place, and those greens may be seen in every conceivable shade in the sea, the hills, the fields and the woods. The main drawback to Wales is that all that green comes at the price of a great deal of rain.

Our remaining time there was wonderful, all the more so because the weather stayed so fine, something which was remarkable in so unpredictable a climate. We were exceptionally lucky in that respect, as normally we could have expected to have rain three days a week, and sometimes more often.

We had been gone more than a month, so we needed to come back to Nova Scotia to touch base and attend to our affairs. Rosalie needed to return to her work at the university, and I wanted to plant my vegetable garden now that summer was here. In addition, I wanted to make sure that my wine store was thriving and running without a hitch.

When we got in, the hall table was piled with mail which our cleaning lady had left for us. Most of it was bank statements, bills, and junk, but one letter stood out because of its distinctive envelope. I recognized it instantly as coming from the Single Malt Appreciation Society. It was from Donald Chisholm, announcing a tasting and dinner to be held in New Glasgow in a few days' time.

After checking with Rosalie and receiving her assent, I phoned him to indicate that I would attend. I apologized for not getting back to him sooner, but explained that I had been away in Wales.

"Not a great deal of single malt there, I dare say."

"Actually, there are four or five distilleries in Wales. All making single malt."

"You do surprise me!"

"I didn't get to try any of them. But we're planning on going to Scotland in about a month and, no doubt, I shall sample some good ones there."

"You will disappoint me if you don't."

"How's Duncan?" I was not really interested in how Duncan was, but felt politeness required me to ask.

Donald sighed deeply. "Ach. Duncan is Duncan. Moody and intense. I fear I may have indulged the boy too much when he was younger and now the damage is done."

"I'm sorry."

"Sometimes I hardly know him. He takes everything so seriously."

"Will he be at the New Glasgow function?"

"Yes. I hope he will behave himself. And Alec MacNeil has recovered, so he will be there, too."

"He's the man who was away sick last time?"

"That's him. I've never known anyone who knows his malt like Alec does. He is a hell of an expert, but..."

"But...?"

"Just between ourselves, Marc. If I had to choose whom I'd least like to spend a weekend in a locked room with, I'd be hard-pressed to decide between Alec and my own son."

He paused, and sighed again, sounding as if the weight of the world were on his shoulders. "Please forget I said that."

"Already forgotten."

"Thanks. *Gun èirich an rathad gus do choinneachadh. Biodh na trioblaidean agad beag.*"

Since I was also itching to get updated on the four unsolved murders in the province, I called Patrick Kennedy.

"You're back?"

"Yes. We got in yesterday."

"Did you have a good time?"

"Very good. What's the latest?"

"Not many developments, I'm afraid. We've been shorthanded. Five officers in my department are out with COVID."

"Were you able to contact any relatives?"

"Some, but none of them could recall ever being told anything about the Wind in the Willows summer camp."

"That's too bad. Is there anything I can do?"

"Not officially. You could go back and question Mrs. Withers without any problem, because she is a client of yours. There is no way you can act for the RCMP, or even leave the impression that you are acting with our blessing."

"I understand that. You know I have my private investigator's license now, so I could conduct inquiries which might be related to my client's case."

"Hmm. Well, we have found Reverend Walter Pettigrew. You could try seeing him."

"Who is he?"

"He's the guy who was in charge of the Wind in the Willows at the time."

"Really? That sounds promising."

"I guess you could call him the Camp Commandant. He's very old now, in his nineties, and long retired from the church."

"Which one?"

"Anglican, I think. Although the camp was non-denominational. Or ecumenical, I guess, would be a better term."

"Where does he live?"

"In New Glasgow."

"I have to be in New Glasgow the day after tomorrow. Why don't I go to see him then?"

"Don't ask me for permission. This has nothing to do with me. I don't even know you're going."

"Right. Understood."

After I had hung up, I told Rosalie that prior to the get-together in New Glasgow I would see Reverend Pettigrew, and that the day following I would go to Halifax. There I would see Mrs. Withers and her sister-in-law, Iris.

"Do you think they have anything more to tell?"

"Probably not, but I have to see if I can squeeze more information from them. They might remember something if I prod them."

"You think this summer camp is the key, don't you?"

"Is has to be. If we can find out what happened at the Wind in the Willows, who did what to whom and why, we can find our killer."

"But you still only have two of the four victims tied to the camp."

"Yes, that's true, but a connection between the camp and at least one of the other victims is bound to turn up sooner or later."

"Good luck with that," Rosalie said in a skeptical tone. "What are we having for dinner? There's not much in the fridge until I get groceries."

"There's a duck in the freezer. If I put it in a bucket of cold water it should thaw in time. Do you fancy a really nice wine with that?"

"Ooh, yes, please. We didn't have a lot of good stuff when were away. What did you have in mind?"

"I have a couple of bottles of 1953 *Vieux Chateau Certan* from

Pomerol. I last had it about three years ago."

"Was it good?"

"Amazing. I remember it smelled of flowers, liqueur, cherry, truffle, and cigar. In the mouth it was incredibly deep, and concentrated. It was lush and opulent—just like you, darling."

"Then that's the one we shall have!"

Rosalie leaned over and kissed my cheek. "You do say the nicest things, Marc LeBlanc."

14

On the appointed day I had a swift, very pleasant run in the Bugatti up to Pictou County. The roads were not particularly busy and there were no speed traps, so I got to Stellarton in an hour and thirty minutes.

I had forgotten to make arrangements in advance, so when I saw the sign for the Holiday Inn, just off the Trans-Canada Highway, I stopped in to reserve a room for the night. Then I headed into New Glasgow and crossed the East River via George Street, then made my way to the High Crest Home on Forbes Street.

The place looked nice and neat in an institutional way, being fronted by a large, dignified, grey mansion, possibly of Victorian origin. I had not called them ahead, because had they refused my request at that point, they would have been alerted and might then have taken measures to prevent my subsequent entry.

So, just turning up out of the blue, I had no idea if they would let me see Reverend Pettigrew. If they did, I did not know whether he would be sufficiently lucid to talk to me. Even then, I could not be sure how good his memory would prove.

The woman at the front desk could not have been more helpful, although she seemed a little dubious when I told her I was a private detective. She asked me to wait while she made sure the reverend wanted to see a complete unknown without an appointment. I thought it unlikely, but she returned smiling, saying that he would be delighted as he had few visitors these days because his children and most of his former friends had predeceased him.

When she told me he was 97, I asked if he was sound in mind enough to converse about the past.

She laughed out loud. "I should say so! He will talk your head off if you let him."

She gave me directions to where I would find him, which turned out to be a large, comfortable lounge with arm chairs. Almost before I could get through the door, a very tall, white-haired old man came bounding towards me, obviously in no way disabled or incapacitated.

"Mr. LeBlanc!"

"Yes, Reverend Pettigrew."

"That's me."

He towered over me by at least three inches. He poked a bony finger in my chest. "Now, I don't think you're one of the Pictou County LeBlancs because I know most of them, and I doubt you are one of the Cape Breton LeBlancs, so you must be from further afield."

"Grand Pre."

"Ah. Of course! You have returned to the place from whence you were ejected in 1755."

"Well, my ancestors did."

"Precisely. Please come and sit down."

He led me to two chairs in the window, waving to several other residents dotted around the room. "No cause for alarm!" He boomed. "Just a private detective to see me. I doubt he is interested in any of you."

"You're full of it, Walter!" shouted an old man in the corner.

"Whatever you say, George, as you wish," called Pettigrew, settling himself in his seat. Then he lowered his voice to me. "They're not a bad lot, you know, but somewhat limited by their life experiences. Few of them did very much of anything before they wound up here."

"Whereas you—"

"I'll have you know, young man, that I served eight different parishes in four provinces."

"You got around."

"Indeed I did. Now, how may I assist you?"

"Do you by any chance, remember the Wind in the Willows summer camp?"

"Of course I do. What about it?"

"I wanted to ask you about an alleged incident which may have occurred many years ago, when you were in charge of the camp."

"Yes?"

"It involved several people who were either employed by, or were attending, the camp."

"Names?"

"The only ones I can identify were called Bill Withers and Struan Robertson."

"Remember them well. Withers was older by a few years. Big, heavy-set fellow. He was a camp counsellor. Struan was young, skinny, and quite athletic."

"Have you any notion of the incident I am referring to, Reverend?"

"Of course I do, I'm not gaga, you know."

He looked around and, noticing that some of the others were listening in, stood up. "Let's go outside. Follow me."

He stalked out of the lounge and led me into the yard where, curiously, he manoeuvred us behind a large tree. I was bewildered until he pulled a pack of cigarettes from his cardigan and furtively lit one.

"They wouldn't approve. I imagine they think that if I stopped smoking I would live to be over a hundred. You want one?" He inquired, offering me the pack.

I shook my head.

"Wise. Very wise. Habits of a lifetime and all that. Now where were we?"

"Withers and Robertson."

"Ah, yes. What about them?"

"The alleged incident."

"Ah, yes. As far as I can recall, one of the boys accused another of the boys of...how shall we put it...an indiscretion."

"What does that mean? I am sorry to have to press you, Reverend."

"Well, if you insist, not to put too fine a point on it, the lad claimed he was raped by another boy. There was quite a to-do about it. Police were involved, that sort of thing. Lawyers, I think. But nothing came of it. It was one boy's word against another, and there were no witnesses."

"Were Withers and Robertson involved?"

"Only to the extent that the lad claimed that they should have helped him and didn't."

"Do the names Alex Gillespie and Leonard Lake mean anything to you?"

"No, I don't think so." He stubbed out his cigarette and frowned. "Gillespie? Lake? The names are not ringing any bells."

"Who was the victim?"

"The lad who claimed to have been raped?"

"Yes."

"Well, I'll be damned!"

"What?"

"Do you know, it's completely slipped my mind."

Pettigrew wandered away from me, pacing up and down the yard, muttering to himself. He wandered back to me. "I'm sorry. I've drawn a blank. Is it important?"

"Very important. The police suspect that the victim, whoever he was, murdered four people."

"Good heavens! After all these years! Well, I'll keep thinking. If it comes back to me, I'll call you. Do you have a card?"

I handed him a business card and thanked him for all his help.

I was effusive, but privately I thought that he had told me nothing I did not already know. The one thing I needed to know, the name of the killer, he had forgotten. He was a remarkable old boy, and I was glad to have met him, but the afternoon had been largely wasted.

When I got back to the Inn, there was a message telling me that the Single Malt gathering would be held at the Little Gull Bistro on Archimedes Street.

While I was changing, the room phone rang to reveal Lachlan (Lachie) MacLeod at the other end.

"Marc, how are you?"

"Lachie, my old breakfast companion! I'm well, thank you. I'm very glad you're here. To tell you the truth I felt my nose a bit out of joint last time. I could use a friendly face."

"You're speaking of that young ass, Duncan, of course. Strutting popinjay! Don't let him get to you."

"I'll try."

"You just about ready? I thought we could share a cab to the bistro. And we'll get together for breakfast tomorrow to do a post mortem."

"Sounds good to me. Give me ten minutes. I'll see you in the lobby."

It transpired that Donald Allister Chisholm, the self-appointed chairman of the group, had arranged for us to have the bistro to ourselves that night, and had also planned the menu for our dinner. He was in fine form, dressed in his kilt and smart blazer, as were Lachie and Murdock MacKay. Duncan was again adorned in full regalia, silver buttons gleaming, preening himself like a peacock. Harold Westwood wore his customary suit.

The one face I did not recognize I assumed belonged to Alex "Sandy" MacNeil, whom Donald had described as a great authority on Scotch whisky. He was a sallow, thin, bald, man in his late sixties, also wearing a kilt but with a Harris tweed jacket.

We each placed our bottles in brown paper bags marked A through G, and took our places. There were no place cards, so I quickly nabbed a seat next to Lachie, who winked at me conspiratorially. Thankfully, I was at one end of the table, while Duncan was at the other.

Placing bags E, F and G on a side table, Donald announced that we would try the first four, then take a short break to "stretch our legs".

The first struck me as an exceptionally strong malt, considerably above the usual 40% average, but it was unfamiliar to me so I had no idea what it was. It turned out to be Glen Scotia, Icons of Campbeltown, The Mermaid, and had been brought by Harold. Sandy said it was around 50% alcohol (it was 54%) and then guessed its identity.

The second was the one I brought and was guessed by Sandy

and Donald as Glencadam, Reserva PX Cask Finish. The fruity, toffee-like aroma and rich, creamy taste was popular with everybody except Duncan, who sneered in his inimitable way.

The next malt was a 25-year-old Ardbeg, brought by Donald, which I detested. I have mentioned before how my palate changed from love to hate of Island malts, which are particularly peaty and smoky. This one tasted as if it had come straight from a burned-out barn.

Seeing me grimace, Lachie gave me a playful dig in the ribs, and whispered, "I see you're still too young to appreciate the good stuff from Islay."

A rather fine 21-year-old Aultmore was next. It was brought by Duncan and was guessed by Sandy. Of all of us, only Harold professed to dislike it, saying he found it too sweet on the front of the palate and too bitter on the back.

On Donald's command, we rose and wandered around the room. Lachie and I went to the front of the restaurant to look out at the street, where the light was just starting to fail.

Suddenly our attention was seized by harsh voices, and we turned to see Duncan and Harold almost coming to blows.

"For Christ's sake, Duncan, just cool down. It's only whisky."

"You would say that, you fucking Sassenach. You people are all the same!"

"What the hell do you mean by that? My people?"

"All you English bastards. You think you're better than us Scots!"

"Both our families have been here for generations. We're both Canadian!"

"You can't hide your pedigree...or, in your case, lack of it. Your people oppressed and exploited us for centuries and you're still trying to lord it over us."

"Duncan!" Donald stepped between them.

"He knows what his people did. He's here in Canada voluntarily. We're here because his crowd drove us out of Scotland!"

"That's enough!" Donald said, "Either stop that or leave the premises!"

Harold had already moved away down the room. Now Duncan

huddled with his father in a corner, where we could just hear them muttering.

At length, Donald turned and grinned. "Ah, these tiny misunder-standings occur from time to time in the best of companies. We won't let them prevent our further appreciation of fine whisky and excellent food later. Gentlemen, please return to your places."

Sandy's malt was a 15-year-old sherry cask Jura, which we all liked, although Duncan only managed to voice weak approval.

Lachie surprised me by bringing a lowland malt, an Auchentoshan Three Wood which, even more to my surprise, was liked by everyone, it being rather dark, sweet and intensely fruity.

We wound up the tasting with a 15-year-old GlenAllachie brought by Murdock. I was alone in this being my favourite malt of the night, Duncan again sneering when I said I loved its mahogany colour, and layers of spices, vanilla toffee and chocolate. I resolved to acquire some of this fine whisky for my cellar.

We again rose so the staff could lay the table for dinner. As we were milling around, Donald announced the bill of fare.

We would start with Merigomish oysters, follow with French onion soup, and then have beef tenderloin with roast potatoes and vegetables. Instead of a dessert, Donald had chosen a savoury of toast spread with farmed and wild mushrooms. As usual, we would drink whisky throughout the meal.

Everything was superb, my only regret being that we could not have wine with the food.

Lachie and I shared a taxi back to the hotel and each went to his room more than a little worse for wear.

"See you for breakfast at eight," he said, fumbling with his door card.

15

I was up fairly early the next morning, wandered around the hotel parking lot, then took a walk down Lawrence Boulevard. It was a fine day which promised to be hot later on. The birds were out in force and competing for attention with their calls. I would have visited the Museum of Industry, but it was not open yet.

I sauntered slowly back and called Lauchie's room from the lobby. He said he would meet me in the breakfast room in ten minutes.

We helped ourselves to the buffet, Lauchie having scrambled eggs and some rather sad-looking bacon, while I took some French toast and very shiny sausages. We found a table by the window and ate in silence for some time.

I looked across at this man, who was a comparative stranger to me, and reflected how much I had come to like him in such a short time. On better acquaintance, I now guessed he was in his mid-seventies. He had an amusing habit of wobbling his head from side to side when eating and talking. This made his thatch of gray hair lollop about in an unruly fashion. His eyes almost always sparkled brightly with amusement or mischief.

"Well," I said when we had satisfied our first pangs of hunger. "What did you think of that performance last night?"

"Not very seemly. I guess Harold was entitled to express his opinion without being molested."

"Isn't that the whole point of these tastings? That we can say exactly what we think of the malts, regardless of who brought them? After all, none of us made the damn stuff, so a negative comment is no reflection on the person who brought it."

"Hmm. You're right there. Young Duncan is an ass to show his feelings so openly, but we Scots feel we have special privileges when it comes to whisky because we invented it."

"So you say, but you can't prove that. There are just as many Irishmen who will claim it was invented in Ireland. And those who say it started with the Babylonians or the Chinese."

"That is a discussion for another time. It certainly didn't originate with the French," he said rather pointedly. "Duncan tends to take everything very seriously, but I can't bring myself to dislike him."

"Well, I can! He's such a prig. You can't think his attacking Harold because his ancestors were English was fair or sensible."

"Old wounds often close the heart to new friendships." He said, his eyes narrowing momentarily. "There is much which can never be forgotten and, for some, cannot be forgiven. Duncan is young and intense. His father has spoiled him to the extent that he has a lot of time on his hands. He has used it to immerse himself in his history and ancestry."

"I guess so. When you put it like that, he doesn't seem so bad. You're a good fellow, Lachie."

"Ha. I don't know about that. What are you up to today, Marc?"

"I have to make a few calls, then head to Halifax to see a few people. How about you?"

"I shall head back to Skye Glen to tend my diminishing stock."

"Why diminishing?"

"I'm getting old, Marc. Livestock requires almost constant attention. And I don't really expect to make much profit out of cows and sheep."

"I think you keep them because you like them. I'll bet you call them all by name."

"Haha! That's true enough. I think I am keeping them because I like them better than humans."

"Well, I hope you have a good ride back. It's always great to see you, Lachie."

"You too, Marc. *Gur math a thèid leat.*"

~

After I had checked out of the hotel, I thought I would take a quick run over to High Crest to see if Reverend Pettigrew had remembered the name of the boy who had allegedly been victimized at the Wind in the Willows.

When I pulled up to the home, I noticed an undertaker's vehicle parked outside the front door. As I strolled up, some men in dark suits were bringing out a body on a collapsible trolley.

As they tried to manoeuvre down the steps, the trolley rocked and the sheet covering the deceased slipped slightly. White and drawn though it was, there was no mistaking the face which was revealed. It was Reverend Pettigrew's.

If he had remembered anything more about Wind in the Willows, he would take it with him to the grave.

From New Glasgow I drove to Valerie Withers' house in Dartmouth. It was a very modest, rather dull house with no front yard or garden, and had a path to the front door from which last year's dead leaves had still not been removed.

I hesitated before approaching because I was dreading meeting the fatuous yet belligerent Norman again. At length I plucked up my courage, picked my way through the rotting vegetation and pounded on the door. I would have used the knocker or bell had there been one, but there was just a frayed hole which might have once housed a bell pull.

Valerie answered the door and looked surprised—alarmed would be a better word—to see me.

Keeping the door partially closed, she peered around the edge, nervously stammering, "Oh, it-it's y-you."

"Yes, hello, Valerie. I've come to give you a report. An update."

"Well..."

"Can I come in?"

"Well..."

"I won't be too long."

"Well...." A look of panic came over her face, before an idea occurred to her. "I'll come out. That'd be alright, wouldn't it?"

"If you prefer, sure."

She closed the door behind her and turned to face me. I noticed first that she had marks on the side of her face which had been hidden by the door. Then I observed that she was shabbily and scantily dressed, and that she had no shoes on.

"If this is a bad time, I can come back. Unless you want to come back to Grand Pre."

"No, no." She looked up and down the street.

"Is Norman around?"

"No. He's gone to the mall."

I resisted the temptation to say 'good', and instead gave her an abbreviated version of what I had, and had not, discovered to date. I felt it necessary to cut my report short because Valerie appeared to be shivering which, it being a hot day, I attributed to nervousness.

Then I asked her if she remembered Bill telling her anything about a problem at the Wind in the Willows camp. She seemed surprised that he had ever been a camp counsellor, but when I pressed her further, she did admit to hearing him mention that once he had been in some trouble.

"What kind of trouble?"

"He didn't say. It was before we were married."

"Did he mention any names?"

"How do you mean?"

"The names of boys who were at the camp?"

"No. Look, what are you trying to get at?"

"I'm not trying to get at anything, Valerie. It's just that if I knew the name of someone who he said had been at the camp, I might have found who killed Bill."

"Oh I see. No names."

"Well, thanks. I must be off. I have to go and see Iris now."

"Wait!"

"What is it?"

"Once when he had fever, he was rambling and kept muttering about some Arthur."

"Arthur? Are you sure?"

"Yes It was only the one time. You know, when he was sick. I never heard him say it after that. Yes, Arthur." She looked at me and frowned. "Or maybe it was Walter."

As I drove away, I speculated on how Valerie had sustained the injuries to her face. As unkind as it seemed, I thought that, given her age and drab appearance, it was unlikely she would have a 'boy friend', especially not this soon after her husband's death.

That left Norman as the leading suspect for the assault. I admit that I was not objective where he was concerned because I had disliked him from the moment I first saw him, but Valerie's facial marks again had me wondering if he could have murdered his father.

I approached Iris Withers' house with a great deal more equanimity than I had Valerie's. Iris was a woman I found to be highly intelligent, articulate and very pleasant company. I also liked her neat, quaint, comfortable home, where it seemed time had stood still.

"Thank you for your message. I'm sorry I didn't get back to you earlier, but I was in Wales when I received it."

"Wales! Lovely place. If you like rain," she said.

"You've been there? I didn't have you as a world traveller."

"Did you not? There's a lot more to me than meets the eye, Mr. LeBlanc."

Her eyes held mine for several seconds. They were steady and steely. I wondered if there had ever been venom or violence in them.

"I'm sure there is. I didn't mean to insult you, Ms. Withers."

"Miss Withers."

"Yes, of course. I'm sorry. Miss Withers, can you enlarge on what you told me in your message?"

"In what way?"

"The nature of the trouble, for instance. I have spoken with a Reverend Pettigrew—"

"Who's he?"

"He was the man in charge of the camp."

"Oh."

"He told me that one boy had alleged that another had, um, raped him."

"Not Bill!"

"No, Bill was the counsellor. The charge was against another boy."

"Ah. Well, you already have the sordid details. What can I provide?"

Her tone had become adversarial, quite unlike at our first meeting, and I felt the interview was slipping away from me. But I no option but to press on.

"Do you recall if Bill mentioned any names?"

"He may have."

"Did he mention an Arthur or a Walter?"

"What?"

"Valerie said she heard Bill talking about someone called Arthur or Walter."

"She's crazy!" She said with unexpected animus. "She doesn't have the sense she was born with."

"Do you remember Bill mentioning anyone by name?"

"This is getting tiresome, Mr. LeBlanc." She sighed deeply. "Let me think."

"Please do. It's very important."

"There was an Ian, I think."

"Ian? Are you sure"

"No, not Ian. Struan."

"Any others?"

"Wait a minute! Don't rush me."

"Sorry."

"Yes, Leonard or Len was one name."

"That checks with other sources."

"And Allan."

"Are you sure it was Allan?"

She glared at me with unconcealed annoyance. She looked out of the window for a second, then turned back to me.

"I apologize, Mr. LeBlanc, it was not Allan. It was Alex."

"Right." Now we were getting somewhere. I needed only one more name. The name of the killer.

"Any more?"

"More what?"

"Names."

"Good heavens, how many do you want?"

"Just one more. The most important one."

"Well, I don't have it. Whose name was it?"

"The boy who claimed to have been assaulted."

"I can see how that would be crucial," she said, rising, "but that's all I have. Now, I think it is time for you to go."

As I walked to the car I realized that, regardless of what the investigation turned up now, I would not be welcome in Irene Withers' house again, and likely not in the house of my own client, Valerie.

At least, I thought, we had established that all four of the murdered men (assuming that Bill Withers was murdered) had been at the Wind in the Willows camp, and probably at the same time, but we already strongly suspected that. Even assuming they had been murdered by one of the boys for their part in a sexual assault on that boy, we had no idea who he was. Unless we got a freakishly lucky break, our only hope lay with Patrick's people findings attendance records of the camp.

I called Patrick on my cell from the Bugatti and related all I had discovered.

He sounded glum. "You don't think the reverend's passing was suspicious, do you?"

"I guess not. He was 97."

"So, it's not likely."

"You tell me. To tell the truth, Patrick, I'm so confused by this bloody case that I am suspicious of everyone."

"Does that include me?"

"Sometimes."

"Haha! I didn't do it."

"That's what they all say."

"Who else are you suspicious of?"

"Norman Withers for one. Even Iris Withers is now starting to look dodgy."

"So we are at a stalemate."

"Not necessarily. Did your people track down any records of who went to Wind in the Willows during those years?"

"Bad news there, too, unfortunately. For whatever reason, all records prior to 2010 were kept in cardboard boxes. Guess what happened to them."

"They were burned in a fire?"

"No. They were 'accidentally' destroyed."

"How accidental do you think it really was?"

"Impossible to say."

"So we're no further ahead?"

"No. You going to be around for a while?"

"Only a few days. Then we're off to Scotland."

"Oh, yes. I forgot. I wish I was going with you."

16

At breakfast the next day, I brought Rosalie up to date on the pro-
gress of the investigation.

We discussed it over some lovely capelin, which one of her
friends had brought from Cape Breton. She had gathered them
from the beach at Baleine and put them in a refrigerated container
before driving to the Annapolis Valley. We fried them in a mixture
of olive oil and butter, and served them with buttered bread. They
were delicious.

"It was very unlucky to lose your reverend before he could remember the name," she said.

"If luck had anything to do with it."

"Do you have any reason—any real reason—to think it was a
suspicious death?"

"No, I don't."

"Then be careful. Otherwise we could be entering the realm of
conspiracy theories."

"Yes, you're right. But I do find it slightly difficult to accept as coincidental that within hours of Pettigrew passing away, Iris Withers could remember three other names, but not the crucial one. Or
that Valerie Withers came up with a cock-and-bull story about an
Arthur or Walter."

"In her case, it sounds more like forgetfulness to me. But I must
say the change in Iris does seem strange. You got on like a house on
fire on your first visit. You said she was really nice."

"She was. Maybe I just caught her at a bad time."

"Never mind. I have two pieces of news which should cheer you
up."

"What are they?"

"First, you'll be glad to know I've worked out our Scottish trip."
"Already?"
"Yes, I'm clear at Acadia until the fall. We leave in two days."
"You're joking?"
"No time like the present! We fly to Edinburgh via Toronto. It's an overnight flight so we should arrive refreshed just as the dawn is breaking."
"How poetic you are. Do go on."
"Two days in Edinburgh. Then we go by rail to Pitlochry for an overnight stay. Then likewise to Blair Atholl to see that lovely castle."
"Oh, nice!"
"Then, also by train to Inverness, where we have two days."
"Are we doing the whole trip by train?"
"We could if we wanted to, because there are rail links to Skye, Ullapool, Durness and Thurso on the western and northern coasts, but we wouldn't have much freedom of movement. So I've arranged for us to pick up a car in Inverness."
"What will it be?"
"What will what be?"
"The car?"
"Marc, it'll be a car. With four wheels and seats. I don't think they rent out Ferraris in the Highlands of Scotland."
"Oh, alright."
"Then we can tootle our way north."
"Tootle?"
"Yes, my love, tootle. Taking our time, we will visit twelve different places, spending two nights at each."
"I hope you've allowed enough driving time between stops. Roads in Scotland can be very slow and winding. It takes longer than you might think to get from one place to the next."
"I did know that, and I have made the appropriate allowances."
"Clever girl! What are the places we shall be going to?"
"I'll let you know tomorrow. We don't have time to go through the list now."
"Why on earth not?"

"That brings me to the second piece of good news"

"Which is?"

"Frank is coming to dinner."

"Frank Wilberforce?"

"The very same."

"Marvellous!"

Frank was one of my favourite people. I had encountered him on my first case, the search for the Holy Grail, and since then we had become fast friends. He was employed as an investigator for the Canadian Art Prevention of Fraud and Theft Agency, and we both liked him because he was excellent company, and always had an immense number of fascinating stories to relate.

Frank was also remarkable for his physical size and for the copious amounts of food he could put away. Whenever Frank visited, we had to make sure that meals were least twice their normal size.

"However, there is a problem."

"What's that?"

"When I invited Frank, I forgot that I had already asked Walter and Joyce Bryden to dinner. And I was so hung up with arranging the Scottish trip that I also forgot to get in supplies."

"That's awkward. What on earth shall we feed them?" I asked.

"Well, you know Frank is not hung up on fancy French cooking, but I think we should do something nice for the Brydens. And serve some good wine."

"Is Joyce still a vegetarian?"

"No, thank God. She got tired of that."

"Good. What food do we have on hand?"

"Not much. We have quite a lot of fresh salmon, but not enough for a main course, especially not with Frank at the table. We have all kinds of stuff in the big freezer, but anything big enough to feed that many wouldn't thaw in time."

"How about veg?"

"Lots of spuds, leeks, carrots, onions, and some mushrooms."

"Bacon?"

"Yes, several packages."

"Any pork?"

"I have a piece of shoulder, and about four or five chops. What are you thinking?"

"I know it's not terribly sophisticated for the Brydens, but why don't I make sausages and we can have them with lots of buttery mash and a mélange of vegetables."

"Lovely. What about a starter?"

"Why don't I delicately poach the salmon, and serve it cold with homemade mayonnaise?"

"Works for me. I guess dessert is my responsibility."

"Yes, but we have loads of ice cream. Why don't you put a long dish on ice and serve scoops of all the different colours and flavours side by side, and let them help themselves?"

"Nice and easy to do. How about wine?"

"I have half a case of *Chateau La Mission Haut-Brion Blanc* 1998. I think that should flatter the salmon while having the guts to stand up to the mayonnaise. Remind me to put lots of dill in cooking the fish."

"Sounds good. Are you sure that wine won't be too old?"

"Maybe, but we have to find out sooner rather than later. With the main course we're going to need a big strapping red. This calls for a *Chateauneuf du Pape* from Chateau Rayas. The 1995 is the one, I think. Anyone who is not impressed by the humble sausage will be blown away by the greatness of the wine."

"And for dessert?" Rosalie asked with a mischievous smile, remembering how she had once shocked me by serving an extremely-rare, fabulously-expensive bottle of *Chateau d'Yquem* without first consulting me.

"All you can serve with ice cream is Champagne. Anything else is murdered by the cold. You can choose whatever you want from the cellar, but not the Krug, the Crystal or the *Salon Les Mesnil*."

"Oh, alright, spoilsport."

First, I got the largest flat pan I could find, laid out the salmon, sprinkled it with lots of dill, seasonings, and white wine and gently poached it for five minutes on top of the stove. I let it cool, then removed the skin. It would stay in the fridge until about twenty minutes before we were ready to eat it.

I made the mayonnaise, adding a tiny pinch of saffron and a touch of cream to thin it, and also put it in the fridge

Next, I took all the pork I had, removed the bones, and ground it finely together with the bacon, then thoroughly mixed in bread-crumbs, eggs, thyme, nutmeg, lard and pepper. Then, taking an ex-trusion die of four centimetres, I pumped the forcemeat into the casings, taking care to tie a knot every ten centimetres to ensure sausages of equal length.

When they were done I plunged them into a big pot of boiling beef stock for three minutes, then pulled them out to dry. These I later fried until they were golden brown.

I put some Yukon Gold potatoes, half in the oven to bake and the other half to boil on the stove. When they were done, I set them aside to cool and, when we were ready to eat, combined their flesh in a large saucepan and mashed them with lots of butter, heavy cream, salt and pepper and chopped chives.

The leeks, carrots and onions I chopped into large pieces, placed whole mushrooms on top, and baked them in the oven with olive oil, dry sherry, sage and parsley. This could be reheated when needed.

Everyone was in an almost party mood, boisterous and full of fun. The food was greatly appreciated, especially by Frank, who, by my reckoning, had a double helping of the salmon and about six of the fat, juicy sausages. He also put away a gargantuan amount of mashed potatoes which I had lightly flavoured with a pinch each of saffron and marjoram.

Although there were no complaints about it, I had made a mis-take with the white wine, which was past its peak and had almost a sherry quality to it. It was not the right accompaniment for the sal-mon, even with the mayonnaise. I made a mental note to drink the rest of the bottles fairly soon with an even more robust dish, pos-sibly a bouillabaisse or brandade.

The red was immense and brought joyous noises of approval from everyone.

"So, what are our amateur sleuths working on now?" Joyce asked as we spooned up the ice cream. "Do you have a new case?"

"Not amateur any longer," said Rosalie. "Or at least Marc isn't. He has his private investigator's license now. And, yes, he does have a new case."

"Congrats, Marc," said Walter. "Does this mean you'll be able to charge now?"

"If I wanted to, but not as much as lawyers," I said impishly.

"Ouch. But seriously, you could make some money at it."

"I work for nothing. Or have until now, and I think it will probably stay that way."

"What is the case?" Frank asked.

Taking care not to mention any names, or to imply I was involved officially with the police cases, I outlined each of the three confirmed murders together with the Withers death, which we supposed to be murder. Then I explained that, as far as we could ascertain, these individuals (I called them A, B, C and D) attended an event where an alleged rape had taken place.

"So did any of A to D sustain the rape?" Walter asked.

"No."

"Then who did?"

"We don't know."

"No idea?"

"None."

"I take it you are assuming that this person—the victim—killed the others?" Frank asked.

"That is the working hypothesis."

"Well, if he did...is it a he?"

"Yes, we think so."

"Okay. If he did, the motive is clear. Revenge."

"Have you come across revenge cases in your legal practice, Walter?" Rosalie inquired.

"Only the Father Mike case, with which you are very familiar, Rosalie. But there have been some very notable historical cases."

"Which ones?"

"The case of Bharat Kakicharan is a good one. He was a notorious Indian gang leader, who was said to have committed more than 40 sexual assaults, and used sexual violence to terrorize residents of a poor neighbourhood. In August 2004, Yadav was scheduled to appear at a bail hearing in court in the city of Nagpur. After word got around that the court might release him, local women decided to take matters into their own hands. After Kakicharan mocked a victim he had raped, a woman struck him on the head with her shoe, then other women first threw chili powder in his face, then pelted him with stones and finally pulled out knives, stabbed him at least 70 times, and hacked off his penis in retribution. The women also threw chili powder in the police guards' faces so they couldn't do anything to stop the crowd. Apparently, it took him almost twenty minutes to die."

"God, Walter!" Rosalie cried. "That sounds a bit like the Bobbett case."

"Yes. That, too, was revenge. Lorena claimed she did it to get revenge for John's having abused her."

"Yes, I read that."

"Then there was the case of the 47 samurai who had sworn loyalty to a member of the Japanese nobility. The problem came when their master slashed another with his sword and the court ruled that he should commit suicide, which he did. So, the 47 went to the home of the complainant and beheaded him."

"Charming!" Said Frank. "Any more?"

"Well, there's always Mrs. Crippen's revenge, although she wasn't an active participant."

"Crippen? The doctor who killed his wife?" I asked.

"He was convicted because the police found her body in the basement and he was hanged."

"And?"

"In 2007 they did tests on the remains and found out it wasn't her!"

"Good God!"

"Finally, there was a really bad case of revenge killing as WWII was ending, when American troops who liberated Dachau concentration camp were so horrified by what they saw that they turned round and gunned down 75 captured German soldiers."

"I never heard that," said Frank.

"The whole thing was hushed up until decades later."

"What about you, Frank?" said Joyce, "You must know of famous examples of revenge in works of art."

"Oh yes. Rubens' *Prometheus Bound* is a good one. It shows the poor man having his liver eaten out by an eagle because he defied the gods and gave the gift of fire to mankind.

"Then there is Michelangelo's getting even with a Vatican official who criticized the nudity in his Sistine Chapel paintings as more suited to a tavern or public bath than the most sacred space in the land. So, behind the Chapel's altar, Michelangelo painted Minos, the despicable judge of the underworld, and put the official's face on him. He included a serpent eating Minos's genitalia and added donkey ears to portray the official as a jackass. When the official complained to Pope Paul, His Holiness replied, 'Had the painter sent thee to purgatory, I would have used my best efforts to release thee; but since he hath sent thee to hell, it is useless to come to me, as I have no power there.'"

"That's a great story, Frank." I said.

"Then there is the sad and very real case of a very great painter, Artemesia Gentileschi."

"She's one of my favourites," Rosalie said.

"She was an Italian artist, famous not only for her paintings, but also because she was successful in a field dominated by men, and was victimized during her attempt to succeed as an artist. Her teacher, Agostino Tassi, was tried and convicted for raping her when she was 19, but because he was a friend of the Pope his two-year sentence was nullified.

"So Gentileschi did a painting of Judith heroically beheading a drunken general. In her rendition, she painted herself as Judith, her mother as her assistant, and Tassi as the general!"

"On that cheerful note, I think we should head off into the sunset," said Walter. "Good luck with your case, Marc."

Jeremy Akerman

17

Once, Edinburgh had some of the worst slums to be found anywhere in Britain, but after World War II there was a massive slum clearance on an unprecedented scale. Areas like Dumbiedykes, Greenside and Leith were among the worst of these working class communities, whose residents had been living in overcrowded and unsanitary conditions for generations. So the districts were razed to the ground in a monumental effort to "elevate" the populace.

The result was the creation of some comfortable suburban areas, but also hundreds of soulless, concrete apartments, most of them in huge towers on large council "housing estates". So-called "experts" in the 1940s had convinced governments that, because of the country's limited space and the cost of servicing with sewer and water, the way to go was "Up not Out."

But in practice, the results failed to live up to the imaginations and intentions of the experts: they created veritable jungles with little sense of community or belonging. In many cases the new inhabitants of these new housing utopias expressed the sentiment that they would much rather be back in the "slums", modern conveniences of apartment living notwithstanding.

All this I was able to learn from Rosalie's laptop and my own eyes, because our flight was unable to land on time and had to circle over the city several times before being allowed to descend.

However, we had no intention of visiting Muirhouse, Dumbiedykes, and West Pilton or even leafy suburbs, but would, like other tourists, confine ourselves to the city's Old Town which, even from the air, promised to be a rare treat of impressive buildings and sites brimming with centuries of dramatic history.

The flight from Toronto normally took nine hours and twenty

minutes, but the delay added another twenty minutes. We did not mind because we were in business class, so had comfortable, flat-out reclining seats, and consequently were able to enjoy a good, long sleep.

Rosalie had booked our hotel for three nights, including the one we spent in the air, because she thought we might be tired and want to rest for some hours before looking around the city. Though we were not in the least tired, in the event it proved useful because it meant we could check in immediately upon arrival, unpack, have a wash and change, and get breakfast in the hotel.

The taxi took less than twenty minutes to get into Edinburgh proper, and drove the length of the Royal Mile, a collection of an-cient streets which run between the Palace of Holyrood and the spectacular castle set high on rocky hill dominating the city. Though it was difficult for us to understand his accent, the taxi driver explained that the route he had brought us was the tradi-tional processional route of Scottish monarchs. The Royal Mile seemed to have everything from pubs, to shops, to restaurants, as well as the country's main law courts.

We drove up streets called Abbey Strand, the Canongate, and the Lawnmarket to Castle Hill, where our hotel was located.

The Witchery by the Castle was indeed well in sight of the castle, and only a short walk from it, but from the outside the hotel looked more like a prison: tall, grey, bleak and made, presumably, from granite. It was flanked on one side by an enormous Gothic church and on the other by another grey, stone building calling itself "The Scotch Whisky Experience."

As our taxi drew up to the curb, Rosalie dug me in the ribs, say-ing, "You better not be spending too much time in there."

As forbidding as it seemed from the outside, the hotel could not have been more different inside. We were immediately over-whelmed by its palatial opulence, every furnishing and accoutre-ment seeming to belong to a by-gone era. Lots of gilt, dark wood panelling, brocade, velvet, gleaming mirrors and ornaments bore down on us from all sides as we moved to our accommodation. As far as I could see, the only things missing were stags heads on the walls.

Our "room" was a suite which was an extravaganza of Victorian comfort and luxury, with heavy wall hangings, a four-poster bed, and an elaborate table in the window. The staff were polite and attentive to the point of obsequiousness.

"Isn't this exciting?" Rosalie said. "It's like being in a romantic fairy tale."

"How is it described on the website?"

"'Hidden in a collection of buildings on Castlehill, the Witchery has just nine fabulously original and indulgent suites,' she read from her laptop. 'Frequently described as one of the seven wonders of the hotel world by *Cosmopolitan*, each has its own unique quirks and charms. Whichever suite you choose you'll find glamour, luxury and roll top baths for two.'"

"It's certainly intriguing," I said, "but I'm not sure I would want to live in the world of Sir Walter Scott and Queen Victoria for more than a few days. It's a tad oppressive."

"The restaurant is supposed to be very good, and apparently has a spectacular wine list."

"Ah, really?"

"I thought that would perk you up. Let's go and have some breakfast. I'm starving."

"Tomorrow we can have it served in our room if we wish," I said, reading from the literature at hand, "but we have to order the night before."

"Maybe tomorrow. Now, let's go down and eat!"

After an exquisite breakfast of everything from smoked salmon to scrambled eggs *en brioche*, to devilled lamb kidneys and fried haggis, and duck eggs with a whisky sauce, we were well satisfied. In a somewhat bloated state we staggered out into the streets to explore this supremely historic city.

We decided to stick to our "own" street, The Royal Mile, today, and save the famous Princes Street for tomorrow.

First we headed to the castle, a hugely impressive structure which had been under siege 26 times in its history, giving it the claim to be the most attacked place in the world. There was a castle on this rocky hill rock since the reign of King Malcolm III in the 11th century, and it was the residence of Scottish kings and queens until the middle of the seventeenth century. Thereafter it served principally as a military garrison.

Of course, we had to see the Cannonball House, where a cannon-ball lodged in the wall which is said to have been accidentally fired from the Castle, and the 16th century house of John MacMorran, who was killed by schoolboys in a riot in 1595.

Then there was the Scotland supreme criminal court Justiciary Building and the great Tron Kirk, which was initially commissioned by Charles I and became known as "The Tron" because of a large weighing beam just outside. It was here that the marriage of Mary Queen of Scots to Francis II of France was wildly celebrated in 1558, although the wedding itself took place in Paris.

On the south side, about one-third of the way down from the Castle toward Holyrood Palace, we saw Parliament Square, where the law courts and parliament had sat before Scotland became part of Britain in 1707; and the Old Tollbooth, which served as a jail and as the administrative centre for taxation and justice.

We saw the famous Mercat Cross where Royal proclamations were read and the summoning of Parliament is announced; the house of that crusty old Protestant curmudgeon, John Knox; and the World's End pub.

After all this site-seeing we were exhausted and were glad to return to the Witchery, have a hot bath, change and go down to dinner.

The dining room was all a-glitter with candles, shining silver, sparkling glassware, and dazzling white napery. The contrast between the bright tables and the dark walls made us feel we were guests of Queen Mary herself.

We decided to start with some Champagne and thought a *Billecart-Salmon Cuvee Nicolas Francois Billecart* 2002 would be just the thing to get us into the right mood.

While we were sipping the exquisite Champagne, we carefully examined the menu. To start, Rosalie chose baked, hand-dived Orkney scallops with pancetta butter; while I ordered the roast crail langoustine with toasted brioche, hollandaise sauce and blue shell mussels. With this course we ordered the *Le Montrachet Marquis Laguiche* 2002.

For the main course we both wanted to risk the intriguing red deer and haggis Wellington with "bashed neeps", and, to go with that, I chose a *Chateau Haut Brion* 1996.

The food and wine exceeded our expectations, and we were happy foregoing dessert and just sipping at the unfinished wine.

I could not remember having slept in a four-poster before and I felt a little like a King of Scotland lying in the vast, comfortable furnishing with my queen by my side.

"*Oidhche mhath mo ghràidh*," I whispered to Rosalie.

"What the hell is that?"

"It's Gaelic."

"How do you know?"

"I looked it up while you were bathing."

"What does it mean?"

"'Goodnight, my love.'"

18

After another sumptuous breakfast, we tottered out into the streets of this uniquely-fascinating city. Before walking the approx-imately kilometre-long Princes Street in New Town, we decided to see more of Edinburgh's Old Town.

Despite Rosalie's mild protest, I insisted that our first stop should be at the Scotch Whisky Experience, next door to our hotel. We were too early for the official tour, so we just wandered around. Even Rosalie was impressed by their 'library', which contained al-most 4,000 bottles, claiming to illustrate 35 years of whisky mak-ing. Despite my being a single malt devotee, the most intriguing item for me was a bottle of Buchanan's blended whisky, made in 1897.

Unlike Lachie MacLeod or Donald Chisholm, I could not honestly say that I appreciated older malt in proportion to its much greater cost. I found I preferred many malts over others which were five and ten years older. It would have been sacrilege to say so at this place (or indeed with the group at home), but I had a sneaking sus-picion that a 127-year-old whisky would not taste all that much different from distillations of a similar style, but of more recent vintages. It would, of course, depend upon when a whisky was bottled, because aging only occurs in the cask and the process stops the minute the cork is sealed.

Before long, Rosalie dragged me away and back into the *Auld Toun*, the name popularly given to the most ancient part of the city, where much of its medieval street plan and Reformation buildings are preserved. We saw the Grassmarket, the Cowgate, the Canong-ate and, of course, Holyrood, including the Palace and Abbey.

The Palace is the King's official residence in Edinburgh, and the home of Scottish royal history, which has associations with some of Scotland's most well-known historic figures, such as Mary, Queen of Scots and Bonnie Prince Charlie (who, I gathered from Lachie, was neither very princely nor particularly bonnie).

The Palace being huge and impressive, we were only able to see part of it. Much of it stems from renovation work started during Charles II's reign; however, he never actually came to see his Scottish palace.

Rosalie loved the amazing collection of furniture and tapestries, while I was rather taken with the portrait of Charles II by John Michael Wright that hangs in the Throne Room. I thought Charles looked rather forlorn, and I reflected that, for all their riches and power, none of the Stewarts seemed to be very happy, at least not in the official portraits.

Adjacent to the Palace is the ruined abbey, which was founded in 1128 by King David I to give thanks to God for his being saved from the horns of death in a hunting accident. The abbey was used as a church until the 17th century, and fell into a state of dilapidation in the 18th.

We learned that, in 1177, the Papal Legate Vivian held a council here, but to achieve precisely what we were unsure. Later, the nobles and prelates of Scotland met here to discuss raising a ransom for King William I (The Lion), who had been kidnapped by Henry II of England at the Battle of Alnwick 1174.

I got a laugh out of the information that a fragment of the 'True Cross' was allegedly brought by King David's mother, Margaret, from Waltham Abbey, and was known thereafter as the Black Rood of Scotland. At the battle of Neville's Cross, in 1346, we were told, this precious relic fell into the hands of the English, and it was placed in Durham Cathedral, from where it disappeared at the Reformation.

"Why are you laughing?" Rosalie asked. "Don't you believe it existed?"

"If all the relics which have been claimed as part of the cross were real it would mean the original had to be at least fifty feet high."

"I guess." She seemed disappointed. "I wonder who took it from Durham?"

"Crazy Protestant fanatics, I suppose."

"Let's leave. Can we go to Princes Street now?"

Princes Street has few buildings on its south side, mainly comprising extensive, rather beautiful gardens. The street was named after King George III's eldest son, George Duke of Rothesay (later George IV).

In the last century, the railway companies created huge hotels at either end, the Caledonian Hotel to the west, and the North British Hotel to the east. In between were the Royal British Hotel, the Old Waverley Hotel, and Mount Royal Hotel.

The Gardens contained a large bandstand, a floral clock and a war memorial in addition to many trees and flowers. It was an entrancing place, especially as the day had turned out warm and sunny.

We also saw two of the main Scottish art galleries, and a huge, intricate Gothic monument dedicated to Sir Walter Scott, fabricator of stories who cast a pseudo-mythological glow on life and culture in the Highlands.

Scott was responsible for popularizing the invented tradition of clan tartans. He falsely thought leading families could claim unique colour combinations and designs. In the Victorian era, clan leaders were delighted to go along with this phony new view of their 'heroic' culture, and many adopted as ancient any plaid they had on hand. Other clan tartans were designs invented by fabric manufacturers for customers who had read Scott's novels and decided they wanted tartans of their own.

"It's a shame," Rosalie commented. "It nice to think of all those romantic highlanders rushing down the braes in their clan tartans."

"They probably did wear some kind of rudimentary plaid, but it would have been coloured only by roots and natural dyes found in the wild."

"How did they know who was who?"

"I imagine by what they shouted and by what kind of sprig of vegetation or feather they wore in their hats."

"Bonnets," she corrected.

"Right, bonnets. Now how about going back, getting cleaned up and having some dinner?"

"Yum." Said Rosalie, running up the bank to the street.

We almost had the dining room to ourselves that night, so they had dimmed the lights at the edges of the room. We decided to have Champagne to start, and to continue to drink it with our appetizer. Rosalie chose *Taittinger Comtes de Champagne Blanc de Blanc* 2007, a choice with which I had no difficulty at all.

She ordered shellfish bisque, and I ordered half a dozen Islay oysters. For the main course she settled on roast rump of border lamb. I went for the dry aged fillet of scotch beef. With that we asked for a bottle of *Georges de Vogue Bonnes Mares* 2008, and watched the sommelier carefully decant it over a candle flame so as to avoid serving the sediment.

For dessert we chose to share *Tarte Tatin* and to have it with a half bottle of *Hermitage Vin de Paille*.

As we were finishing our dessert, the maître d' sidled up to the table. "Mr. LeBlanc?"

"Yes."

"There is a telephone call for you."

"Where?"

"Just outside the door. At the small table in the alcove."

"Thank you." Then to Rosalie I said, "It must be Patrick. I won't be long."

I went out and picked up the phone. "Hi, Patrick."

"Where are you?"

"Edinburgh."

"Nice."

"Has there been a breakthrough in the case?"

"Kind of. You know, neither we nor any police department in the province has any record of the incident at the Wind in the Willows because no charge was laid?"

"Yes, I guessed as much."

"Well, I've got good news and bad news."

"Give me the good news."

"One of my detectives unearthed a brief reference in an old regional weekly. Unfortunately the page has no date, but it does identify a boy who was reported as having made a complaint to camp officials. I guess that would be your Reverend Pettigrew."

"Great! What's the bad news?"

"He has rather a common name."

"Not John Smith?"

"No, worse."

"What?"

"Robert MacDonald."

"Holy shit! How many Robert MacDonalds are there in Nova Scotia?"

"Five hundred and thirty three have listed phone numbers. We don't know how many have unlisted phones on land lines, or how many have mobiles, or how many don't have phones at all."

"But don't forget that if the incident took place around 1985, we would only be interested in the ones born, say, between 1966 and 1968."

"Yes, I'm well aware of that, Marc. But the task of finding out the birth dates even of the 533 with listed phones is immense."

"I can see that."

"When we can get around to it, my guys will go to the Registry of Births, Deaths and Marriages and work it from that end."

"What do you mean, 'when you can get around to it'?"

"We've had a number of crimes recently which take priority due to their—ahem—political sensitivity."

"Damn!"

"And I still have some people off sick with COVID."

"When do you think you might have a list of possibles?"

"I'm guessing a week for a list of all eligibles. Another week, maybe two, for a list of those within a reasonable catchment area of the camp."

"Remember, Bill Withers was from Dartmouth."

"Marc, please stop trying to teach me how to do my job."

"Sorry."

"I was about to say that, because of Withers, the catchment area has to be everywhere east of Halifax."

"Wow! That's likely half, possibly two-thirds of the total."

"I had thought of that, Marc," Patrick said with a sigh. "So, that means it will be at least three weeks to a month before we have a short list of possible suspects. It is a gargantuan task involving a great deal of time and a lot of shoe leather."

"Yes, I understand. You'll keep me in the loop?"

"Yes, of course. Enjoy your trip."

19

The next day, we were sorry to be leaving the Scottish capital, wishing we had arranged a longer visit.

We caught the train from Waverley station for Perth. It took more than an hour to get there, taking in stretches of the Fife coast. As we rolled over the bridge across the River Tay, Perth presented itself as such an attractive city that we regretted we were not stopping there.

Rosalie got to work on her laptop and soon was regaling me with information about this ancient place, whose history extended back to prehistoric times.

Not far away from Perth, she told me, was Scone Abbey, which formerly housed the Stone of Destiny, on which the Kings of the Scots were traditionally crowned. Although it was long before my time, I recalled hearing the story that in 1950 four students from the University of Glasgow stole the Stone of Scone from Westminster Abbey in London and smuggled it back to Scotland. I made a mental note to watch the movie which was made about the event so I could find out how they accomplished such a daring deed.

Rosalie told me that King James I was assassinated in Perth in 1437, and in 1559, the irascible old curmudgeon John Knox began the Scottish Reformation with a sermon against 'idolatry' in the burgh kirk of St John the Baptist.

A violent mob quickly destroyed the altars in the kirk, and attacked the Houses of the Greyfriars and Blackfriars monks. Scone Abbey was attacked shortly afterwards.

In 1651, Charles II was crowned at the Abbey, the traditional site of the investiture of Kings of Scots. Later on in the year, Oliver Cromwell came to Perth following his victory in the Battle of Dunbar. But eventually Charles II was restored to the throne, and the Act of Settlement in 1701 led to the Jacobite uprisings.

Soon the train started to roll again, and in about half an hour we pulled into Pitlochry. Here we disembarked for a two day visit.

This is a charming little town which became fashionable when Queen Victoria and Prince Albert visited the area. They bought a highland estate at nearby Balmoral, which is still the King's residence in Scotland. The town still has many grey stone Victorian buildings, the high street having a strange cast-iron canopy over one side.

We stayed at Fonab Castle, an impressive brownstone building with slate roofs and a pointed turret. Here we were made very comfortable and spent our time walking among the fine scenery of the area.

~

It was only a matter of twenty minutes on the train from Pitlochry to Blair Atholl, where we were quickly installed at the Atholl Arms, a 19th-century building across from the famous castle. Blair Atholl is a village built at the confluence of River Tilt and River Garry, and is surrounded by the majestic Grampian Mountains.

Right after checking in, we made a bee-line for the fairy-tale, white-walled castle with its conical towers.

This was the last castle in the British Isles to be besieged during the last Jacobite Rebellion in 1746, and was the traditional home of the Dukes of Atholl, who, we learned, are the only people in Britain permitted to raise a private army, consisting of workers on the extensive Atholl estates.

The countryside hereabouts is idyllic, so we spent the rest of our time walking. Those walks, and the simply, scrumptious salmon from the local rivers, were among our fondest Scottish memories.

~

It took an hour and half for the train to travel the 50 miles to Inverness, entering it by way of the Culloden viaduct, a vast structure, 600 meters long with 30 arches, which spans the River Nairn. To my mind, this was almost as impressive as the famous Glenfinnan viaduct which Harry Potter's train crosses on its way to Hogwarts.

As informative as ever, Rosalie told me that nearby was the site of the 11th-century battle of Blar nam Feinne, in which the Scots fought the Norwegians, and the field of the renowned Battle of Culloden in 1746.

Inverness is the northernmost city in the United Kingdom, lying within the Gleann Mòr (Great Glen), at its northern end. It is said that Shakespeare's MacBeth ruled here in the 11th century.

Mary Queen of Scots was once denied admittance to Inverness Castle by the governor, but Mary later took her revenge by hanging him. The house where she lived stood in Bridge Street until the 1970s, when it was demolished, a matter of acute disappointment to us.

Our hotel, The Beaufort, was only a short distance from the train station and was an old-fashioned, comfortable place on a pleasant street. Once we were settled in our room, Rosalie examined all the literature provided by the hotel and checked out local sites of interest on her laptop.

Among other snippets, she found a reference to one Cionneach MacCionnich, a poet born nearby, who had composed the poem *The Lament of the North*, mocking the Highland gentry for being absentee landlords who spent their wealth uselessly in London rather than locally. She also stumbled through some Gaelic names for various prominent features in the vicinity which she said translated into Lamb Hill, Yellow Hill, the Hill of the Fairies, the Hill of the Wind, the Great Hill, and the Hill of Peat.

From this, I foresaw we would be doing a fair amount of climbing the next day.

Later, in the rather nice dining room, we both had smoked mackerel to start and a lobster each to follow. Both were extremely good. We drank Chablis with the fish and an undistinguished Sauterne with some delicious Dundee cake with whipped cream.

Back in our room, I thought it was time to discover what my wife had planned for the rest of our vacation. "How many more places are we going to?"

"Oh, dozens and dozens."

"How can we? We'll be here for months."

"You mean how many places are we staying at?"

"Yes, what did you think I meant?"

"All the places we'll be seeing."

"Well, how many of those?"

"I don't know yet. I figured we would kind of follow our noses from glen to glen."

"That sounds nice. They do tend to run into one another. And where will we stay?"

"I picked eight places which we can use as bases to explore from."

"How did you choose them?"

"I chose them because they're scattered around the Highlands in a kind of circle which will bring us back here in a little over two weeks. And because..."

"Because what?"

"I liked the sound of them!"

"That's seems like as good a reason as any. What are they?"

"First we're going to Beauly. That's a few miles up the coast from here. Then at a place called Bonar Bridge, which is about two hours north of here on Dornock Firth."

"That sounds lovely."

"Then we go up the coast another fifty miles to Helmsdale. It's a seaside place on its own river. After that, I thought we had to go to John O'Groats to see the most northerly point in Scotland."

"I agree."

"Then round the top and down the western side to Achiltibuie."

"What?"

"I think that's how it's pronounced. It's a remote spot opposite the Summer Isles on a bay called Badentarbet."

"I've heard of the Summer Isles. It's where the movie *The Wicker Man* was set."

"I never heard of that movie."

"The original starred Edward Woodward and was very scary. The remake was with Nicholas Cage, but they set it somewhere in the states."

"Anyway, from there we'll be going to Loch Torridon. Isn't that a terrific name?"

"Yes, it is."

"I've seen pictures of it. It's spectacular and there's a lovely old castle-style hotel."

"Nice."

"After that, we go to the Isle of Skye, which I've heard is a must-see for everyone, and finally to Inverlochy. Then we will drive up the Great Glen, along the shores of Loch Lochy and Loch Ness, until we get back here."

"Marvellous. You've done a great job."

"Yes, I have," said Rosalie with complete conviction.

20

Our trip around the Highlands was both enjoyable and enlightening for both of us. We picked up our car, an MG ZS compact SUV, in Inverness, and drove north feeling like young newlyweds, out for adventure. Despite the fact that for nine of the twenty-one days the winds and rains howled round us, we relished every minute of the time we spent in this amazingly beautiful country.

From Beauly we explored Strathglass, a long, meandering glen with many little lochs and offshoots. For much of the way, the Glen is heavily tree-lined, but extensive, idyllic grassy areas were evident.

The nearby Glen Strathfarrar was in some ways more impressive, as the river twists and turns, revealing small islands along the way. Other, smaller, glens poked here and there into the mountains and where there were roads, we pursued them as far as we could go.

We discovered that this area, today so deserted and sparsely populated, had had its population reduced by over 50% in the nineteenth century, when the Laird had evicted his tenants to make way for Cheviot sheep farming.

Further north, from Helmsdale, the long and lonely Strath of Kildonan winds some 20 miles inland to the tiny settlement of Kinbrace. The scenery here is impossible to describe other than to overuse the term "lovely."

Again, we ventured into smaller valleys where car travel was feasible. And, as earlier, we were struck by how few people lived here. Apart from the occasional small town and tiny village, only a few dwellings dotted here and there testified to human habitation.

Talking to a local man, Ruary Mackay, we learned that in the

1830s over 250 crofters' houses were burned in order to force them to leave the land.

We found John O'Groats to be entrancing, with its huge, jagged cliffs. Because this day was fine and clear, the Islands of Stroma and Ronaldsay were visible far out to sea. Like children, we swung around the famous signpost, pointing to Orkney, Edinburgh, Land's End and New York.

Here we had fresh mackerel, which we both adore, fresh out of the sea.

Although its remoteness had a certain rugged appeal, we found Achiltibuie, on the west coast, rather bleak. This little community lies on the Coigach Coast just west of Loch Broom. The weather was appalling and we could barely see the Summer Isles across the bay through the rain.

We were impressed with huge hydroponic greenhouses, which produce fresh fruit and vegetables all year round. We were told that they actually grew bananas, but we didn't see any.

Another sumptuous feast of lobster at the hotel was certainly very welcome after a day of being tossed and blown about.

After dinner, Patrick called. The line was terrible and we had to shout.

"Where are you?"

"Achilitbiuie."

"Where the hell is that?"

"Never mind."

"What?"

"I said, never mind."

"Mind what?"

"Patrick, the line is rubbish. Just tell me what you have."

"We've narrowed down the list. I have two guys working on it around the clock. They're worn out."

"Good."

"What's good about that?"

"I meant, good that you've narrowed down the possible suspects."

"Yeah. Well the list is under a hundred."

"Great."

"No, it isn't."

"Why? How many are on the list?"

"Seventy-eight."

"Shit!"

"Exactly."

"I guess each one will have to be visited and questioned."

"You got that right. I'm so strapped at this end, some of them will have to wait until you get home."

"But I—"

"Yes I know, I know. You have no official status, but I'll have to turn a blind eye to your activities."

"Oh, alright. I'll do what I can."

"Okay, buddy. Love to Rosalie."

~

Loch Torridon was as dramatic as the pictures had suggested. It was a bay, enclosed by towering mountains on each side. Sadly, the weather did not cooperate, so we could not do as much walking as we had wished.

The food and accommodation were very good, and the hotel had a fine selection of single malts. In conversation with the manager, I learned that in the 19th century, evictions of tenants had also occurred in nearby Strathcarron, a few miles south of Torridon.

Two days later, when we headed over the bridge to Skye (Rosalie singing *Speed Bonnie Boat*), the clouds cleared and the sun beat down. The bridge, not built until 1995, was located at the Kyle of LochAlsh (which we were told is pronounced Kylahosh) where previously a ferry was required to get to the island.

We stayed at a very fine place called Carter's Rest in Glendale, which is at the most westerly part of the island. Skye is a very special place, with so many notable attractions, so we were glad that the weather remained good until we left, two days later.

The second day we took a long walk, and in Dunvegan we were astonished to find a museum to the Cape Breton Giant Angus

MacAskill.

As we were coming out, we met an old man who said his name was John MacDearmid. Obviously, he loved company, and insisted we sit on a wall by the harbour. He became extremely garrulous, one minute lapsing into Gaelic, and another making rude suggestions to Rosalie.

We were not sure how far we could believe anything he said, but he told us that between 1840 and 1850 Lord MacDonald had evicted 30,000 of his tenants and that the valley of Lorgill, which we could go to see, was totally denuded of its people.

The following day brought us to Inverlochy, our last stop before driving up the Great Glen to Inverness and getting the train back to Edinburgh. Inverlochy is a small place joined at the hip with Fort William, long a garrison town.

The day before we left, Rosalie instructed me to drive south under the shadow of Ben Nevis, the tallest mountain in the British Isles. We made our way up a tiny road until we reached a place called Orchie, an abandoned village of which only the shells of two cottages and a ruined church still existed.

We clambered out of the car and she led me to the church. There, amid a tangle of bushes and weeds was a small graveyard.

"What are we looking for?" I asked.

"You'll find out."

We pulled sticks out of an overgrown hedge and thrashed around in the grass for at least twenty minutes.

Finally, I heard Rosalie utter a cry of triumph. "Here it is! Come look at this, Marc."

It was an extremely weather-beaten tombstone, about two and a half feet high. The inscription was worn but just legible:

Here Lies
ARCHIBALD WILLIAM FLETCHER
Died age 62, 1858
The Lord knoweth his deeds
And holdeth him to account

"Who is he?"

"My great, great, great grandfather," Rosalie replied. "I may have left out a 'great' or have used too many. It's hard to figure."

"What was he doing here?"

"I'm not entirely sure. As far as I can discover, he was some kind of servant or manager for Lord Cameron, the local laird."

"Well, how about that? Good for you. You couldn't find your Welsh ancestors, but you've found your Scottish roots."

"Yes, I'm rather pleased about that. Now, let's go and pack for tomorrow. We should make an early start for going up the Great Glen, because we'll probably want to stop several times to take pictures"

"Okay. Only two more days and we'll be home again. Sorry to be leaving?"

"No, three weeks is plenty. And we did have our Welsh trip, too."

"Back to the grind. Patrick and I are still nowhere closer to finding our killer."

21

The weather was now superb in Nova Scotia and we were glad to be back. Our hill looked lush and green, and my small vegetable garden had undergone a dramatic transformation which had seen all plants up and growing fast.

The peas and beans were already forming on the stems, and herbs were in full flower. The basil, sage, lavender, thyme, and rosemary filled the air with an exotic perfume. Tomatoes and peppers were still in their infancy, but looked healthy and, if the weather held, promised to produce a bumper crop. Rosalie's roses, peonies, pansies, hydrangeas, iris and freesia were in magnificent form, making the property a spectacular blaze of colour.

Rosalie had to return to the university to teach her summer courses, and have meetings with students and administrators. I had two glorious but back-breaking days weeding my garden in blazing sunshine. More the once I reflected on the difference between these conditions and the cold, rainy, blustery days in the Scottish Highlands.

Notwithstanding, I missed those vast, beautiful, lonely glens and mountains, and part of me longed to be back there among the wind-swept heather and giant, grey rocks.

The third morning, I had just pulled some radishes and was wiping the dirt off on my jeans when I heard the phone ring. I went into the kitchen but, before answering, I quickly rinsed the radishes under the tap and stuck one in my mouth. It was amazingly good.

"Marc, is that you?"

"Yes."

"You sound funny."

"I'm crunching radishes."

"Are they good?"

"Terrific. Just picked from the garden."

"That's nice. So you're back?"

"Obviously."

"This is Patrick."

"Yes, I know. Any news?"

"You remember I said I would need you to check out people on the suspect list?"

"I remember."

"Well, I want you to get stuck in."

"When?"

"Now, today."

"Where? In the Valley?"

"No. Halifax area."

"Oh, no! We only just got back and haven't settled in properly yet."

"No time like the present."

"Surely it could wait until tomorrow."

"Better get up there right away. You might be able to get a dozen done this afternoon and evening."

"I have to work in the evenings?"

"Of course. Makes sense. That's when most of the men will be home. I wouldn't be surprised if at some calls you make in the afternoon they tell you to come back later."

"Do I get paid by the hour or on piecework?"

"Funny guy! Marc, please remember that you make it clear that you have no connection with any arm of law enforcement."

"Yes, I know. We've been through this."

"You must say you are investigating on behalf of a client—which is true—and that you would like to know if the person you're seeing had any association with the client."

"Yes, yes. I know the drill."

"I'm glad you do. It's important that you stick to it."

"Patrick, what do I get out of this?"

"The satisfaction that you have been a good friend to me and…"

"And what?"

"Half a case of *Sassicaia* 1975"

"Really?"

"Yes. I was keeping it for Ruth's and my silver anniversary."

"Patrick, I don't know what to say."

"Don't say anything. Just pack your bags."

"I'll get on the road right away."

"I thought that might clinch it. If you've got some paper, I'll give you the list of names and addresses."

There were nine names and addresses on the list, most of them being within the Halifax-Dartmouth area, but two were out in the country. One was in North Preston and the other in Glen Margaret.

If the man in North Preston turned out to be black, which was highly probable, it was very unlikely he would have attended the Wind in the Willows camp in the early 1980s, but I had to check him out. I left him until last, working my way from west to east.

The man who answered the door in Glen Margaret was in a wheelchair. He told me he had been disabled from birth, so was unable to "go gallivanting around to summer camps". I thanked him and drove into the city.

In Fairview, a fairly dingy-looking house produced a man at the door who was clearly drunk and spoiling for a fight. His comprehension was so impaired it took me a long time to make him understand what it was I wanted.

"Yeah, yeah I was at the camp," he slurred.

"Please tell me what happened with Lake, Robertson and Gillespie."

"Who the fuck are Lakie, Gilbertson and Roberts?"

"Lake, Robertson and Gillespie," I corrected, speaking slowly and clearly.

"Never heard tell of them. Say, you don't have any liquour on you, do you?"

"No, I'm sorry, I don't. But why don't you remember Lake, Robertson and Gillespie if you were at the Wind in the Willows?"

"Who says I was there?"

"You did. You told me so."

"I said I was at camp, but not that one." He pushed me with his elbow. "Move over. I need a piss so bad I can taste it."

Immediately he started to urinate on the stoop. I quickly jumped out of the way and beat a hasty retreat to the car. As I moved off I saw him swivelling around, spraying in all directions.

The next two addresses were fruitless, in that one was empty and had a large Realtor lockbox on the door, and at the other an old lady told me that, to the best of her knowledge, no Robert MacDonald had ever lived there. Nobody was home at the next three, so I scribbled notes on the back of my cards, asking them to get in touch with me.

The light was starting fade when I reached the penultimate address. I was getting tired and was ravenously hungry.

A tiny woman answered the door, listened patiently to my introduction, then called back into the house. "Bob! There's a detective here to see you."

The light from inside the house was almost blocked out as an enormous man, almost a giant, appeared before me. He had to step outside to avoid the door lintel obscuring his vision. He was red faced and bald, with a smile, almost from ear to ear, revealing several yellow teeth. He put out his hand for me to shake and, with great trepidation, I took it. It was akin to putting my hand into an industrial vise.

"Hey there, buddy. Come on in." He shouted over his shoulder, "Josie, get out the whisky and a couple of glasses!" Then he turned back to me. "How can I help you?"

"Mr. MacDonald—"

"Bob. Call me Bob."

"Thank you. Bob, about forty years ago, do you remember going to a summer camp called the Wind in the Willows?"

"Sure do. Great place. I had a terrific time there. There were woods, a big hill and a lake where we swam and could sail little boats."

At this point Josie came in with a tray bearing two glasses and, to my great surprise, a bottle of Glen Moray Port cask-finished single malt.

Apparently, Bob caught my eyes lighting up. "Ah I see you're a single malt man, Mr. LeBlanc."

"Marc, please. Yes, I am."

"I never got the taste for the high life, with the one exception of single malt."

"How did you acquire that?"

"Years ago, I was in Scotland and got a job at the distillery."

"Really? Which one?"

"This one. Glen Moray. I've been faithful to it ever since. They took one look at me and said, 'Laddie, I can see that you could roll more barrels in a day than three of our lads. You're hired.'"

"That's great. Now to the Wind in the Willows."

"Yeah. What do you want to know?"

Before it came out of my mouth, I knew something was not right. Even had Bob been only half his present size, no other kid would have dared to try to rape him. Still, I pressed on.

"Did you have any trouble at the camp?"

"No. I loved every minute of it."

"You knew Reverend Pettigrew?"

'Sure. Old Petters, we called him."

"Why was that?"

"There was a rumour—that's all it was—that he played hanky panky with some of the younger boys."

"You never saw anything like that?"

"Me? No, never."

"How did you get along with Leonard Lake, Struan Robertson and Alex Gillespie?"

"Who are they?"

"They would have been at Wind in the Willows when you were there."

"Not when I was there. I didn't know everyone, '.specially not the younger boys, but I knew those in my own age group."

"How many years did you go to the camp?"

"Three."

"In succession, or was there a gap between any of them?"

"No. They were in succession."

"And in none of those years did you come across anyone called Lake, Gillespie or Robertson?"

"There was a Robertson, but he was a Trevor."

"Thank you very much, Bob," I said, rather dazed by what he had told me. "And thanks also for the dram. If I wasn't driving I'd be tempted to stay with you and finish the bottle."

It was well into evening by now, and I was starving, so I decided to put off the North Preston visit until the next day. I headed to my hotel, had a quick wash and change, and then went out in search of some dinner.

22

After breakfast, I decided to visit the three people who had not been home the previous day, and then to drive out to see the Robert MacDonald in North Preston.

At the first house, the lady who answered the door told me, tearfully, that her husband had died only a few months before. I waited patiently, leaning against the door jamb, while she went into great detail of how her Robert had been as fit as a fiddle and never had a day's sickness in his life.

"Never even been to a doctor," she sobbed. "Then, pow! He just dropped like a stone."

"I'm very sorry, Mrs. MacDonald."

"Right there. Exactly where you're standing."

"That's awful," I said, instinctively moving away from the spot.

"And when I checked with insurance company, they said the premiums had not been paid for over a year."

"I am sorry."

"So I got nothing. Zero. Nada. Zilch."

"I'm very sorry for your loss, madam, but I must be going."

"Yes, you're just like the rest of them. So, go! Go! Fuck off!"

At the next address on the list, a small, thin, unshaven man came to the door. He was wearing a threadbare robe over obviously-dirty pyjamas, and down-at-heel slippers on his bare feet.

"Aha! Come in, come in. I've been expecting you."

"You have?" I asked, wondering how on earth he could have known I was coming.

"Oh yes, sooner or later. In the fullness of time. In due course. Come in, come in!"

I followed him, through an assortment of cardboard boxes and piles of old newspapers and empty bottles, into a back room containing an old television and two battered arm chairs.

"Sit down. Do you want a cup of tea?"

"No thank you."

"Coffee?"

"Thank you, no. You are Robert MacDonald?"

"Am I? That's the fifty thousand dollar question."

"You mean, your name is not Robert MacDonald?"

"Did I say that?"

"No, but you implied it."

"Ah, did I imply it, or did you infer it?"

"I'm in no mood to play games, sir."

"Now, now, no need to get all snarky. You see I am a smith."

"Your name is Smith?" I was getting angry.

"No, no I am a wordsmith. I play with words."

"Well, I wish you wouldn't do it with me. I'd be grateful if you would just answer a few questions."

"Fire away!"

"Please could you confirm that your name is, in fact, Robert MacDonald?"

"Guilty as charged. Since you insist."

"Did you attend a summer camp in the early 1980s?"

"That was long ago and far away. Beyond the primrose path of youth."

"None the less, did you go to summer camp?"

"Some might call it that."

I was becoming thoroughly annoyed with this wretched little man, and was fighting hard to control my temper. "Please, sir!"

"Others might call it the involuntary imprisonment of youthful persons."

"What did they call it?"

"Who?"

"The people who ran the camp?" I was almost shouting.

"What about the people who ran the camp?"

"Reverend Pettigrew and the others. What did they call the place?"

"Who is Reverend Pettigrew? Was he an adherent of the Church of Rome, or was he wedded to the heretical views of the Protestants? Or maybe a spiritualist?"

I took a deep breath, and waited several seconds while MacDonald sat there, smiling complacently. Finally, I spoke quietly, but with an unmistakable menace in my voice. "Look, Mr. MacDonald tell me now, and tell me simply, what was the name of the camp you attended?"

"It was called Rainbow Haven. It's been closed now for some time—"

I jumped up and stormed out leaving him talking to himself.

At the third address, an old woman invited me in and pressed me to have some dubious-looking cookies together with a glass of some unidentified cordial. She made a big production over carefully taking off her apron, folding it and putting it into a drawer.

Then she sat down and put her gnarled, red hands together. "Now then," she said, "we can get down to business."

"Business?"

"Yes, aren't you the man come about the roof?"

"The roof?"

"Yes, the tiles that were blown off in the storm last week."

"No, I'm sorry, I'm not here about the tiles."

"Then why are you here? Who are you?"

"My name is Marc LeBlanc. I'm a private investigator."

I thought her eyes were going to pop out of her head. She stood up quickly. "What are you investigating? Not me?"

"No, no. I was inquiring about a Robert MacDonald."

"Oh, Bobby!" she said, retaking her seat.

"Is he your son?"

"Yes, he is."

"Where is he, Mrs. MacDonald? May I see him?"

"Sure, if you've a mind to go to Moncton."

"He lives in New Brunswick?"

"Yes, has done for some years."

"You don't happen to remember if he attended a summer camp when he was younger, do you?"

"Yes, I do. Look, what's this all about?"

"My client is trying to get in touch with others who were at the camp."

"Oh, I see. Well, yes. He went to the Wind in the Willows camp several years running."

"Did he enjoy it there?"

"Look, Mr. LeBlanc, this line of questioning is becoming very strange. What are you trying to get at?"

"Nothing. It's just that my client had some difficulties there and I wondered if others did, too."

"You'll have to talk to Bobby about anything like that," she said, getting up. "I think you'd better go now."

"Certainly. But could you give me his address, please?"

"I can do that."

She walked over to an old bureau and scribbled on a pad. She tore off the page and handed it to me. "There you go."

The look on her face indicated that I should tarry no longer.

My final call was to North Preston. The gentleman there was a big, hearty, black man with a wide smile and sparkling eyes.

"We don't get many private investigators around here," he said with a laugh. "'Course, we gets some of the other kind, if you know what I mean. Now, what can I do you for."

He laughed again and, when his laughter had subsided, I explained my mission.

"Sure, I was at that camp. It was what they call ecumenical, so all sorts was there. Not many of us black Baptists, but there were a few of us."

"Did you have any trouble there?"

"Like what?"

"Any kind of trouble."

"Oh you mean the 'R' word."

"The 'R' word?"

"Yeah racism. In them days there was a lot more of it about. Today there's a good deal less of it, but a damn sight more talking about it."

"So there was racism at the camp?"

"Not that I noticed. Maybe a little name-calling, but we all got on."

"And nothing happened to you when you were there?"

"What you mean, happened?"

"Did anyone assault you?"

"Hell, no! I'd have like to see them try. But nobody tried because they knew I could handle myself in a scrap."

"Did you know Bill Withers, Len Lake, Alex Gillespie or Struan Robertson?"

"Where? At the camp?"

"Yes."

"Can't say the names ring any bells. Maybe Withers. Would he a guy older than me?"

"Yes. One of the counsellors."

"I think I might just recall him. Not the others."

Before I drove back to Halifax I called Patrick from the car.

"Mission accomplished," I said. "All but two on your list are accounted for."

"Well done. Maybe you should join the police force. Who are the two?"

"One was an empty house up for sale. The other is living in Moncton."

"And none of the others are likely suspects?"

"I wouldn't think so. They are either weirdos, people who couldn't have been at the camp, or guys who'd beat the shit out of anyone who tried to rape them."

"The one in Moncton. Does he sound like a suspect?"

"Not on the face of it, but..."

"But what?"

"I got a strange feeling about him from his mother."

"Really?"

"I think you should get your colleagues in New Brunswick to check him out."

"Or maybe we should take a run up there."

"You think?"

"I'm not sure I trust guys to do the interview who don't have all the background."

    "Makes sense. When do you want to go?"

    "How about tomorrow. Where are you staying?"

    "The Muir."

    "You got the Bugatti?"

    "Of course."

    "Well, you know where I live. Pick me up at six."

23

Patrick was standing, bag in hand, outside his house when I pulled up at six o'clock the next morning. Ruth gave me a wave from the open door, which I returned with a smile. She was a wonderful woman, a perfect mate for Patrick, and one of my and Rosalie's nicest friends.

"I hope you've told Ruth to take good care of my Sassicaia," I said to Patrick as he squeezed into the passenger seat.

"It's not yours yet," he grunted as he buckled his seatbelt.

"But you promised!"

"And I'll make good on that promise, but it is contingent on your behaving appropriately today."

"That wasn't mentioned at the time you made the promise."

"It should have been."

"Chiseller. And what does 'appropriately' mean in this context?"

"Doing what I tell you. Following my lead. Not saying dumb things. And not pretending you are the police."

"If you're not careful, you'll have to walk to Moncton."

"Just drive!"

"If this guy isn't the one, we've got nothing," I said as the Bugatti sped over the Trantramar Marshes into New Brunswick.

"That's about the size of it, I reckon," Patrick replied. "So, that being the case, we must be extra careful to be objective and not try to make something out of it if nothing exists."

"Yes. I'm afraid I may already have done that by exaggerating the vibes I got from his mother."

"Now you tell me! What exactly did she say? Run the entire conversation past me."

"If I can remember it."

"Try hard."

"After I told her who I was, I asked her if her son had attended a summer camp when he was younger. She said yes, he had, and asked me why I wanted to know. Then I told her that my client was trying to get in touch with others who were at the camp. She confirmed that he went to the Wind in the Willows camp several years running."

"Then what?" Patrick asked.

"Then I asked her if Robert had enjoyed it there."

"That's a weird question. What did she answer?"

"She said something about my line of questioning becoming very strange."

"Uh-oh. That was a red light. I hope you backed off."

"Should I have? I said that my client had some difficulties at the camp and I wondered if others did, too."

"Big mistake. Schoolboy error."

Out of the corner of my eye I saw Patrick sadly shaking his head.

"So, what happened then?"

"She said I'd have to talk to the son and that it was time for me to go."

"Well, I agree that's suspicious, but the way you botched it almost certainly means she will have called her son and that he will have pulled up the drawbridge and be on the defensive."

"Sorry, Patrick."

"Live and learn."

The Bugatti was purring along at a good rate, averaging 130 kph. The traffic was not very heavy and Patrick kept an eye open for police.

"What would you do if we were stopped?"

"Tell the truth. I'd produce my badge and warrant card and say that we were pursuing a case the details of which I was not at liberty to discuss with his rank."

"Deceit! Corruption!"

"Not at all. A gentle, very minor bending of the facts to get the job done."

"If this guy MacDonald is as pure as the driven snow, what do we do then?"

"Widen the net. We still have roughly another 70 Robert Mac-Donalds to check out."

"God, I can't imagine having to visit that many."

When we got into Moncton, Patrick directed me to RCMP headquarters, where he asked me to wait. Some fifteen minutes later he reappeared and ordered me to drive on.

"What was that all about?"

"A courtesy call. I had to clear with my opposite number that I was on his patch, and let the local guys know that I would be doing some sniffing."

"Sniffing?"

"Yes, I thought we should do some sniffing with a number of MacDonald's neighbours before we go in to see him."

"Makes sense. When do we start?"

"Right now. Park at the end of his street, if you can, and we'll proceed on foot."

From the neighbours we learned that MacDonald was some kind of provincial civil servant. Nobody knew what department he worked for, but several thought it was "something scientific", and one told us it was in atomic energy supervision and regulation.

None of them described themselves as friends of MacDonald, and none of them said they knew him well, despite his having lived on the street for some years and the street having had a stable population. Three or four described him as 'weird', two said he was a 'kind of loner' and one woman actually shuddered when she spoke of him, saying, "He just gives me the creeps." Some of the men intimated, without actually saying so, that he was gay.

All were agreed that MacDonald lived alone, had a responsible position with a good salary and drove an expensive car. But the overriding characteristic communicated to us by his neighbours was that he was tetchy, ill tempered, spiteful, petty and officious. None of this information boded well for our forthcoming interview, something which prompted Patrick to insist once more that I say nothing throughout the encounter.

The man who answered the door appeared to be in his late

fifties, was about five feet seven inches tall, slender ('willowy' was the term which occurred to me at the time), and expensively dressed in a grey silk polo-necked sweater, dark grey flannels, and soft leather shoes with tassels.

"Ah yes," he said in a whining tone before we had spoken. "The Heavy Mob. I've been expecting you. First you intimidate my 85-year-old mother and now you come here to browbeat me."

"Neither of those assertions is true," said Patrick. "Will you let us in so we may speak in private?"

"No, I don't think I will," MacDonald said petulantly.

"Then we will have our conversation out here, where all your neighbours will be able to hear it."

MacDonald looked around and noticed, as I had, that several heads had appeared above the hedges and fences in adjoining properties.

"Bastards!" he almost spat at us.

"Or, alternatively"—Patrick deliberately raised the level of his voice—"you can follow us down to RCMP headquarters, where we can conduct a formal interview."

"Come in, then." MacDonald wailed like an animal. "You'd only force your way in if I don't invite you."

"Sir, please—"

"Sit down if you must, but do not sit on that blue couch. The material is delicate and easily soiled."

Patrick sat on an elegant rosewood chair of quite modern design, while I had to make do with a huge, white bean bag which was remarkably uncomfortable and made squeaking noises whenever I moved.

On the walls were abstract paintings in a variety of pastel colours, mauve predominating, and the furniture was blue or white. On the floor was the biggest, thickest, fluffiest, white carpet I had ever seen.

"I'd ask you to take your shoes off, but I know you'd refuse," MacDonald whined.

"Now, sir, I'd like to ask you a few questions if you don't mind."

"Well, I do mind! Should I have a lawyer here?"

"I think that would be quite unnecessary. However, if you want a lawyer, by all means have one, but that would mean our all going downtown."

"Oh, alright, then."

"Right—"

"First, let me see your credentials."

"Certainly, sir." said Patrick, producing and handing them over. I was earnestly hoping he would not ask for mine, for if he had, I would have had to leave.

"A superintendent! Oh, I am honoured. And what can be so important to require such a senior officer?"

"This doesn't have to be difficult, sir. I'm just making preliminary inquiries."

"About what crime?"

"Who said there's been any crime?"

"There must have been, otherwise you wouldn't be here."

"First, let me establish that you are Robert MacDonald."

"Don't you know?"

"I just want to make sure I am speaking to the right person."

"And who is that person?"

"Robert MacDonald. Is that your name, sir?"

"Am I obliged to tell you?"

"No but I could construe that as hindering police inquiries and we would need to go downtown."

"Alright, then."

"Alright then what?"

"Alright. I am Robert MacDonald."

"Thank you, sir. That wasn't too difficult, was it?"

"Whatever."

"Can you recall if, in the early 1980s, you attended a summer camp called the Wind in the Willows?"

"What if I did?"

"Please, sir, just answer the question."

"I don't remember."

"Is that really true, sir? It's not something anyone would be likely to forget."

"I may have."

"May have? Or did?"

"Alright, did."

"Thank you, sir. Do you recall William Withers, Alex Gillespie, Struan Robertson or Leonard Lake?"

"God knows, I may have met people with those names somewhere along the road in my lifetime."

"We're talking about the Wind in the Willows summer camp."

"You want to know if I remember those people at the camp?"

"Yes."

"Well, I don't."

"Are you sure? None of those people?"

"I can't remember."

"Think hard, please."

"Well," MacDonald sighed deeply, rose form his chair and started pacing up and down the room. "I may have."

"May have?"

"May have met them at the camp."

"I'm unclear what you are telling me. Are you saying that you now recall these people, but that you did not know them well enough to have remembered them when I first mentioned their names?"

"Brilliant!" MacDonald laughed and clapped his hands. "That's brilliant, Superintendent. You have put the case succinctly."

"Is there anything else about the Wind in the Willows that you had forgotten, but which is now coming back you?"

"Maybe."

"Memories becoming clearer?"

"Maybe."

"Would you care to elaborate?"

"Yes, I will elaborate. For your information, it was a fucking hell hole! I hated it!"

"The camp?"

"Yes, of course the camp. Are you stupid?"

"Really, sir, there's no need to be abusive—"

"Not only one year. I had to go back for another year." MacDonald was openly crying. "I begged my mother not to send me back, but the bitch said those were the happiest days of my life and that I would have fun there."

"But you didn't have fun?"

"No, by Christ, I did not!"

"And was that because of interactions with others at the camp."

"You could say that, yes."

"I see. Did you at any time have any actual altercation with anyone?"

"That depends upon what you mean by 'altercation.'"

"Specifically, I was referring to any attack, assault, bullying, intimidation...that sort of thing?"

"Plenty of that." He sobbed loudly.

"I beg your pardon, sir. Are you saying one or more of these individuals—namely Withers, Robertson, Lake or Gillespie—did assault or attack you?"

"No, no."

"No? But you just said—"

"Not them. I was assaulted, but not by any of them."

Patrick sat back in his chair as if he were winded. He looked at me, obviously puzzled, and slowly shook his head.

"Then if not by those individuals, by whom were you attacked or assaulted?"

"By fucking Pettigrew, of course!"

"The Reverend Walter Pettigrew?"

"Who else? God knows how many lives that man blighted."

"Do you know that he died recently?"

"No, I didn't, but I'm glad to hear the news. I hope he rots in hell!"

"I know this has been an unhappy experience for you, Mr. MacDonald, and I'm sorry if I've upset you. I don't think we need take up any more of your time."

As I started up the Bugatti and pulled out into Moncton's tree-lined streets, we said nothing, each trying to distill what we had heard and witnessed.

Finally, Patrick broke the silence. "Well, I'll be fucked!"

"We sure didn't expect that."

"It never even crossed my mind."

"When we went in, he was a suspect, and when we came out he was a victim."

"Sure looks like it. Of course, it could have been an act. If it was, it was a brilliant piece of acting."

"Do you think he's capable of it?"

"Hard to say. I've seen criminals with an IQ of close to zero who fooled me into thinking they were as clean as a whistle. And others, really smart types, who couldn't fool a child."

"Patrick, let's not dismiss him out of hand. If he did succeed in fooling us, it would put us completely off the scent. It would send us in a hundred other directions which is precisely what the killer would want us to do."

"You're right. He stays on the list."

"What list? There is no list until dozens of other prospects have been interviewed."

"You're a proper Mr. Sunshine, aren't you?"

As we were approaching Shubenacadie, I envisaged the enormity of the task ahead, and I wondered if there was some other approach which might find our killer in less time and with less effort. It occurred to me that maybe Patrick's officers had missed something in their initial investigations.

"Patrick, do you think there is anything to be gained by going back to the beginning?"

"What do you mean?"

"Us concentrating on the summer camp end by looking for someone who may or may not be called Robert MacDonald—"

"May or may not?"

"Yes, I've just thought that he could have changed his name years ago."

"Why the hell would he do that?"

"I don't know. May be it was prompted by the shame of being known as someone who had been raped."

"Jesus! You're right. Why didn't I think of that?"

"So, even if we see every Robert MacDonald in the province, we still might never come across our guy."

"Right. So we go back to the scenes of crime."

"I think we should."

"Alright. We're getting close to Dartmouth. Let's see your Mrs. Withers as soon as we get there."

"It's getting late. I'll need somewhere to stay tonight."

"I call Ruth. You can crash at our place."

"You're on."

Much to my relief, Valerie Withers looked a great deal better than she had the last time I saw her, and this time there was apparently nothing in the house she did not want us to see. Any reluctance to talk to me again was more than compensated for by Patrick's presence. She seemed overawed and flattered to have a police superintendent visit her.

"Please go in and sit down. I'll put the kettle on," she said, scuttling to the kitchen.

As directed, we went into her living room, only to find Norman sitting there like some gross oriental potentate. He looked more evil than ever; even more overweight, even more arrogant.

"Hello, LeBlanc. You here again?" he said. "Who's your little friend?"

"Hello Norman," I said, just managing to be civil. "This is Superintendent Kennedy from the RCMP."

Visibly shaken by this news, Norman instinctively got up, looking around for a way out, but I blocked the doorway.

"Oh no, you don't, Norman. Superintendent Kennedy has a few questions for you."

"Me? What about?" Norman asked. "Why would he want to ask me questions?"

"If you'll kindly sit down again, you may find out." Patrick's voice was smooth, even oily, but carried an unmistakable hint of menace.

"What's going on?" Valerie asked, coming into the room with a tray of tea things.

"Nothing to worry about, Mrs. Withers," Patrick said. "Why don't you and Norman sit down on that sofa? This won't take too long."

They sat down, at first with difficulty because of Norman's size.

When they were finally squeezed in, Patrick pulled his notebook from his jacket pocket, and took out a ballpoint pen. In silence, he made an elaborate, but totally unnecessary, show of shaking the pen, clicking the button and scribbling on the notebook.

At length, he looked up. "Now then! I am going to ask a series of questions. In each case I want you to answer first, Norman, and then your mother. Is that clear?"

"Yes, I guess so," said Valerie. Norman mumbled something and briefly nodded.

"Right. On what day of the week did Mr. Withers die?"

"It was a Tuesday."

"No, it wasn't. It was a Wednesday, Norman."

"I think you've got it wrong, Mom."

"Maybe I have. Please go on."

"So Mr. Withers died on either a Tuesday or a Wednesday, but most likely the former. That can easily be checked. For how long was he home alone that day?"

"I went out around eight-thirty in the morning. I don't know what time Mom went out."

"It was about quarter after nine."

"And when did you return?"

"I came back around six. Mom was already here. So was the ambulance."

"I got home about four-thirty. I found Bill after I had put my shopping away and went upstairs to change."

"Now, think very carefully about my next question. When you left the house, what did you see when you went out into the street?"

"How do you mean?"

"Just tell me what you saw."

"Just the street. And cars parked."

"What cars?"

"Let me see....there was Hugh Parker's Chevy, Mrs. Williams' Fiat, Fred Walker's car wasn't in the yard....."

"Any strange cars?"

"Well, I think there was van going up the street and a couple of cars coming the other way—"

"I mean cars which were stationary."

"You mean parked?"

"Yes."

"It's hard to remember." Norman gazed off into the corner of the room, obscenely chewing his tongue. "I think there was a blue Pontiac, and another hiding behind it."

"Hiding? Why do you say 'hiding'?"

"Did I?"

"Yes, you did."

"I guess what I meant was I couldn't see much of it because it was behind the Pontiac."

"Sedan or SUV?"

"Sedan."

"What colour?"

"Black."

"Size?"

"Big."

"Bigger than your standard sedan?"

"Yeah."

"Mrs. Withers, what did you see went you went out?"

"I can't say as I took much notice. I guess I would have seen the cars I usually see."

"You mean neighbours' cars which you see every day?"

"Yes. That's right."

"Any others?"

"Well, I'm not sure about this, but when I heard what Norm said, I got to thinking and, now I cast my mind back, I'm pretty sure I saw a big black car, too."

"Had you ever seen it before?"

"No. I'm pretty sure of that."

"Norman. How about you?"

"Yeah. I'm almost positive it was there the day before."

"Were you out on the street?"

"No. I looked out the front window."

"Parked in the same place?"

"No, I'd say one space closer to the house."

"Okay. I have one last question—for today—and think before you answer. Was there any point in the day prior to Mr. Withers' death that both of you were gone from the house?"

"I know I didn't go out," said Valerie. "I had cleaning and ironing and baking to do that day."

"Norman?"

"Same. I thought I had a cold coming on, so I stayed in."

"All day?"

"Yeah."

"Thank you both. You've been most helpful."

"Now let's go home and see what Ruth has rustled up for dinner," Patrick said, when we were back in the Bugatti.

"Patrick, I have to say, that was a masterly interview."

"Why, thank you, Marc."

"Having Norman go first was a stroke of genius. That way he didn't have time to think up an answer, and if he told lies, the chances were his mother would have contradicted him."

"There's method in my madness."

"So, it looks as if the killer stalked him for at least two days."

"Yes, he was prepared to try the first day, but had to give up because Valerie and Norman stayed home."

"But the next day he got lucky."

"Yes."

"So we're looking for a big, black sedan. Not many of those in Nova Scotia."

"Only a couple of thousand. But it narrows it down a bit. If any of our suspects have black sedans we can move them up the list.

"What do you think of Norman?"

"As a suspect?"

"Yes."

"Odious creature. He's a possible. He could easily have made up all the stuff about the car. His mother's corroboration wasn't particularly strong."

"I still think he could have killed his father but, obviously, he can't be considered for the other murders."

"Two killers! It makes my head hurt. I'll call Ruth and tell us to expect us momentarily."

He dialed and then said to his phone, "Hi, darling. We'll be there in five-ten minutes. What's for grub? Roast chicken? Lovely! Just go down and bring up a bottle of *Gaja Barbaresco* 1985. See you soon."

"*Gaja Barbaresco* 1985!" I said. "A marvellous way to end an interesting day."

24

The next day being a Saturday, Patrick did not have to go into his office, so we had a late breakfast. Unfortunately, Ruth had made pancakes, something I utterly despise. Occasionally I can run to crepes—as *Crêpes Suzette*, or very thin ones wrapped around Bayonne ham—but otherwise I avoid the stodgy things like the plague.

"I hope you like pancakes, Marc," Ruth said cheerfully as she plonked a huge stack of them on the table. My face must have shown my disappointment, if not disgust, for she immediately added, "Oh, I am sorry. Shall I knock you up some crispy bacon and a few eggs?"

"Yes, please, Ruth. I'm sorry to be a nuisance."

"Not at all. Patrick will probably clean the plate."

"Yes," he said eagerly, "all the more for me!"

The bacon was delicious and the eggs were perfect, over very easy. I wiped my plate clean with Ruth's excellent homemade bread.

"That *Barbaresco* last night was stupendous," I said.

"Wasn't it just? I was afraid it might still be too tannic, but it was one of Gaja's more forward vintages."

"You must have bought it some years ago. The prices he charges now are ludicrous."

"You're right. I bought it in 2013. Even then the price was astronomical."

"I think most of the world's top wine producers are being greedy and irresponsible. They know there are a few millionaires, neurosurgeons and high-flying corporation executives who are prepared to pay any amount to be ultra-fashionable, so they absolutely milk the market."

"I agree. Sure, the wines of Gaja, Domaine de Romanee Conti and Chateau Petrus likely are among the best in the world, but there is no way they are twenty times better than the excellent wines in less-fashionable categories. This usually means that poor slobs like me can never get to drink the best."

"It's a shame, but that's capitalism, and the producers will over-step the mark one of these years. They almost went to the wall about sixty years ago. It could happen again."

"Marc, if you're finished eating, why don't you bring your coffee into the den? We can figure out what to do next."

We made ourselves comfortable and Patrick flipped through a number of files which he had put on the table in front of him.

"It seems to me that we could look at Leonard Lake and Struan Robertson within the same time period."

"Remind me where they lived."

"Lake lived in Ogden, near Guysborough, and Robertson lived in Lakevale, Antigonish County."

"They're still some way apart, so I wouldn't plan on doing them and getting back here on the same day."

"You may be right. The last one, Alex Gillespie definitely couldn't be done at the same time."

"He's the one in Cape Breton?"

"Yes, Northern Cape Breton. South Harbour. That's near Ding-wall."

"We could do the first two on one day stay overnight—say somewhere near the Strait of Canso, then go on down north the next day."

"Sounds right, but there may be a problem."

"What's that?"

"I really can't go running around as if I was an ordinary in-spector. Mine is basically a desk job, and I have dozens of cases to supervise."

"What are you suggesting?"

"It may have to be another officer who takes these three invest-igations. I could give them the wink so they let you tag along."

"No! Patrick, it's likely, because they didn't have the full picture, that other officers may have missed important stuff in the first place. And to be honest, if you assign this to some other guy, I think I would step away and let him or her get on with it."

"I'll have a word with my chief super. But even if he does okay it, we'll have to put it off for a few days. I have a lot of catching up to do on other cases."

"I understand. Do what you can and let me know. Now, I must be getting back to Grand Pre. Rosalie hasn't seen me for a while, and my garden has been neglected."

"I've just had a thought. Could we do it on a weekend?"

"I don't see why not. We'd go up early on Saturday and come back Monday morning."

"Yeah, I can wing that. Maybe we could all go. Ruth and Rosalie, too. While we're interviewing they could be hiking and stuff in the vicinity."

"And stuff?"

"I don't know what women do when they get together," Patrick said with a laugh. Then he went to the door. "Ruth! Sweetheart!"

"Yes, what is it, Pat?"

"How do you fancy a trip up country, to Cape Breton with Rosalie and Marc?"

"That'd be nice. What's the catch?"

"Marc and I have to do some interviewing. You and Rosalie could do whatever you want."

"Where would this be?"

"First day, somewhere in Antigonish and Guysborough counties. Next day, Dingwall in northern Cape Breton."

"I imagine we could find something to amuse ourselves. But, Pat, I warn you now, if the weather is bad, Rosalie and I get the car. You'd have to do your interviewing on foot, in the rain."

"Alright, darling. If worst comes to worst, I 'll get the local plod to send us a car."

I was already on the phone to Rosalie, who readily agreed, and suggested the following weekend. The Kennedys saw no difficulty with this, so Ruth said she would make some calls and book us rooms in both locations.

"Why don't Rosalie and I come here on Friday evening?"

"Good idea. We can't use the Bugatti. You alright with my car?"

"We'll bring our BMW SUV. There'd be more room."

"Sounds fine. Now come with me."

I followed Patrick down the hall to the basement door, then down the steps into the cool, dark cellar. He pulled a hanging cord and a light came on.

He led me along piles of old carpets and boxes to the end, where his wine collection was neatly laid out on shelves. He picked up a half case and put it into my welcoming arms.

"One half case of Sassicaia 1977, as promised."

"That's wonderful, but I can't take all six. Three is quite enough."

"You sure?"

"Yes"

"Thanks, Marc. I confess that parting with six would have been a wrench."

Gingerly he put three bottles back on the rack. The labels were faded somewhat, but the blue and white star was unmistakable.

I think it was back in the 1960s that the Marchesi Incisa Della Rocchetta planted Bordeaux grapes on his property at Bolgheri, ignoring all warnings that only the Italian Sangiovese grape would thrive in Tuscany. The result was a triumph and those who bought the earlier vintages got bargains which would bring them infinite pleasure in the years ahead. Those who could afford to purchase Sassicaia since the 1980s had to pay stratospheric prices.

I carried my treasured reward out to the Bugatti and gently tucked it away. Then, tossing my travel bag on the passenger seat, I waved goodbye to the Kennedys and made my way homeward to Rosalie.

25

It rained most of the following week, which was very depressing. I could see through the window that the garden was coming on in leaps and bounds, and I regretted being unable to get out and deal with the weeds which somehow always seemed to grow at a faster rate than my plants.

Rosalie was tied up at the university most of the time, and I had little to do which was particularly interesting or productive.

I drove into Wolfville a couple of times with no determined purpose, so I wandered into the book shop and chatted with Gerald. Both he and the stock were noticeably changing each time I saw him. Now that he was out of the closet, he was unrestrained in his dress and manners, his clothes all seeming to be flouncy, silky and purple, and his gestures more pronounced, so that he looked as if he were permanently conducting an orchestra.

The shelves told a similar story, tomes on local history and bird-watching giving way to a variety of gay publications. I just hoped he wouldn't go too far and put off most of the customers, who were fairly traditional and had conservative tastes. But he seemed very happy, and I was glad I had made the decision to give him the store when I inherited it from my father.

Across the street, I went into the wine store which I jointly owned with Louise, who managed it on a day-to-day basis. Even though I was the major shareholder, I tried to interfere as little as possible except on major decisions.

I saw that Louise had engaged an assistant, called Jill, who appeared to be intelligent and cheerful.

I told Louise about my acquiring three bottles of the 1977 Sassicaia and she gasped.

"Will it still be good, do you think? It's almost fifty years old."

"I'm going to find out soon. I'm guessing that the tannin will have subsided and that it might be quite soft. The question is whether the fruit will have faded."

"It will be interesting to find out."

"I'll make sure you're there."

"Ooh, thank you, Marc."

"In fact, why don't you come to dinner on Wednesday? We're having our friends Ray and Rachel Bland over, and the Marshalls. Do you know them? Gary and Jane?"

"Yes, they're frequent customers here."

"Alright, then. About 6:30?"

"Fine."

When I got home, I tried to figure out what to serve on the Wednesday. Feeding seven people is not easy, especially if you wanted to serve intricate dishes.

Bearing in mind that Rachel observed Kashrut, I decided that simple would be better and that we could not do much better than a huge roast with lots of vegetables for the main course. For the first course, I thought soup would be easiest, and, to end the meal, my pear tart, which was one of the few desserts I can make adequately.

I went back into town to see what I could find, and by sheer chance ran into Bob Taggart, a local farmer.

"Hello, Marc, how's it going?"

"Good, Bob. Say, you haven't slaughtered any of your lambs lately, have you?"

"Matter of fact, I have. What're you looking for?"

"I guess I'm looking for two large legs, but I don't want hogget."

"Hogget? As if I would sell you hogget! The very idea!"

"Just so you know. What can you do for me?"

"Two large legs. I will drop them off at your place tomorrow morning."

Then I went to the supermarket to get whipping cream, Bon Maman apricot jam, big yellow potatoes, yellow onions, green beans, garlic and fresh herbs: mint, thyme, rosemary. I wasn't entirely happy with the pears they had, so I got some nectarines and peaches, too.

I was putting my purchases away when the phone rang.

"Marc, this ia Donald Chisholm."

"Donald! How are you?"

"On top of the world. Listen, I know this is short notice, but could you come to another tasting in the next few weeks?'

"I guess so. This week would be a bit difficult. But I could do the following week, if it is in the latter half of the week."

"Good. That can be arranged."

"Where will it be?"

"Arisaig. At my place. I'll have the dinner privately catered, in case you were worried I was going to cook."

"You'll have to give me instructions on how to get to your place."

"They will be forthcoming."

"Where will I stay? Is there a motel close by?"

"You can stay here. We have several guest rooms."

"Thank you, Donald. I guess Lachie will be staying over, too. I like him."

"Yes, he's a fine fellow, but I rather think he'll be giving this one a miss."

"Not sick, is he?"

"No, not sick. His fortunes have taken a turn for the worse this last year."

"He didn't mention anything when we last met."

"He wouldn't. He's proud. I bet he told you all about his animals and how he calls them all by name."

"Well, yes, he did."

"All gone. He had to sell what was left."

"Left?"

"Most died. I don't know if it was from neglect or disease, but his farm is empty now. The tractor and most of the other machinery has had to be sold. The land is going to be auctioned next week."

"God, I'm so sorry."

"All he has left are the house and his car."

"I was really getting to know him quite well. I thought he was such a nice guy."

"Always was. Turning bitter now, sadly. Anyway, I'll be back to you to confirm the date and give you directions."

After I hung up, I set about preparing something for dinner that night. I had some thinly-sliced Serrano ham in the fridge, which I thought we could have with not too-ripe honeydew melon for a starter. I had seen fairly good-looking rainbow trout in the store, so I got one each for Rosalie and me. We would have that with some lovely, fresh, chunky asparagus and a simple *beurre blanc.*

I reflected that good asparagus was very hard to find, the stores being full of skinny, stingy stuff which had been picked too soon. The best asparagus has to be perfectly fresh and green and be at least an inch and a quarter in diameter. I had some macaroons for dessert, which we would eat with some of the peaches I bought today.

My planning was again interrupted by the phone ringing.

"Marc?"

"Yes."

"Patrick. Bad news."

"What? Are you cancelling our trip next weekend?"

"No, nothing like that. It's MacDonald."

"What MacDonald?"

"Robert MacDonald. The one we were talking to the other day."

"What about him?"

"Moncton Division just called me. He was found dead yesterday."

"Dead? *Merde*! How did he die?"

"Appears to have been suicide."

"Appears?"

"You never know. I wasn't there. I'm just going by what the local guys tell me."

"I'm flabbergasted. Gobsmacked."

"That's putting it mildly. I don't think there's much point in our trying to poke around in Moncton. Who knows if he was our man? Personally, I don't think he was."

"Either way, we can scratch him off the list."

"Only another seventy to go."

26

Wednesday dawned grey, wet and cold, so I was looking forward to a pleasant evening with friends. I went down into the cellar and snooped around, looking for suitable wines for the evening.

One of them had to be the Sassicaia, which I had promised to Louise, so I put two of those in my basket. I found two of *Chateau Pichon LaLande* 1996, which I would have on standby in case the first choice was over the hill.

I was stumped about what to serve with my golden soup, but finally settled on *Chateau Grillet* from the 2010 vintage. Personally, I was not fond of the Viognier grape of which this wine was made, but it had a great reputation and a price to match.

To go with the tarts I chose a *Tokaji Aszu 6 puttonyos*, an intensely sweet wine from Hungary.

Having brought the wines up, I set about preparing the meal. In a large pot I sautéed some finely-chopped onions and garlic until soft, and then added a half bottle of Riesling, some orange juice, and some chicken stock.

Into that went chopped carrots, turnip, and butternut squash, and it was gently simmered until everything was completely soft. Then I added salt, pepper, chopped parsley, basil, nutmeg marjoram, a little sage, and a very generous pinch of saffron, and whisked it until it was thoroughly blended and was the consistency of thick cream.

The finished product was not quite as golden as I had hoped for, so I added more saffron and a spoonful of turmeric. I checked it to see if the seasoning needed adjustment, then set it to one side. When reheated, it would be ready to serve.

Then I got out my pastry. If Rosalie had been home I would have asked her to make the pastry because I am hopeless at that task, so I had bought two large, frozen, shortcrust pie shells. These I baked briefly, then, when they had cooled somewhat I slathered the apricot jam over the pastry and arranged half pears, nectarines and peaches and sprinkled brown sugar over the top.

These went back in the oven until the pastry was fully cooked, then I put them aside to reheat when the time came. I would serve them with whipped cream.

I cut the potatoes into roughly two-and-a-half inch cubes, par-boiled them until they were half soft, then put them into a baking pan with a mixture of olive oil, butter, and rosemary.

I seared the legs of lamb until they were a medium golden brown and stuck them with pieces of garlic. Then I sprinkled them with salt, pepper, thyme and more rosemary. These would roast until pink; then, while they rested, the potatoes would go in to roast.

Into a medium-sized pot I sliced four large, yellow onions and slowly cooked them in oil and butter until they were very soft, then added heavy cream and cooked them on low heat until I had a thick sauce. For Rachel, and those who preferred mint sauce, I finely chopped the mint leaves and mixed with sugar, salt and malt vinegar.

My preparations were complete.

Our guests started to arrive around seven and, judging by the number of taxis, I guessed they all expected to drink a lot of good wine. The loud noise of laughter, greeting and hugging as they arrived was, I thought, one of the most joyous sounds imaginable, as it promised happy times to come.

It was very good to see Rachel and Ray Bland again. We had not known them long, but we became close friends after Rosalie and I investigated Ray's ancestors. That was a tough experience, as we were unprepared for what we discovered, but our friendship more than compensated for the distress any of us felt. Subsequently, we were happy to have been asked to stand at their wedding as matron of honour and best man.

As she always did, Rachel made her presence felt without even trying. She was so radiant and good-looking, and her voice was so sweetly commanding, that she always became the centre of attention.

Gary and Jane Marshall were friends of longer standing than the Blands, as I had known him before I left for England, almost twenty years ago. Truth to tell, our friendship with them was more of a habit than anything else because, although we both liked Gary a great deal, we had discovered that Jane was a malicious gossip who could not be trusted to keep a confidence.

We would have invited my lawyer, Walter Bryden and his wife, Joyce, but they were away, checking out potential universities for their daughter, Jennifer.

When everyone was seated, I poured glasses of Champagne. Gary had quietly asked me for scotch (maybe to brace himself for any indiscretions by his wife), but I persuaded him that the bubble was superb, so he acquiesced.

I chose *Pol Roger Cuvee Sir Winston Churchill* 2004, of which I had bought several cases, partly from considerations of taste, but also because I had always admired Churchill and his achievements. In an age of 'deconstructionism', Churchill's reputation was being savaged by those seeking to make their books sensational; but for all his faults and peccadilloes, what he did for Western civilization against the Nazis was undeniable and indelible.

We sat down around our large rosewood table, Rosalie and I at each end, the Marshals and Louise on one side and the Blands on the other.

"Rachel," I said. "You should be alright with everything until the lamb, when you should have the mint sauce because the onion sauce has cream in it. Also, for dessert we have fruit tart, but the whipped cream is separate."

"Thank you so much, Marc. It is good of you to go to the trouble."

"What...?" Louise looked around the table, mystified.

"I'm Jewish. I keep kosher as much as possible," Rachel said.

"Oh. I see."

"I didn't know that," said Jane. "Gary, did we know Rachel was Jewish?"

"Yes, sweetheart. I told you that."

"I don't remember."

"Well, I did."

I don't think so," said Jane. "I think I would have remembered that."

Rosalie served the soup piping hot, with little biscuits she had made. As she ladled it into the bowls it glowed a deep yellow. Judging by the comments, it seemed to meet with everyone's approval. The *Chateau Grillet* went well with the soup, but, while I recognized its quality, I still couldn't warm to it.

When I took out the legs of lamb, the odour wafted through the room to "oohs" and "ahs" from our guests. I set the meat to rest while I roasted the potatoes and put the green beans in the steamer.

When all was ready, I asked Gary to carve, which pleased him. The meat was nicely pink and the sauces complemented it perfectly.

Louise and I approached the Sassicaia with trepidation. The aroma was an amazing combination of black currant, vanilla, violets and a trace of coconut. On the palate it was still intense, somewhat tannic, and slightly sweet, with hints of cinnamon. We agreed that it was truly remarkable for a wine which was considerably older than we were.

When we told the others its age, there were cries of disbelief.

"What a surprise!" said Rachel.

"Speaking of surprises, I have been reading an extraordinary book written by a group of academics and investigative journalists," Ray said.

"Oh yes? What was it about?"

"About all those native children who were reportedly buried in mass, unmarked graves a while back?"

"Wasn't that terrible?" Jane said. "So sad."

"It really showed us up badly to the world," Louise said.

"How did it all start?" I asked.

"It started when an anthropologist who was working for a local band in British Columbia said she'd done a series of tests on the humps and lumps in the ground near one of the former residential schools. She said her work had detected a number of graves."

"Of children," Rosalie said.

"That what she said, but no excavations were done to find out. They assumed that there were bodies; and if there were bodies, they must have been those of children who attended the school. And because there was nothing to be seen on the surface, they said the graves were 'unmarked'."

"I remember there was a huge hue and cry. The prime minister even went out to B.C. and was photographed kneeling down, holding a teddy bear," Gary said.

"Then the hue and cry was taken up by other native bands, which said they too had lumps and bumps in the ground which also must be unmarked graves."

"Everybody and his brother got in on the act," I said. "The entire news media were preoccupied with the story for many weeks."

"Canadian flags on federal buildings were flown at half-mast for months," Ray said. "They only came down when Remembrance Day approached and the government realized that they couldn't lower the flags on November 11th if they were already down. So they asked the natives if it was okay to haul them down so they could put them up and haul them down again."

"Ray, is that really true?"

"As God is my witness."

"Anyway it was an awful thing," said Louise.

"The thing is this. These professors and journalists looked into the whole affair over a considerable period of time. How many children's graves do you think they discovered?"

"I'd say two hundred," said Gary.

"More," Rosalie said.

"I doubt they could have excavated that many in the time," I said, "so I'll say twenty or maybe thirty."

"Not one," said Ray solemnly.

"No!"

"You're joking!"

"Not one solitary grave. Not one body of a child. And the report which the anthropologist said at the time would be released soon —when do you think she released it?"

"I don't know. I imagine there must have been a delay."

"Never. The report has never been made public. The whole thing was a gigantic hoax!"

"I don't believe that." Louise said.

"Why not?"

"Because it was on the news."

"And the news always tells the truth?"

"If they got it wrong, why didn't they correct their stories afterwards?"

"When did any of the media ever admit their errors on any major issue?"

"I don't know what to say." Louise shook her head.

"Just one more comment and I'll let this go," said Ray. "Remember the story that Trump colluded with the Russians?"

"How could anyone forget?"

"We now know it was a total fabrication from beginning to end. But has any of the media said, 'Sorry, we misled the American people and fed them total bullshit for months on end'?"

The table fell into silence, and we all sipped our wine.

Suddenly Jane Marshal turned to Rachel. "So, Rachel, you're a Jew," she said in an accusatory tone. "Why didn't Israel allow more aid to the starving Gazans when it was needed? And, while I'm at it, do you think the International Criminal Court should have issued arrest warrants for Netanyahu?"

"Are those genuine questions seeking information, Jane? Or is there something you expect me to say?" Rachel's voice was kind, but in the way one would be kind to a child.

"I don't know. I just asked because—"

"Because you've been told on the news that Israel prevented aid from getting through?" The tone was still kindly.

"Well, yes. I guess so."

"There is so much to unpack in your question, but I owe it to you to try my best."

"Thank you Rachel. I'd appreciate that."

"First, Israel did not prevent aid from getting through to where it was needed. Before the war, the number of trucks containing supplies which entered Gaza from Israel on a daily basis were actually exceeded by those which entered during the war.

"Second, much, if not most, of the aid which was sent into Gaza was stolen by Hamas, and either stored for their own purposes or sold.

"Third, there was a multitude of photographs and video footage out of Gaza, particularly Southern Gaza, which showed market after market laden with fruit, vegetables and meat. There might have been those who were hungry, but very few who were starving.

"Fourth, may I ask you if you knew that the ICC were going to issue arrest warrants for Ukraine's leader, Volodymyr Zelenskyy?"

"No. Is that true?"

"No. Why do you think that was?"

"Because he was defending himself against an invading force."

"Just so," said Rachel very quietly. "And did you at any time worry about aid getting through to help the poor Russians?"

"Of course not."

"Of course not. Did you worry about aid getting through to help the starving Iraqis when the allies invaded that country?"

"No."

"No. How about aid to the poor Afghans when America and its allies invaded there after 9/11?"

"Er...no."

"No. Why not? What were the essential differences between those cases and the Gaza war?"

"Well....er..."

"Stop picking on poor Jane," said Gary, swiftly coming to his wife's assistance.

"Why do you put it that way? Why don't you say that she shouldn't pick on me?"

"Because—"

"Because she should be excused on account of her being ill-informed?"

"That's not fair. She's only repeating what the media tells her."

"Indeed she is. I apologize to her and forgive her. The media I will never forgive."

"They're not that bad, are they?" Louise asked.

"Aren't they? Haven't we already established that previously, in reference to the supposed 'unmarked mass' graves?

"Why, in hundreds of news reports, have CNN and CBC never referred to Hamas as 'terrorists' but only as 'militants'?

"Why, when NBC, BBC and the others know full well that statistics from the so-called Gaza Ministry of Health are invented propaganda, do they continue to cite them time and time again anyway?

"Why did they always call for a ceasefire when they were well aware that Hamas would use it to regroup and rearm? Why did they call for Israel to release hundreds of murderers—yes murderers from prison—in exchange for a handful of hostages? Why did they never call for Hamas to release the hostages and surrender?

"Why did they never acknowledge the truth that the war could have ended at any point had Hamas surrendered? Answer me that!"

"I think you've made your point, sweetheart," said Ray, putting his hand on hers. "They know they can't answer, because it would reveal their hypocrisy."

"Wait one minute!" Gary shouted.

"Hold it!" I shouted even louder. "Rosalie and I understand the pressure of a relentless media. There was a time when we would have echoed their lies and distortions, but Rachel has helped us to overcome them. I think everyone should calm down and enjoy dessert and this wonderful wine. You're all friends of ours and we want you to stay that way. That's why I am declaring this particular discussion closed!"

"That's right," said Rosalie. "Marc made these beautiful tarts. I had a nibble earlier, and I must say I'm surprised how good they are. Besides, he needs your advice on a case he is working on."

In fact, I neither wanted nor needed advice on the murders Patrick and I had been investigating, but it neatly served to steer the attention away from controversy.

After Rosalie's comment, I felt I should say something. "I have a case involving one suspected murder, and our good friend Superintendent Kennedy is looking into three definite homicides."

"Wow!" Louise exclaimed. "Four murders!"

"Now here's the thing. They say the main motive for murder is always one of the following: Love, greed and revenge. I'm not sure which is the strongest motive. Gary?"

"It would depend upon one's circumstances. If you had no money at all, you might be driven to committing murder."

"Jane?"

"Love. I think people can become so obsessed with another person they would do anything to protect them."

"Louise?"

"I'd say love, too, although it would be a distorted sort of love."

"Rosalie?"

"Same here. Love."

"Ray?"

"Greed every time. Even some of those who have all kinds of money and possessions are so determined to get more, they would kill for it."

"How about you, Rachel?"

"There's no question in my mind. It's revenge."

27

As planned, Rosalie and I stayed that Friday night at the Kennedys' house in Halifax's South End.

In the evening we had a delicious lobster salad, simply prepared with chunks of lobster meat, romaine lettuce and mayonnaise. With the salad Patrick served a *La Scolca's D'Antan Gavi di Gavi*, aged on the lees in stainless steel tanks for ten years. It was not usually one of my favourite wines, but this one was remarkably good.

After that, Ruth had cooked us a magnificent dinner of roast chicken with chestnut and sausage stuffing, roast potatoes, mashed turnips, Brussels sprouts and lashings of gravy. Patrick produced a *Biondi Santi Brunello di Montalcino* 2004 which went very well with the main course.

"The weather forecast is excellent for the whole weekend," said Ruth, "so even if you don't find what you are looking for, it won't be a total loss."

"I'm not sure we really know what we're looking for," Patrick said. "If anyone had seen anything material they would probably have already reported it to my people."

"We might just pick up something, like we did at the Withers place," I said.

"But my people never investigated the Withers case."

"That's true, but still we live in hope."

"I haven't been up around Cape George—which is where Robertson came from—for many years, so I'm not sure what to expect. But I was in the area of Guysborough—where Lake was— abut ten years ago and my recollection is that it is pretty deserted around there, most houses being set way back from the road."

"Does that mean that if there was any suspicious activity, the chances are that nobody would have seen it?" Rosalie asked.

"That's what I'm afraid of. But we must try."

We got away fairly early in the morning, Ruth having packed a picnic basket in case we got peckish around midday.

There was quite a bit of traffic in the Metro area, so it took us a little over three hours to get to Antigonish on the Trans-Canada Highway. There we branched off on Highway 7 to South Lochaber; then on to the 276, the 316 and finally the Salmon River Lake Road, which wound across the country from west to east.

Patrick had been right. Although some of the scenery was very attractive, it seemed a desolate and lonely road, much potholed and patched. Little human habitation was apparent, with no indication that would change until the road emerged on the Atlantic coast at a place called Cook's Cove. Patrick had also been correct about there being very few dwellings close to the road; a rather nice Catholic church and one or two large old houses being the exceptions.

However, Leonard Lake's house was hard to miss, being on the left of the road, now a burned-out shell. We got out and climbed up the bank to take a look, but it told us nothing. It still stank of burning, but any sign of Lake's execution place had been eradicated by the police and fire department.

We saw several dirt roads which, from the evidence of old, weather-beaten mailboxes, led to houses and farms beyond our vision. The first real sign of modern civilization we came to was a hardware store at the junction with Larry's River Road. There were two pickup trucks parked outside. The drivers were smoking, leaning on the hood of one of the vehicles.

As Patrick and I went up to them, they gave us suspicious glances.

"Good day, guys," Patrick said cheerfully. "Do you mind if we have a word with you?"

"What if we do mind?" This came from a very large man with a huge belly.

"Then, I would have to insist." Patrick produced his badge. "But

I'm not looking for trouble. Just want to revisit what happened to Len Lake."

"Ah, poor Len," said the other man, a tall, rangy individual in tattered coveralls. "If I got my hands on the bastard who did that to him, I'd cut his balls off with my teeth."

"You've absolutely no idea who that could have been?"

"Nobody around here, that's for sure," said Big Belly. "Len was well liked in these parts."

"Yes, sir. Indeed he was," said the other man. "We all been racking our brains since it happened and we can't think of nobody who would want to do that."

"Now tell me this, guys, and I want you to think very, very carefully before you answer. On the day it happened, or on the days before, did you see any strangers about?"

The men drew on their cigarettes, threw the butts on the ground, ground them out with their boots, and then looked off into the nearby trees.

"Well?" Patrick asked.

"We're thinking," said Coveralls.

"Yeah," Big Belly said. "We're thinking."

There was a profound silence, broken only by the sound of the birds and by Patrick jiggling his car keys in his pocket.

Finally, Big Belly spoke, not to Patrick, but to his friend. "Don't know if I should say anything about that car. What do you think?"

"May as well. I seen it, too."

"A car?" Patrick probed.

"Yeah. You wouldn't think so, maybe, but we do get quite a few on this here road, but it was just that this was, well, kind of swanky."

"Swanky, yeah, I guess so. If we hadn't seen it a coupla times, I wouldn't have made anything of it."

"You didn't get its license plate, did you?"

"Nah. We only seen it from a distance both times."

"What make was it?"

"Couldn't see. One of them expensive cars. Big."

"What colour was it?"

"Black."

"Black. Are you sure?"

"Yeah," said Coveralls.

"Or navy," said Big Belly. "Could've been navy."

"Yeah. There is a lot of dust around these roads. Could've been navy."

We retraced our steps to Lochaber and Highway 7 and north to Antigonish. There, we had to drive through the university town and out onto Highway 327 which would take us up the coast to Cape George's Point, should we wish to go that far. This route was a far nicer drive than the forlorn stretch across the interior of Guysborough County, and it gave us frequent views of the sea.

It took us less than half an hour to reach Lakevale, then another twenty minutes finding out where Struan Robertson's widow lived. It was a small, dirty yellow bungalow at the end of a side lane called MacNeil's Road.

Since the weather was perfect, and we could see the Northumberland Strait, Patrick suggested that Ruth and Rosalie go for a walk while we went into see Mrs. Robertson.

We walked through a rather neglected garden to a front door which had clearly seen better days, its paint peeling to reveal a previous coat of garish turquoise

The door was answered by a short, faded woman in her sixties, but still with red hair which seemed to be natural. She showed us into her living room which, to my discomfort, was occupied by at least eight cats.

She bade us sit down, an invitation Patrick accepted, but I could not, so remained standing, trying not to brush against any surface from which I could pick up hair.

Patrick offered our regrets and condolences at her husband's passing and repeated the questions she must have been asked by the original investigators. No, she said, Struan had no enemies of whom she was aware. She had no idea why anyone would have wanted to kidnap her husband and starve him to death.

"Mrs. Robertson," Patrick said gently, "you're fairly isolated from the main road here, aren't you?"

"I guess so, Superintendent."

"So you would notice if any strangers had been hanging around?"

"Sure."

"And were there?"

"Were there what?"

"Strangers hanging around."

"Oh. Not that I can recall."

"No strange vehicles?"

"Well, we do sometimes get people who've taken the wrong road, and come up here to turn around."

"Did anyone come up here to turn around in the weeks before Struan went missing?"

"Let me see." Mrs. Robertson closed her eyes. For a minute we thought she had gone to sleep.

"Mrs. Robertson," Patrick said, a little sharply.

"What?"

"You were trying to remember if you saw any strange vehicles."

"Two or three, I guess. Maybe four. Or five."

"What were they?"

"Ooh, I don't know much about cars, sir."

"How about their colours?"

"Well, the usual, I guess."

"The usual?"

"Well, white and grey. Maybe a green one. A red truck, maybe."

"Any black cars?"

"You don't see so many of them these days. When I was a girl every third car seemed to be black."

"And in the weeks before Struan disappeared?"

"Could have been. Anyhow, not so as I took particular notice."

"Like getting blood out of a stone," muttered Patrick as we strolled back to the car.

We could see our wives walking in a field, so he blew the horn to let them know we were ready to move on.

We drove back along the highway to where we had seen a large handsome church, a big white house (presumably the glebe) and a cream and red community centre. Though we knocked on all three doors, we could not raise anyone so we drove up the Sunrise Trail until we saw the sea on our right, and a number of houses on our left. However, these were some way from the road and we wanted to find people who lived closer to the traffic.

Eventually we found a number of dwellings only yards from the road, so we pulled off.

There was nobody home at the first two, but a man was in the yard of the third. He introduced himself as 'Chucky' Gillis.

"There's not much misses these eyes or ears," he boasted when Patrick had told him why we were there. "No, sir, if any monkey business is going on, Ole Chucky is the man you want to see."

"That's excellent. How about strange cars?"

"Lots of them. George has got the strangest. It's painted four colours, all of them different. Then there's Walter, who turned his Buick into a truck by just cutting the back off—"

"No, no. I meant cars which are not local."

"Huh." Gillis seemed highly displeased at being interrupted. "You should've said. We're always getting cars through her that aren't local. What do you expect? This is the Sunrise Trail, for God's sake."

"I'm sorry to have bothered you Mr. Gills," said Patrick, moving away.

"Wait, now. No need to get all huffy. Tell me what you're looking for, and I'll tell you if I've seen it."

"Large, black cars."

"Oh, plenty of them."

"This would have been very large, and might have been seen in the vicinity just before Struan Robertson went missing."

"Oh, that! Sure I seen that, alright."

"Really?"

"Sure! Got the number plate too!"

"Wonderful. What was it?"

"Could have been a Mercedes."

"No, the plate number."

"That's easy," said Gillis, chewing his lip and looking at the sky. "GDK 283. Yes, sir, that's what she was."

A few hundred yards down the road, Patrick pulled over, took out his phone and called H Division headquarters. "Hi. This is Superintendent Kennedy. Who's in 706? Okay put me through. Stan? Do a CPR on GDK 283. Yes, I'll wait. Yes, thanks, Stan.....Mother-fucker!"

"Pat! Watch your language!" Ruth said.

"Lying prick. I knew he was a bullshitter the minute I saw him."

"Gillis?" I guessed.

"Who else? The plate belongs to a red Hyundai Accent."

"Are you going back?"

"No point. He'd just say he was confused or couldn't remember."

"So, is any of his testimony worth anything?"

"No, not much." Patrick sighed deeply. "We knew this was a long shot. Ruth, honey, where are we staying tonight?"

"The Cove Motel. It's in Auld's Cove."

"That's about an hour's drive from here. We'll be in time for dinner."

28

Even though the journey to South Harbour would take us about three hours, we left Auld's Cove early the next day so Rosalie and Ruth would have time to see the sights. Neither had been on the world-famous Cabot Trail before, so Patrick decided we would drive up Highway 19 to Margaree Forks, up the Cabot Trail on the western side of the Island and come back down the eastern coast.

We crossed the Canso Causeway and headed north, the bright sun creating billions of sparkling, flashing lights on the crest of each wave. Fortunately, the weather remained excellent and we yielded to numerous temptations to stop and gaze at the wonderful seascapes and mountains.

We were just coming into Judique when Ruth surprised us. "You guys aren't the only ones with special mysteries. I've got one for you."

"Yes," said Patrick. "No doubt it's the mystery of why you have stuck with me all these years."

"That one is insoluble," Ruth said. "This one goes back to 1914 in Sarajevo, Bosnia and Herzegovina."

"Aha! The start of World War One," cried Rosalie.

"Exactly."

"What's the mystery, darling?"

"The mystery is this. Archduke Ferdinand, heir to the throne of Austria-Hungary, had a chauffeur."

"That's hardly a mystery. All the royalty and rich had chauffeurs."

"Quiet. Let me finish! On the morning of June 28, various observers said that the chauffeur didn't 'quite look himself'."

"What does that mean?"

"I'll tell you. Some said he looked older than usual, some said he looked ill and others said he appeared to be drunk."

"So?"

"That morning he drove the Archduke and his wife Duchess Sophie from their hotel into the city. Along the way he took a wrong turn, bringing the car to a corner where Gavrilo Princip was within point blank range of the car."

"I smell a rat," said Rosalie.

"A huge rat. Princip opened fire and killed them both."

"Thus throwing the world into four years of war, resulting in 20 million dead and 21 million wounded," I said, showing off.

"Right." Ruth said. "Now, here are your questions: One, was the driver the real chauffeur or was he replaced, either voluntarily or by bribes or threats? Two, if he was the real driver, did he take the wrong turn by accident because he was drunk or sick? Three: If the driver was a substitute and he purposefully took the wrong turn to take the car near Princip, why couldn't they find him afterwards? He just disappeared. Four: The authorities went on a rampage, capturing and executing many suspects, but why weren't these important questions addressed? Five: Was Princip really a Bosnian nationalist who acted out of idealism, or was he secretly working for some other individual or organization?"

"That's a good one, Ruth," Patrick said. "What do you think, Marc?"

"Rosalie's the historian," I said.

"I've never had this scenario put to me in this way," said Rosalie. "But it doesn't strike me as very likely that the driver, real or not, just happened, by pure accident, to turn into a street where an assassin just happened to be waiting."

"It's possible it was an opportunistic crime," said Patrick. "If Princip was the revolutionary we're told he was, it's likely he would be carrying a gun at all times. Then one day when he sees the Grand Duke coming round a bend in the road, he can't believe his luck, hauls out his gun and blam blam!"

"You're very quiet," Rosalie said to me. "It's not like you not to have an opinion."

"Well, because there doesn't seem to be any doubt that an incident of that magnitude would lead to war, I ask myself who really wanted a war the most."

"And your answer?"

"The Kaiser. He was just itching, salivating for war. So I think Princip was working for the Prussian Secret Police."

"Is there any evidence for that, Rosalie?" Ruth asked.

"Not that I'm aware of."

"It's as good a theory as any," Patrick said. "We're just coming into Port Hood. We should get out and take a look at the beach."

We stopped eight more times before reaching our destination, the various look-offs along the trail offering spectacular views of the ocean, steep cliffs, and dizzyingly deep valleys. The women were hugely impressed, and more than once expressed amazement that they had lived in Nova Scotia all their lives but had never seen, only heard of, this wonder of the natural world.

At one of these look-offs, Patrick was able to get a signal and called the RCMP detachment at Ingonish Beach. He said the constable had been surprised to get a visit from a superintendent, but said he would gladly meet us in Dingwall and place himself at our disposal.

We started the long, dramatic descent to Aspy Bay.

"I have one for you," Rosalie piped up.

"Another mystery?" Ruth asked.

"Kind of."

"Go ahead."

"This one is in Russia in the summer of 1918."

"Okay."

"At the start of WWI Russia had the third largest reserve of gold in the world, but it was in vaults in St. Petersburg and the Tsarists thought that it might be too close to Germany for comfort. So they shipped 500 tons of it to Kazan, 1500 kilometres away to the east, where they thought it would be safe."

"By rail?" Patrick asked.

"Oh yes. There wasn't any other way. Motor vehicles or pack horses were impractical."

"I doubt they even had a road which went from St. Petersburg to Kazan in those days."

"No, I don't think they did. Anyway, the gold sat happily in Kazan until, in 1918, the Bolsheviks got the upper hand and Lenin ordered Trotsky, who was the army commander, to lay siege to Kazan and get the gold. There was a vicious battle, but eventually the Communists overran the city and joyously marched in waving the red flag. But when they opened the vaults, they were empty."

"Uh-oh!"

"The White Russian forces had spirited the gold out of Kazan and sent it even further east to Siberia, an area the Communists didn't control. Trotsky was furious and went after them in his own train. About 1800 kilometres from Kazan the gold was taken over by the White Russian General Alexander Kokchak, who took it even further east until he came to Irkutsk, north of the Mongolian border, which was in turn another 2,500 kilometres to the east. There, apparently, the gold sat in trucks on a railway siding at the shore of Lake Baikal."

"What happened to Kolchak?"

"When the Bolsheviks finally got to Irkutsk, they shot Kolchak as an enemy of the people. They grabbed the gold, and sent the train 3,360 km back to Kazan," Rosalie said.

"So what's the mystery?" Patrick demanded.

"Ah. When the train arrived in Kazan and they counted the gold, some sources say it was as much as 200 tons shy."

"Phew! What was that worth in today's money?" Ruth asked.

"About $240 trillion."

"Holy cow!"

"Where did it go?"

"Some say it was taken by returning Czech troops. Others that it fell into a lake. Still others said that a special task force went in later and recovered it."

"That's a hell of a mystery, Rosalie," Patrick said. "What do you think happened to it?"

"My guess is that if it did fall into a lake, it's still there. But..."

"But what?"

"Because of hydroelectric power plants constructed over the in-tervening years, the water area has been receding."

"Meaning that something which is irretrievable now may one day become retrievable."

"Precisely."

"I'm guessing that Lenin and Trotsky would have had kittens if there was any amount missing," said Ruth, "and would have moved heaven and earth to get it back, even if that meant the loss of thousands of lives."

"What was the official Communist Party version of events?" Patrick inquired.

"Not an ounce was missing. Everything was tickety boo."

We drove slowly into Dingwall, a small country town of about 600 souls, and parked at the harbour. There was no sign of the RCMP constable, since it would take him four times longer to get here from the detachment as it had for us to drive from Cape North.

We all got out and strolled around in the wonderful heat of the afternoon sun. Ruth and Rosalie wandered off, looking at fishing boats on the wharf.

Impatient with waiting, Patrick decided we should go into the store where Alex Gillespie had been employed.

A middle-aged woman was leaning on the counter. "What can I do for your gentlemen today?" she asked with a big smile.

"I'd like to ask you some questions about Alex Gillespie."

As soon as Patrick mentioned the name, she recoiled in anger. "No! Go away. I'm not talking to you."

"I'm sorry, but you don't have a choice," said Patrick, producing his identification.

She folded her arms and stared at him defiantly. "How do I know who you are? You could be anyone. One of them reporters from Halifax."

This stand-off was settled when the local constable came into the store. He took his cap off, then hurriedly put it back on again.

"I guess you must be Superintendent Kennedy."

"That's right. Will you please tell this woman to answer my

questions?"

"Alright. Alright. I wasn't to know who you were for sure. You could've been anyone," she said, "What do you want to know?"

Patrick took her through the questions he had asked all the others in the areas where the victims had lived, and received similar answers. When he came to questions about cars, she shook her head.

"I can't see much 'cause I'm stuck in here most of the day."

She shouted to somebody in a room at the back of the store, but I didn't catch the name. A voice acknowledged her.

"D'you see any strange vehicles around the time Alex went missing?"

"What d'you mean, strange?" the voice asked.

"Not from around here."

"Can I get back to you on that?"

"No, you can't get back to me. The man is here now and wants an answer."

"What?" A grizzled head peered around the door. "Who the hell is he?"

Then he noticed the constable. "Oh. Okay. What was the question?"

As the woman was repeating the question, I had a weird feeling that I was living in a Monty Python sketch and, not being able to stand it any longer, left the store. After about ten minutes, Patrick and the constable came out.

"Any luck?"

"Big black car."

"That's something."

"No plate number. Uncertain about the dates."

"No, I guess it isn't much after all."

"Constable, could you please take us to where Gillespie was discovered, and then to where he was staying?"

"Sure, but his lodgings will be locked."

"Could you phone the landlord?"

"Yes. I could do that."

"Why don't you do that now while we find our wives and tell

them what's happening?"

"Now?"

"Yes, now."

He moved to his car while we walked down to the wharf to find Rosalie and Ruth.

"How do you do it?" I asked. "It would drive me mad."

"Do what?" Patrick asked.

"Put up with the inanity. Asking the simplest questions which have to be explained time and again."

"It goes with the job. If you're going to carry on with this private detective lark, you'd better get used to it."

We found our wives and told them we were going in the constable's patrol car but would be back soon. Patrick gave Ruth the car keys, but asked that if they went anywhere not to be gone too long.

We climbed into the cruiser and our driver took off down the road to the south.

"Where we going?" Patrick asked.

"To see Gillespie's lodging," the constable said.

"I thought we were going to the place where he was discovered first."

"We can do that after. George has to go to work, so he wants us to meet him now."

"Okay, right." Patrick said in an undertone to me, "We can't have George be late for work."

George was waiting for us outside a tall red house across from a gallery selling art and sweaters. He was a man about thirty-five, tall and severe. He ostentatiously twirled a large key on his forefinger.

"Nothing to see now," he said flatly. "I cleaned it out for the new tenant."

He was right. We slowly went from room to room, but there was nothing to see. Patrick stood there, thinking.

"I gotta go to work," said George.

"Go ahead. We'll lock up. You can get the key from Constable Martin."

George scowled and stomped off.

"He has to get to work," said the constable.

Patrick nosed about the apartment, looking behind chairs and lifting books and newspapers.

"Okay. Let's go."

Constable Martin drove us back up the road by which we had arrived, and a few kilometres beyond Cape North pulled the cruiser over and jumped out.

He led us up a steep bank into the woods. He pointed to a tree which was indistinguishable from a thousand others. "That's where he was tied up."

"Why was he here so long?" Patrick asked.

"If you'll take a look back, Superintendent, you'll notice that this spot can't be seen from the road."

"Then how was he finally found?"

"Harold MacMillan's dog kicked up a row, so Harold went to take a look. There he was."

We went back to the car and the constable drove us back to Dingwall. We thanked him for his help and got out. He drove off at a fast clip.

We looked around, but there was no sign of the women. We sat on some rocks and waited.

"A pretty disappointing trip," I said morosely.

"Yeah. But the girls are having a good time."

"And maybe we can get a good dinner tonight. Where are we staying?"

"Haven't got a clue. Ruth made reservations, but I don't know where."

"If they don't come soon, we may be too late for dinner."

"With our luck, we'll have to go to McDonalds."

"I hate to tell you this, but the nearest McDonalds is about two hour's drive from here," I said.

"Fuck it! After this case I'm definitely going back to my desk. My underlings can do all the field work."

"Here they are!" I cried as I got to my feet. Patrick's car was coming down the street. "Saved by the cavalry."

29

We stayed at the Kennedys' again the next night, having returned from Cape Breton without incident.

Once more, Ruth performed miracles in the kitchen that evening, using produce we had bought at stalls and markets along the way. She had got some fine-looking, fat, pork sausages from the Whistleberry Market in Salt Springs, just outside New Glasgow, and cooked them in a gravy made from hot mustard, Worcestershire sauce, onions, tomatoes and red wine. She served this with heaps of fluffy mashed potatoes, sautéed mushrooms, and broad beans tossed in butter.

Hearing what the menu would be, Patrick descended into his cellar and emerged with two bottles of *Monfortino Barolo Riserva* by Giacomo Conterno, of the 2004 vintage. Since this was reputedly one of Italy's most revered and sought-after wines, I looked forward to an enjoyable meal.

I was not disappointed, and we cleaned our plates, sitting back well content.

"Not everyone appreciates Barolo," Patrick said, holding his wine glass up to the light.

"I think that's because it can be very tannic and unforgiving, especially when it's young," I ventured.

"Yes, the wines of good vintages, when there has been a lot of sun to thicken the skins of the grapes, can last for 40 years or more."

"And few of those are ready to drink before they are 15 years old," I added.

"I have to say," Rosalie piped up, "that while I think this wine smells divine, I find it a tiny bit hard and bitter on the palate"

"Did you notice that when we were eating?"

"No, only now the meal is over."

"That's because the fat in food masked the tannin in the wine," I said.

"Does that mean you don't want any more, Rosalie?" asked Patrick.

"Ah, Patrick, I didn't say that! I don't mind suffering, so you may pour a little more."

Patrick took a sip of the Barolo and swished it around in his mouth before swallowing. He had his eyes closed and looked so relaxed and contented, I was hesitant to break the spell.

"Sorry, to bring up the case at a time like this, but where do we stand, really?" I asked him.

"In a nutshell, nowhere."

"We know a little."

"What? What exactly do we know?"

"We know there is a black car common to all districts where the murders took place."

"Do we?"

"Sure."

"We know that there may have been a car in those vicinities, that it may have been a big car, and that it may have been black, or navy or some other dark colour," he said.

"That's something," said Rosalie.

"Is it? Even if there had been a big, black car in all four places, how would we even begin to find such a vehicle among thousands of other big, black cars in the province?"

"I admit it does seem a tall order," I said.

"And if, as is quite possible, the vehicle may have come from outside the province, it would vastly increase the pool of big, black cars which we would need to search," Patrick added.

"I hadn't thought of that."

The table had fallen silent while we sipped the lovely wine, swirling it around in our glasses to bring out the extraordinary aroma of roses and something resembling autumn leaves.

"So, we're back to finding Robert MacDonald..." I said.

"Who may or may not have changed his name, and who may or may not still live in Nova Scotia," Patrick replied glumly.

"So, we really are—"

"Nowhere."

"Let's not go to bed on such a gloomy note," Ruth intervened. "There have been tougher cases than this which you solved."

"Thank you, darling. I know you mean well, but right now I can't think of one such case."

"Pat, you always say: 'You win some, you lose some.' Maybe this is one you lose."

"Having been thoroughly cheered up by my wife," said Patrick, rising, "I think I'll turn in. Are you off to the Valley bright and early?"

"I want to do some shopping," Rosalie said, "We're not in any hurry to get back."

"Okay, Well, goodnight, all."

When we awoke and came downstairs the next morning, Patrick had already left for work and Ruth was doing laundry. She had laid out some croissants, fruit and cereal and put on a pot of coffee.

When we had eaten, we bade her goodbye and headed into the city, where Rosalie spent an hour visiting several stores.

"It's too soon to head back," she said. "Why don't we leave the car and walk to the Public Gardens. I've only ever seen them once, and that was when I was a little girl. I can't remember anything about them."

"What a sheltered life you've led!" I said. "Let's go. I'm sure you'll love them."

In summer, the Public Gardens in Halifax are among the best places in the province. They were established in the 1860s and cover about 15 acres, the style being Victorian with many statues, extensive flower beds, fountains, bridges, and ponds. The gardens also feature a fine bandstand used for concerts on Sunday afternoons during the summer.

It is also a good spot for seeing ducks, herons and the occasional eagle.

As I anticipated, Rosalie was ecstatic when she entered through the great wrought-iron gates and saw the array of flowers, trees and shrubs. Although it was too late in the year for us to see them in bloom, I pointed out to Rosalie a particular concentration of rhododendron bushes where Patrick and I had an exciting encounter with a villain, which I have written about in my book *The Plot to Kill the Premier.* Despite its having taken place only a year ago, it now seemed like old history.

Although Rosalie and I have been private detectives for fewer than four years, it felt as if we had been involved in investigations for much longer. We had experienced some nasty shocks and frightening moments in our previous three cases, and some dramatic surprises, but we found it hard to imagine our lives in which we were not looking, probing and digging for answers.

Its now being early August, Rosalie was able to see wonderful rose beds in many colours, splendid hydrangeas, different types of lilies, echinaceas, bee balms, peonies, amazing dogwoods, and many others. Dahlias, for which the Public Gardens is especially famous, were just coming into their own, but would need a little more time before being at their best.

We strolled around the gardens in a clockwise direction, then turned and circled the opposite way, constantly encountering new delights in the flower beds and among the trees.

As we approached the bandstand, I thought I recognized a figure coming over the bridge not far from the main entrance. He was elderly, but tall and upright, wearing shorts and a tee shirt.

I squinted in the bright sun and, as he came closer, I could see that it was my old acquaintance, Akerman, who had been of some assistance to me on previous occasions. He had been, in his time, an archaeologist at the Fortress of Louisbourg, a Member of the Legislature, a radio announcer and a newspaper editor, in addition to acting in a large number of film productions.

He grinned broadly as he came towards us. "Marc LeBlanc! Well met."

"Indeed. This is my wife, Rosalie.

"Very nice to meet you, Mrs. LeBlanc."

"Rosalie, please."

"Rosalie it is. Shall we sit somewhere, or are you in a hurry to leave?"

"No, let's find a bench," said Rosalie, clearly curious about this stranger who had materialized out of nowhere.

We searched around until we found a bench which was unoccupied, then made ourselves as comfortable as possible on hard slats. We exchanged pleasantries, during which he told us he had just past his eighty-second birthday.

"I heard somewhere that you are now official," he said. "I understand that you have your private investigator's license?"

"Yes, that's right. Although I don't do it for money, I could if I wanted to."

"Always useful. We none of us know what misfortune lies round the corner."

"It's particularly handy when seeing people at their homes. Being able to produce identification seems to make them more willing to talk."

"I read something about your role in the Premier's difficulties last year. Are you working on a case at the moment?"

"Yes" I replied, "but, alas, we're not getting very far with it. In fact, we're at a standstill."

"Are you allowed to tell me about it?"

"Not some of the details, but I can tell you the broad outlines. It involves four murders—"

"Four!"

"Well, three for sure, and another which is almost certain. That one concerns my client. I became, unofficially, involved in the others through my acquaintance with a senior RCMP officer."

"I think I know who you mean. Is he the one who was mentioned in the news in connection with your last case?"

"Yes."

"Superintendent Kelly, was it?"

"Kennedy."

"Oh, right. Please continue."

"Well, in general terms, the murders seem to have been committed in revenge for an indignity the killer suffered when he was a teenager."

"I would guess that motive is a lot more common than most people might think."

"I can talk fully about my client because I have the widow's consent, and because, as far as the police are concerned, it is not officially a crime, let alone a murder."

"How did your client's husband die?"

"He was drowned in a bathtub. But some of the circumstances are suspicious, to say the least. However Halifax police didn't see anything amiss."

A strange little man wearing a white shirt and bright blue trousers sat down, squeezing into the end of our bench. Surprised, we stopped talking and looked around. Seeing several other benches empty nearby, we looked quizzically at the man. He smiled back at us.

We weren't about to continue talking about the case in his presence, so we all fell silent. I wondered if he was a crew member on one of the cruise ships who neither spoke English nor understood our customs. The little man stared straight ahead, still smiling.

We looked at the sky, the birds and the riotous display of colour presented by the flowers. Finally he got up, bowed to us and moved on.

"That was weird," said Rosalie.

"Are you being spied on?" Akerman asked with a grin.

"I shouldn't think so. They wouldn't learn anything of value, anyway."

"You were telling me about your victim. You said it was a revenge killing. What was he supposed to have done to elicit that degree of vengeance?"

"Apparently, there was an incident when one teenager was assaulted by another. My client's husband was in what you might call a position of trust, and we think the killer believed that by not acting he betrayed that trust."

"I'm guessing that one of the other victims was the perpetrator of the assault."

"Yes. That's what we assume."

"So where do the other two fit in?"

"Seemingly they were thought to have been in a position to help the lad who was assaulted, but either did nothing or maybe even assisted or egged the perpetrator on."

Both Rosalie and I noticed that our companion was frowning deeply and rubbing his chin.

"What is it?" she asked.

"This is beginning to ring some bells," he said.

"Bells? What sort of bells?"

"Can you tell me where these events were alleged to have taken place?"

"I don't see why not. They occurred at a summer camp for boys —"

"The Wind in the Willows!" Akerman slapped the bench. "Am I right?"

"Yes, but how did you know?" I asked.

"When I was editor of the *Metro Weekly*, we ran a story about the person who claimed to have been assaulted—"

"Robert MacDonald."

"No, that wasn't his name at the time. He had changed it some years before. I can't remember the name he was using at the time of his death."

"*His death?*" Rosalie and I exclaimed in unison.

"Why, yes. The story was about his dying. His death raked up the original story."

"He's dead?"

"Yes, that's what I said. He jumped from the MacDonald Bridge."

"My God, when was this?"

"In the early 1990s, I think. I'm guessing this throws your case completely into limbo."

"You can say that again!"

As soon as Akerman had left, I called Patrick. I had never heard him swear and curse the way he did that afternoon.

"This means we have nothing! Sweet fuck all!"

"Certainly, we have no motive."

"No motive for any of them! Now we don't even know if the

cases are connected in any way."

"Except for the black car."

"Oh, fuck the big black car!" he shouted. "You always have attached too much significance to that bloody car. We don't even know if it was the same car in any two of the places. And what if it was? It means nothing!"

"And I guess the fact that they attended the camp is totally coincidental."

"Yes, and therefore irrelevant!"

"What are we going to do?"

"You do what you like." He was in the foulest mood. "I'm going to concentrate on other cases. Ones that have some chance of being solved."

"Shall we be in touch?"

"Who knows?" he snarled, and hung up.

Rosalie and I sat there, staring into the distance. I felt terrible, not least because so much time and effort had been expended for nothing.

"You look like a wrung-out dish rag," she said. "Let's head home, get a shower, cook a nice dinner and get a very special wine from the cellar."

"You usually manage to say the right thing. Just another of the many reasons why I love you."

30

The days following the revelation that our prime suspect, Robert MacDonald, was dead were as depressing as they were long. Without any investigation to pursue, life seemed both listless and pointless. Rosalie was not as affected as I was, because she was required to busy herself with work at the university, but even she moped when she was at home.

I tried to concentrate on my garden, which had shown significant growth, with some of the crops, like radishes, more than ready to harvest while others, such as leeks and celery, seemed still to be in their infancy.

But the most remarkable feature of the garden, having been neglected for so long, was the extraordinary proliferation of weeds. I wondered where they had all come from. Had their seeds been mistakenly mixed with the ones I had planted, had they all blown in from other areas, or had their roots existed in the earth before I dug it? In any event, removing them was a soulless job, not to mention a back-breaking one.

All the while I was labouring among the rows, throwing dandelions, chickweed, dock, spurge and Creeping Charlie into my bucket, I could not stop thinking about the case. What had we missed? Was there any avenue we had overlooked? What had we done wrong?

Although I asked myself these questions over and over, the only conclusion I could come to was that even if I, as an amateur, had missed a clue, Patrick, with his years of experience, would not have failed to detect it.

That Patrick and I had parted on uncertain, if not unpleasant, terms and that I had not heard from him since our last phone call, increased my despondency. Over the past few years, he and Ruth had become rather special friends, and I felt sad that circumstances might have conspired to bring that to an end.

In an effort to take my mind off our lack of success in the investigation, on the days it rained I went into town and hung around the wine store. I do not think Louise was entirely comfortable with my poking my nose in, but since I own 51% of the business's shares she could hardly evict me.

One day, she showed me a copy of a newspaper bearing the news that a well known industrialist, Victor Ransome, had died at the age of 95. I did not know Ransome, other than by name and by the many charitable donations he had made during his lifetime, and I was not aware that Louise had any personal contact with him.

"Ninety-five is a grand old age," I said, "He had a good innings. Why are you showing me this? Was he a friend of yours?"

"No, I never met him, but I've heard on the grapevine that Ransome had an incredible cellar."

"Ah!"

"And it is still quite large."

"I see where you're going with this. But won't his children inherit the cellar?"

"He had no children. His only son was killed in an accident some years ago."

"Sad. But won't his widow want to enjoy the wine in her golden years?

"I've heard that Mrs. Ransome doesn't drink."

"Aha! How old is she?"

"Eighty-nine."

"Where does she live?"

"Just outside the town of Pictou."

"I have to go to Antigonish—Arisaig, actually—the day after tomorrow. I could call on her the day after that, on my way back."

"I'll see if I can locate her by phone and arrange for you to visit. She might be willing to sell some of her cellar."

"And because she's already as wealthy as Croesus she might not ask a high price."

"My thoughts exactly," said Louise with a broad grin.

This news perked me up a little, and when Rosalie later suggested we have a dinner party with Frank Wilberforce and Walter and Joyce Bryden, I felt my depression decidedly lifting.

So, the next day, while Rosalie was at college, I set about planning the dinner. I thought that for the first course we would have simple fresh lobster with a Hollandaise sauce, then follow with a roast turkey and end with strawberries and cream. I went into town and managed to find everything except, to my great surprise, the turkey, so I returned home via Carl Humbolt's farm and had him kill and pluck two geese for me.

Then I went down to the cellar and selected some Krug Champagne, two bottles of 2010 *Meursault Coche-Dury Genevrieres* to go with the lobster, two of *Chateau Figeac* 1949 for the geese, and a bottle of *Chateau D'Yquem* 2001 to match the strawberries.

To avoid the trouble and potential mess of guests having to crack lobsters at the table, I steamed them until almost cooked, cooled and shelled them, cut them into chunks and put the chunks in a casserole which went into the fridge until later. The sauce would be a simple version of Hollandaise, made with slightly more lemon, less butter and wine instead of cream or milk. This I would pour over the lobster and then cook it in the oven for just a few minutes.

I painted the geese with a blend of honey and soy sauce, and stuffed them with a mixture of breadcrumbs, sausage meat, mushrooms, butter, Cognac, and chestnuts. Because of the richness of the geese and stuffing, we would have them with plain boiled potatoes and peas.

Later, our guests arrived and all seemed to be in good spirits; Frank because he always glowed at the prospect of food, and the Brydens because they had got a place for their daughter, Jennifer, at a very good university, albeit at a distance further away than they would have liked.

As we sat drinking the Krug, Walter asked about the case. I had to tell him the truth, that our theory about revenge killings seemed to have crashed and burned.

"That's too bad," Walter said, "because I did some more research on classic cases of vengeance, and came up with some doozies."

"You may as well tell us about them," said Rosalie.

"Yeah. Don't let them go to waste," Frank said.

"Well the first is a very famous story about Hitler. Almost 22 years after the signing of the first armistice which ended WWI by the Germans surrendering in a railroad car, he got his revenge by ordering the same car to be taken out of a museum, and then made the French go into it to surrender to him."

"Isn't that when he did a little dance for the cameras?" I asked.

"That's what it looks like," said Rosalie, "but the film was doctored."

"Really? I didn't know that." Joyce said.

"Yes. Hitler had come out of the rail car and when he was talking with some of his generals, he took a step forwards, raising his right knee higher than usual. The newsreel cameras filmed it, but when the Brits got hold of it they realized that the clip of Hitler's step could be looped, repeated, and turned into a little dance step that would make the Fuhrer look ridiculous. So that's what the world remembers."

"Darling, you are a mine of fascinating information," I said.

"The story of King Clovis is also a good one," Walter said. "He got the Franks together as a single nation, and is generally thought to be the founder of the dynasty which ruled France for hundreds of years.

"Once when he was leading an assault on Soissons, the Franks stormed the city and stole everything in sight. The Bishop of Rheims sent Clovis a message saying that in the cathedral there was a sacred vessel and begged for it to be sent to him.

"So Clovis went over to where the loot was being collected, found the vase, and told the looters to make it went into his share. They all agreed, except for one soldier, who lost his temper and smashed the vase with his axe.

"A year later the Frankish army was assembled for review, and when the king was inspecting the troops he came upon the man who had broken the vase. He snatched his weapon from him, said it was in terrible condition, and threw it to the ground. As the man bent down to pick it up, Clovis drew his axe and in one motion split the man's skull, yelling: 'That's for what you did to my vase!'"

"That sounds like a shaggy dog story to me," Rosalie said. "I don't believe a word of it."

"Yes, why didn't he kill the man when he first broke the vase?" Joyce asked.

"I didn't make it up," Walter said, "I am merely the conveyor of what has been handed down the centuries."

"Do you have any more?" Frank asked.

"Just one more," said Rosalie, "and then we must eat."

"Alright. Here's one you'll like. Around 400 BC in China, there was a war between two kingdoms, Yue and Wu. A princess of Yue was married to a nobleman of Wu, but she ran back to Yue. Wu demanded her return, but Yue said 'no'.

"Wu invaded. The fighting was hot and heavy and both kings of Yue and Wu were killed.

"When the fight passed to their sons, Goujian of Yue was defeated, captured, forced to be a servant of the king of Wu. For three years he was humiliated. Convinced his spirit was broken and was subservient, the king allowed Goujian to go home to run Yue as a vassal state of Wu."

"Does this go on for much longer, Walter?" Rosalie called from the table, where she was filling wine glasses.

"Not much longer. Have patience. Anyway, Goujian returned, but would not be a vassal and quietly strengthened his kingdom, all the while, undermining Wu by bribing their officials. He refused all luxuries, forcing himself to drink bile in order never to forget the bitter humiliation he suffered under Wu. Goujian developed an iron discipline, and instilled it in his people and his soldiers.

"After ten years of reforms, when Yue was totally rebuilt and disciplined, Goujian marched on Wu, led the army of Yue to the capital of Wu and took it. Fuchai committed suicide, and Goujian took control of both kingdoms. His revenge was complete."

"My appetite won't be complete unless I get sustenance soon," Frank said. "Can we eat now, Walter?"

"Certainly. I have one more revenge story, but it can wait until after dinner."

"Alright, everybody, to the table!" Rosalie ordered.

The lobster and Meursault were great hits with everyone, especially Frank, who could hardly wait for the rest of us to say we had had enough.

"Shame to waste it," he said as he scraped the remaining food onto his plate and then drained the wine into his glass.

The goose was also well received, and I was glad that the honey I had used on the glaze was not too dominant, but just gave a hint of sweetness to cut through the fat.

The two bottles of *Chateau Figeac* were quite different from one another, even though they came from the same vintage. One bottle tasted beautiful, with a wonderful bouquet, but was clearly past its best and was like a faded old lady. The other, however, was amazingly robust and full-bodied and tasted like a much younger wine. The first bottle did not surprise me at all, since it had been made 75 years ago, but the second stunned me. Clearly, they had been stored differently, the one in a much colder, damper cellar than its mate.

Both Walter and Frank wanted to know more about the case and why it had collapsed, and peppered Rosalie and me with questions. Since our main line of inquiry was now gone, I felt I could tell them much more than I had been able to do the last time they had dined here. This inquisition took us through the main and dessert courses. Then they sat back thoughtfully.

"You know, you've overlooked an important possibility," Frank said.

"Oh. What's that?"

"That even though the victim at the camp is dead and therefore couldn't be the killer, a relative of his could have been doing the killing on his behalf."

"God, you're right!" Walter exclaimed.

"That doesn't seem at all likely," Rosalie said. "Who would go to those lengths, and take such risks, for someone who was dead?"

"I admit it's a long shot, but it's a possibility, nonetheless."

"I hadn't thought of that," I confessed, "but I'm sure Patrick has."

"I think you'd better call him, just in case," Walter suggested.

"Okay, but he'll probably bawl me out. He wasn't too pleased with me the last time we spoke."

"Go on, Marc." Rosalie prompted. "Do it now."

I went into the kitchen and called Patrick at home, but to my surprise Ruth told me he was still at the office. I then called the private line number and he answered after the first ring.

"Kennedy."

"Patrick, it's Marc."

"Ah, Marc. I was going to call you. I'm afraid I gave you the rough edge of my tongue when we last talked."

"That's okay. Forget it."

"What do you want? I have to brief my chief super in a few minutes."

"I'll be quick. Could the killer be one of Robert MacDonald's relatives?"

"Aha, so that occurred to you, too? I thought of it yesterday."

"Oh, good. Have you done anything about it yet?"

"Still telling me how to do my job, Marc? Of course I have. I've had several people working on it all day."

"And...?"

"His only living relative is an uncle—"

"A good suspect?"

"Who is 84, and living in a nursing home."

"Damn!"

"So, it's back to the drawing board, although, to be honest, I can't give the case a high priority now."

"I understand. Thanks, Patrick, I'll let you go."

Walter and Frank were disappointed when I told them, but accepted that the case was now well and truly at a dead end.

"Yes, that's that," I said. "Walter, did you have another revenge story for us?"

"Just one more. This illustrates how revenge is a dish best served cold."

"Go on."

"This is about a man who waited ten years to get his revenge, and then did it in a brutal, bloodthirsty way."

"Walter, maybe you shouldn't tell these horrible tales this late at night," Joyce intervened.

"No, go ahead, Walter," Frank and Rosalie said in unison.

"Alright," he said.

This is the story of François Picaud who was a 19th-century shoemaker in Nimes in France. Some say he was the man on whom Dumas based the character of Edmond Dantes was based in the novel *The Count of Monte Cristo*.

In 1807, Picaud was engaged to marry a rich woman, but three jealous friends, Loupian, Solari, and Chaubart, went to the government and accused him of being an English spy. I don't know why they did it, but they did. Another friend, Allut, knew of this, but did not tell Picaud about it. Again, I don't know why.

So, poor Picaud was thrown into jail for seven years, not even learning what the charge was until he had been there for two years. During his time in jail he tunnelled into a neighbouring cell and befriended a wealthy priest named Father Torri.

A year later, when Torri was dying, he bequeathed to Picaud a treasure he said he had hidden in Milan.

When the government fell in 1814, Picaud was released and went to Milan, found the treasure, changed his name, and returned to Paris. There he spent ten years plotting revenge against his former friends.

Then he swung into action. First he murdered Chaubart, then he turned his attention to Loupian, who had married Picaud's former fiancée. Picaud tricked Loupian's daughter into marrying a criminal, whom he then had arrested, and the poor wife promptly died of shock. Picaud then burned down Loupian's restaurant, bankrupting him. Next, he manipulated Loupian's son into stealing some gold jewellery and framed him for committing the crime and the kid was sent to jail. Then Picaud stabbed Loupian to death.

Then he fatally poisoned Solari.

He tried to get even with Allut, but he was too much for Picaud, who was injured and turned over to the cops. Before he died of his injuries, the police recorded his confession.

End of story.

"I guess the moral is that revenge is not good for you," said Rosalie.

"I agree," Walter said, "but just imagine how delighted he would have been had he managed to kill them all!"

"Seems to me we have been too hung up on revenge," said Frank. "The motive for the murders Marc and Kennedy have been investigating might not be revenge. They say that if the motive for killing someone is not revenge it must be love or money."

"Yes, a friend recently said that to us," Rosalie said, "but I can't see how love could be the motive in this case. It strains credulity to think that a man would....wait!"

"What?"

"Could it have been a woman?" she asked.

"A woman? Why not?" I said.

"Maybe a woman who was wronged by each of these men... either sequentially or together."

"It doesn't bear thinking about," said Joyce.

"We could still be dealing with a rape," Frank said soberly. "Just not the kind we thought."

"Maybe not that dramatic." Walter said. "She could have been slighted in other ways. Breach of promise comes to mind."

"Come on!" Frank cried. "You mean four guys proposed to her then wouldn't go to the altar? All four guys? That's ridiculous!"

"It's more likely that each of them slighted or offended her in a different way," Rosalie said, "although I can't imagine what they could have been."

"I'm sorry," I said, "I find this theory so utterly unlikely that I think we have to set it aside."

"On balance, I have to agree with you," said Walter.

"Which just leaves money," I said.

"Maybe you should find out if anyone benefited financially from the deaths of these four guys," Frank suggested.

"It's a thought, but how that could happen I have no idea."

"Maybe they were in a....whatyoumecallit," Joyce said.

"What do you mean, darling," Walter asked.

"You know, like a lottery when the last man standing gets the money."

"A tontine!" Frank shouted.

"Joyce, you're a genius!" Rosalie clapped her hands.

"A tontine," Walter murmured. "That's an interesting thought. But there's one problem with that theory."

"What's that?"

"If all these people died so the survivor could collect the money...who is the survivor?"

"Yes, he...or she...could be anybody," Joyce said.

"Literally anybody," said Frank.

"So, what you're telling me," I said, "is that we are back to square one."

"Rather looks that way," Walter said. "Is there any more of that wine left?"

31

I had never been to Arisaig. And it was not until I looked at a map that I realized it was situated on the same Cape George peninsula we had recently visited when we investigated Struan Robertson at Lakevale. Whereas we had been on the eastern side of the cape, Arisaig lay on its western flank. Since we had all thought the scenery thereabouts quite special, I looked forward to seeing more of it.

Lachie MacLeod had told me that Donald Chisholm owned a large property, complete with a farm, a house and many outbuildings. As Lachie had grandiloquently put it, "Donald is lord of all he surveys."

The Bugatti took less than two hours to reach Sutherland's River, then a further 20 minutes to get to Arisaig. On the way I thought about our dinner conversation the previous night, and considered the various theories advanced by Frank and Walter, but it was Joyce's idea of a tontine which was the most intriguing.

I recalled that, many years ago, I had read Thomas Costain's 1955 novel *The Tontine*, which began with the Battle of Waterloo and ended at the end of the 19th century. It embraced the stories of kings, sailors, artists, and soldiers, and was packed with action and romance.

As Costain described it, the tontine was a form of gambling which was part lottery, part insurance. Each subscriber paid a sum into a trust, receiving a periodical payout. As members died, their payout went to the others in the scheme. The amount of each payout went up with each death, and when all but one had died off, the pot went to the survivor.

I looked it up before I left Grand Pre and found that it was named after Lorenzo di Tonti, who invented it in 1653, although some say a Nicolas Bourey was its creator in 1641.

The English, French, German and Dutch governments all had public tontines in 1693, but by the end of the 18th century, the tontine had fallen out of favour as a revenue-raising scheme, but smaller-scale and less formal tontines continued to be arranged between individuals or to raise funds for specific projects throughout the 19th century, and, in modified form, to the present day.

I drove up through Merigomish, Lismore and Knoydart, thoroughly enjoying the sunny day and marvellous views of the Northumberland Strait, with Pictou Island a blue spot in the distance.

As I had been told that the Chisholms were prosperous, there was no mistaking Donald's place, because it was both extensive and conspicuous. His large, white house was up a lane off the high side of the road, while his farm, barns, greenhouses and fields lay on the shore side, extending for several miles in either direction.

As I went up the driveway I noticed a number of vehicles in the spacious forecourt. Since I did not know who drove what, I guessed that the big Bentley Bentayga SUV belonged to Donald himself and the flashy Mercedes AMG GT to his son, Duncan. There being only five cars present, I deduced that the missing vehicle must mean that Lachie's financial difficulties had prevented him from attending.

Donald came out to meet me as I pulled in. He was wearing a kilt in ancient Chisholm tartan of subdued brown and green with discreet, thin, white and red lines. He sported a dress shirt with tartan tie and a Harris Tweed coat.

Duncan, who was lurking in the doorway, again wore his kilt in so-called "hunting" tartan of dark green and maroon, but had a black dress coat with silver buttons on its sleeves, a matching waistcoat, tartan sash, and an elaborate sporran. He was some distance away, but I thought I saw him scowling. I guessed that Duncan scowled at almost everybody, but today his look appeared to be particularly malevolent and intended for the world in general.

"*Latha math! Fàilte. Ciamar a tha thu, Marc?*" Donald called as I alighted.

"*Bonjour, Donald. Je vais bien. Comment vas-tu?*" I replied, pulling my travel bag out of the car.

I said hello to Duncan, who grunted and led us into the house.

It was clear that Donald had lavished a good deal of money on the place, as there was a massive wooden staircase, panelled walls and, as I expected, the obligatory, mounted bucks' heads, their polished antlers glinting in the light. There was a suit of armour standing in one corner, and various paintings and proclamations hanging in prominent locations.

Donald took me upstairs to a long landing on which there was an extensive array of guest rooms. "This one is yours," he said cheerily, "Murdock, Sandy and Harold arrived some time ago."

"No Lachie?"

"Alas, no. Poor fellow's troubles have multiplied. In his present condition, I think he would be embarrassed to see us."

"That's too bad. He's such a great guy."

"Indeed he is. And a good palate for the malt, too. I'm afraid we will have to get along without him."

I stopped halfway into the room, turned around and hesitated.

"What is it, Marc?"

"Maybe I shouldn't mention this, but I have to say, Donald, that if Duncan has another go at Harold for being English, I won't feel inclined to stay."

"I understand." Donald sadly shook his white head. "I can't deny that I expect him to assail the Sassenachs in general, but I have laid it on the line that he is not to make any incendiary remarks directly to Harold."

"Good. Thanks. Provided he doesn't get personal, he can rant about the injustices visited upon the Highlanders all he wants."

"You have to appreciate, Marc, that he feels this stuff very deeply. As, indeed, do I. After all these years it still rankles, you know. You must feel the same way about the expulsion of the Acadian people, being one of their descendants."

"As a matter of fact, I don't, Donald. I understand why others might, but to me it is ancient history. It's buried in the past and should stay there."

"Hmm." Donald seemed perturbed by my response and frowned, scratching his ear. "We shall have to agree to disagree. Settle yourself in and then come down to the dining room. Take a sharp right at the bottom of the stairs. We start tasting in half an hour. If there's anything you need, ring this bell and the housekeeper will bring it to you."

The room was well, if not luxuriously, appointed and there was nothing I needed, or would need, that was not already provided. I had a quick wash, changed into my lightweight cream suit and Sea Island cotton shirt, grabbed my bottle of malt, and tripped down to the dining room.

The others were already there and I shook hands with each of them in turn. I may have allowed my prejudice to overrule my judgment, and I imagined that Duncan had deliberately squeezed my hand more tightly than custom dictated.

I was not about to be intimidated by him, so I returned the gesture. He winced a little, glared at me, pulled free, and then moved away.

"Gentlemen, pray be seated, if you will," Donald boomed. "Please place your bottles on the table."

We did as he instructed and he then marked the concealed bottles 1 to 5 with a pen. Donald sat at the head of the table, with Harold at the foot. Duncan and I were on one side, Sandy and Murdock on the other.

I had brought a 15 year old Macallan, Sherry cask, which most of them guessed. Sandy's malt was an obscure Island malt I had never heard of and did not much like. Neither was I much impressed with Donald's malt, a 21-year-old Balvenie, Port wood, although the others did like it and most guessed its identity.

Murdock had brought a Bunnahabhain 20-year-old, which most liked, although it was much too smoky for my taste. As in the past, Duncan trumped them all with a Dalmore King Alexander III, which I thought utterly delicious and guessed right away because I had drunk it recently. It was everybody's favourite.

"I have a question which has long bothered me," I said, "which is: Does age automatically confer quality?"

"Certainly, to an extent," said Murdock.

"I'm inclined to agree," Harold said.

"I'm sorry if I appear to be a Philistine," I continued, "but I frequently find I prefer some malts which are younger."

"Isn't that because you prefer the style of those malts?" Donald asked. "For instance, you don't like Islay or other Island malts because your palate has turned against peatiness and smokiness, so naturally you would prefer a gentle 12-year-old Dalmore over a 40-year-old Laphroig."

"Maybe, but that's only part of it, I think. I may be committing blasphemy, but I simply cannot see how adding, say, ten years to a malt's age warrants increasing the price tag by $100."

"The price is high because the distillers have had to keep the whisky longer in the cask," said Harold. "While the malt is sitting, aging, in the warehouse, it is not earning any income, so when it is finally released naturally the price is going to be high."

"I agree with both Marc and Harold," said Murdock judiciously, "if the malt is scarce and hard to find, then naturally you are paying for the rarity, but paying much more simply because it is old only makes sense to me if the product is of high quality in the first place."

"Yes. And I have to say," I said, risking opprobrium, "I can't often tell if a malt is very old. I can tell if it's very young, but not if it is very old."

"Ah," said Sandy, "that is something which comes to you only after you have been drinking for as many years as the whisky is old."

Everyone but Duncan laughed. Old Sandy said very little, but when he did his comments were wise or funny. And, of course, he knew single malts like the back of his hand.

At the beginning of this exchange, Duncan had been preening himself over his whisky having been the most popular, but as it progressed he became surly at having lost the attention. He sneered frequently at my comments, and when we rose to allow the housekeeper to lay the table for dinner, he was positively hostile.

"Of course," he said, "we couldn't expect any real appreciation of the aging of whisky from a Frenchman."

"Excuse me, Duncan, but I am a Canadian. I may be of Acadian descent but I am not a Frenchman."

"It's the same difference. Not even all Scotsmen can appreciate malt. Only Highlanders can. Certainly the Sassenachs cannot come close."

"Don't start that again!" Harold said sharply.

"No, indeed, Duncan," Donald intervened, "We will have no personal attacks. But, surely, the rest of you will concede that general comments about history should be allowed."

"So long as he doesn't single me out as responsible for all the perceived wrongs visited upon the Scots by the English—who in most cases were ordered to carry out their actions by men who were Germans from Hanover." Harold was indignant.

"Hanover?" Murdock inquired raising an eyebrow.

"Certainly. All the kings between Anne and Edward VII were Hanoverians. The later monarchs, such as William IV and Victoria, could be said to be diluted and were as much English as they were German, but the three Georges were full-blooded Huns."

"I might point out," I interposed, "that the French were the Highlanders' greatest friends and allies. They sent them money (and wine, of course), and several times tried to land armies to support them. James Stuart, your 'Old Pretender', lived most of his life in France, and when he finally set foot in Scotland in 1715 he could barely speak English and certainly not Gaelic."

"And," said Harold, "Your famous Bonnie Prince Charlie spent all but a few of his 68 years living in Italy."

"None of that changes the brutal way the Highlanders were treated by English armies, no matter who ordered them," rejoined Duncan, seething with rage. "If it happened today, England would be condemned by the United Nations and the International Criminal Court as having committed genocide."

"Nothing those kangaroo courts did would cut any ice with me," I said, my temper rising. "They have assiduously ignored the most heinous human rights transgressions on earth, only picking on small, weak countries such as Israel."

"Whoa!" Donald called. "Enough! Let us call a halt to these arguments and move back to the table. We have roast tenderloin of venison, which I shot myself, served with vegetables I grew in my own garden."

"Sounds wonderful," I said, glad of his intervention. "What are having to start?"

"A broth of seafood—what Marc would call potage—containing items I got from the wharf this morning, and some I collected from the beach and foreshore this afternoon."

"What did you find on the beach, Donald?" Harold asked.

"Razor clams, mussels and limpets."

"Razor clams!" I exclaimed. "They're delicious."

"Yes, aren't they? But you have to cook them right."

"What did you get from the wharf?" Murdock asked.

"From the fishermen I got snow crab, flounder, and lobster, but don't tell anyone outside this room."

"Why not?"

"The season doesn't reopen until next week."

"Ah! So, we are dining with a poacher?" Sandy said.

"Yes, and as soon as you take a mouthful you are all accessories after the fact to the crime!"

~

The food was exquisite, although to my mind it cried out for appropriate wines rather than whisky. However, the Glen Moray Phoenix Rising, which had recently won awards for the best single malt, was excellent, especially with the homemade shortbread Donald's housekeeper provided for dessert.

While we were having coffee, Duncan, who by now was more than a little drunk, started again on his theme of the perfidious English and their alleged crimes against the Scots. Some of what he was saying rang some bells with me, because it was along similar lines to what Rosalie and I had learned on our recent visit to Scotland.

But because I was tired and because Duncan was making his points in a belligerent manner, I made my excuses and headed off to bed. Harold quickly joined me.

When we were up on the landing he turned to me before going into his room. "I don't know how much more of this I can take, Marc," he said.

"I know what you mean."

"I wouldn't say I actually hate the guy, but he makes me feel so uncomfortable. These occasions were supposed to be fun, but now they're becoming a drag."

"Yes, and all because of him."

"He is such a fanatic, so filled with hatred and bitterness."

"It's not as if he has anything really to be bitter about. His father seems to have given him everything he would want."

"Maybe that's part of the problem. If he'd had to work for a living, he wouldn't have had the time to immerse himself in this ancient history."

"I agree. To tell you the truth I don't think I'll be coming to another of these tastings. I'm not really enough of an expert anyway, not compared with you and the others."

"Let me know if you do decide to quit," said Harold. "If you do, I'll join you and we can have our own tastings."

"With wine as well as malt?"

"Certainly. Why not?"

"Okay, Harold. I'll see you at breakfast."

"No you won't. I have to be away a first light." He handed me a business card. "Call me some time."

32

When I went down the next morning, I was surprised to see that the dining room was laid out for breakfast rather as it would be in a movie about an English country house in the 1900s.

There was a dazzling, starched cloth on the table, which was covered with gleaming bone china and glittering silverware. On a long sideboard were numerous chafing dishes over small flames which kept their contents hot. These contained eggs—scrambled, fried, boiled and poached, and as omelettes—sausages, ham, bacon, kedgeree, mushrooms, grilled tomatoes, fried bread, steaks, kippers, fried potatoes and even haggis. On platters were smoked salmon, pickled mackerel, sliced ham and a variety of cheeses.

Alongside were huge bowls of fruit, cereals, and yogourt, and jugs of cream.

In addition, there was a huge toaster with a wide variety of breads, and an urn at either end holding coffee and tea. This was more like a five star-hotel, and I could scarcely believe that Donald (or his housekeeper) had gone to such lengths for our benefit.

Under the circumstances I thought it would be churlish if I did not do justice to this feast, so I helped myself to more than I had eaten at a single meal in a very long time.

As he had indicated, Harold had left early, so there were just five of us for breakfast.

Duncan was somewhat improved in temper over the night before, and was quiet, busily tucking into his potatoes, eggs and haggis. He still wore his hunting tartan kilt, but had abandoned his frilly shirt and dress coat for a more sensible shirt and sweater, although that, too, sported the Chisholm tartan.

I looked around the table, to make sure I was not being rude and eating more than others, and I was amazed to see that Sandy and Murdock had shovelled down astonishing amounts of food, going to the sideboard as many as three times.

"I'm very sorry Lachie couldn't make it," I said, when our plates were empty and we were draining our coffee cups. "I've grown rather fond of the old boy."

"Ah yes, he's always been a charmer, has Lachie," said Murdock. "It's a very sad case."

"You mean about his financial difficulties?"

"Yes, that too," Sandy butted in, "but they were caused by the other problem."

"The other problem?"

"Yes," said Donald, "Lachie has a brain tumour. Inoperable, so I've heard. You didn't know?"

"No. He didn't say anything to me on the occasions we were together. That's awful. I had no idea."

"Indeed it is very dowie, but there's no sense kicking yourself over spilt milk," said Murdock, standing up. "Donald, I must be away. I thank you kindly for your hospitality."

"Me too," said Sandy. "You are an incomparable host, Donald."

While Donald was seeing them out, I was taken aback when Duncan came up and sat beside me.

"You don't have to go right away, do you, Marc?"

"Er...no. I have to be in Pictou at 11."

"That less than an hour from here. You have lots of time."

"For what?"

"To see my wing." He had a sickly kind of smile hovering about his lips.

"Your wing?"

"Yes, I have a wing of the house. It's kind of a cross between a museum and a library. It's where I do my research."

"Your research?"

"Yes into the history of Scotland."

"Oh yes, of course!"

"So, are you up for it?"

During this exchange, Duncan had been unctuously solicitous, almost wheedling, something I found remarkably unpleasant, so much so that I felt my flesh crawling. But Donald had not come back into the room and I did not know what to do. To my horror I heard myself feebly agreeing to accompany him to his "wing".

He had described it well by saying it was a cross between a library and a museum. The whole wing was depressingly dark and was lit by old-fashioned brass lamps. The shelves carried hundreds of books, some of them quite venerable and, as far as I could gather, all were about Scottish history and the clans.

He also had innumerable charts, maps, scrolls and defiant declarations decreed by various clan chieftains. Very prominent were the presence of the two kings James I and II, and of Charles Edward Stuart, all of whom Duncan clearly held in deep and devout veneration.

As he led me through this labyrinth of old Scotland, both real and imagined, he touched—I should say caressed—the various items on display, sometimes talking to himself in undertones, sometimes cackling with laughter. If the surroundings had been different, I would have thought I was in the workshop of a mad scientist.

He waved, rather too dismissively I thought, to his work desk and tried to head me away from it. But I caught glances of documents he was illuminating in red and gold which announced a new age in which Scotland would rise again and Clan Chisholm would occupy a rightfully major role.

I thanked Duncan as politely as I could, and hastened upstairs to pack my bag. As I came down, Donald appeared.

"Sorry to have deserted you, Marc, but Murdock wanted to discuss a little business with me. He wants me to take a bull off his hands, but I'm no too fussy about the prospect."

"That's okay. Duncan has been showing me his...wing."

"Ah," he said. "Been showing you his wing, has he?"

"Yes."

"Well, I guess you must be off. I'll see you to your car."

~

It took me forty minutes to get to Pictou.

As I was crossing the Harvey Veniot Causeway and noticing the cormorants which live there, Louise called me. She said she had received a call from Mrs. Ransome's maid, saying that her mistress would like to put off our appointment until noon because she was finding it difficult "to pull herself together" that morning.

That gave me over an hour to fill, so I parked the Bugatti and walked up Water Street to Grohmann Knives. My 6-inch filleting knife was old and worn, so I needed a replacement. I found a nicely balanced one and bought it for a little over $100.

Still having time to kill, I carried my purchase along the wharf to *Hector*, a replica of the 18th-century ship that carried Scottish settlers to

Nova Scotia. I lined up, paid $8, left a donation of $20, then after a little performance from a guide, I went on board.

Apparently, *Hector* was built in Holland and was used for the immigrant trade to North America. In 1773 she carried 189 Highlanders who were required to quit their tenancies in Scotland and emigrate to Nova Scotia. To induce them to undertake the arduous passage, they were offered free passage, a year of free provisions, and a farm. The voyage took almost four months, disease claiming the lives of 18 passengers.

Apparently it turned out to be something of a dreadful scam, because the free provisions were never produced and the new settlers faced a terrible winter with no shelters ready for them. There was also, I gathered, misrepresentation of the extent and quality of the land they received.

I found the history of this escapade and its presentation so engrossing that time passed quickly and I nearly forgot my appointment. I had to run back to the Bugatti and only got to Mrs. Ransom's place outside town with minutes to spare.

Her house was a handsome, old, wisteria-covered mansion set at the top of a grassy bank, and reached by a flight of stone steps. Flanking the steps were a myriad of sweet-smelling flowers, many of them crawling with bees.

The maid answered the door and ushered me into a very large room with many tall windows. The furniture was very old, but of the very best quality, much of it being antique. Clearly, this had been the home of very wealthy, but not ostentatious, people for many years.

On the walls were beautifully-framed paintings of notable Nova Scotians, some of which I could name. Joseph Howe and Charles Tupper were much in evidence, as were Angus L. MacDonald and Robert Stanfield. Apparently, the Ransomes had been admirers of outstanding premiers, and were not partisan.

After a few minutes, the maid pushed in a frail, white-haired, old lady and parked her wheelchair facing the windows, through which the sun was now streaming.

"Mr. LeBlanc, I'm Evelyn Ransome," she said in a much stronger, deeper voice than I had expected. "I'm sorry I had to delay our meeting, but I find that in the mornings it is increasingly difficult for me to get my body to do what my mind tells it."

"That's quite all right, Mrs. Ransome. I filled in the time going over *Hector.*"

"Ah. Very interesting, I believe. I have not been on it myself for many years. Not since I was incapacitated."

"I'm sorry," I said, then added, "It is very good of you to see me."

"Not at all. Now, straight down to business. I think you are interested in getting some of Victor's wine."

"Yes, if that's possible. Of course, I am willing to pay the market value."

"Pouf, don't be foolish, man! What would I want with more money at my age? You can take your pick, and welcome to it. Please leave some cases for my nephew, who fancies himself as an aficionado and expert. He doesn't fool me. I know he'll sell the stuff as soon as he gets his hands on it, but he's my only heir."

"That's most extraordinarily generous, Mrs. Ransome. I promise not to take more than three cases. In any event, I couldn't get more than that into my car."

"Well, then, three cases it shall be. Mix and match as you please. I know nothing about wine and never liked it. For years I pretended to enjoy it, and to the day he died Victor didn't know that I always had my maid put syrup in my wine. It's the only way I could stand to drink the stuff!" She shrieked with laughter. "Fancy that, Mr. LeBlanc. You must think that was heresy!"

"Well..."

"Off you go. Carter will take you down to the cellar and provide you with empty cases, which you can fill as you choose. Now I must go and lie down for a little while before my lunch. You must see yourself out."

With that, she wheeled herself to the doorway, where Carter, the maid, took over.

"I'll be right back, sir," she said as she took her mistress away.

As I waited for Carter to come back to escort me to the cellar, I felt strangely agitated. Something, I did not know what, was preying on my mind. I thought it had something to do with *Hector*, and I resolved to go back and have another look as soon as I had taken my wine.

When I followed Carter down the steps, I was astonished at the extent of the late Mr. Ransome's cellar. It was enormous, covering the whole under floor of the house, with many rows of glinting bottles, and many others with the dust of time upon them. It was immediately apparent to me that the nephew would net hundreds of thousands of dollars when he sold the collection.

That thought, and my limit of three cases, focused my mind. If, as Mrs. Ransome had said, I could fill my three cases with anything I liked, I was determined that it would be the very best.

Making my decisions was difficult because there was so much incredible wine from which to choose. In the end, I selected *Chateau Mouton Rothschild* and *Vieux Chateau Certan* from the 1945 vintage; *Chateaux Palmer, Lafite* and *Latour* from 1961; Burgundy's *Romanee Conti* from various vintages including 1999 and 2005; *Krug Clos d'Ambonnay Blanc de Noirs* from Champagne; Penfolds Block 42 2004 from Australia; *Vega Sicilia* and *Sierra Cantabria Teso La Monja* from Spain, and *Giacomo Conterno Monfortino Barolo Riserva* from Italy. This last wine I resolved to give to Patrick soon, as I knew it to be his favourite.

As I squeezed my selections into the Bugatti, I felt as if I were secreting a stolen treasure trove, and looked furtively about to make sure nobody was watching. Feeling foolish, I drove away.

Near *Hector*, I locked the car and made my way back to the Heritage Quay, still not knowing what was impelling me there.

Inside the exhibit again, I looked carefully at all the photographs and information displays. I noted the capacity of *Hector*'s hold, how many passengers she could carry, the complement of her crew, and then I came to this: The ship was owned by Mr. John Pagan and Dr. John Witherspoon.

I straightened up, my mind reeling. That was it! That was what I had seen the first time before my visit to Mrs. Ransome, but it had not registered.

I cast my mind back and then I realized the connection. Bill Withers' sister, Iris, had called her antecedents "the Spoons" because several generations before the family had changed their name from Witherspoon.

Why had they done so, I wondered, if not to expunge the opprobrium the name had attracted over Dr. John's cruel exploitation of the Highlanders in 1773? And if this circumstance was known to someone else, someone nurturing a centuries-old grudge, would it not provide an ideal motive for murder?

I went out onto the wharf and immediately called Patrick.

"Kennedy."

"Patrick, it's Marc."

"Hi Marc, what's up?"

"I think I've finally cracked it."

"Cracked what?"

"The case. The four murders."

"Go on," he said warily.

"It is about revenge, but nothing to do with the Wind in the Willows summer camp."

"Oh?"

"But about grievances hundreds of years old."

"Marc, what are you talking about?"

"The clearances."

"Clearances? Marc, are you okay?"

"Never better. I'm coming in to see you. Are you in your office?"

"Yes. When should I expect you?"

"I'll be there in an hour and a half. Have some expert computer re-searchers standing by."

"Marc—"

"Trust me on this, Patrick. I not only know why, I also think I know who."

"Okay, but you better not be shitting me on this."

~

The elevator was not working, so I arrived at Patrick's office out of breath.

He sat on the edge of his desk, flanked by two young officers. "There you are," he said, almost accusatorily. "This better be good."

"It will be."

"These are Corporal Jennie Habib and Constable Randy Hancock. What they can't find on computers isn't worth knowing."

"Thanks for coming," I said, rather weekly. "I appreciate it."

"Alright," Patrick said firmly, "the floor is yours. We don't have all day."

"Okay. Iris Withers—she is sister to one of the murdered men—told me that the family had changed their name from Witherspoon. That was also the name of the owner of the ship *Hector*, which transported half-starving settlers from Scotland. Stop me at any point if you are not following."

"Carry on."

"Right. Jennie, Randy, please look into the people responsible for the forcible clearance of the Scottish highlands between, say, 1750 and 1880 and see what names you come up with."

"What names are you looking for?" Jennie asked.

"Gillespie, Robertson, and Lake," I said.

The two officers' keyboards immediately started chattering.

Patrick stood up and walked to the window. He stared outside for a few minutes before turning around. "Marc, I have to tell you that this is a supernumerary use of resources for a less than palpable lead."

"Just wait, Patrick. Don't be so pompous."

"Let's go get a coffee. Do you guys want any?" he asked the officers.
They both shook their heads.

"You're sure about this, Marc?" he asked as we strolled down the corridor to the coffee machine.

"I think so. We have nothing else, so surely this is a worthwhile inquiry."

"We shall see."

He put money in the machine, but no coffee came out. He thumped the side with similar results. Finally, he kicked it, cursed and turned back toward his office.

"Superintendent!" Randy's voice called.

"That was quick," I said.

"These guys are spectacular."

"I have a William Robertson, Laird of Kindeace who cleared his land at Strathcarron of Highlanders in the 1840s. Strathcarron is in Ross and Cromarty, on the west coast of Scotland."

"And I've got a Thomas Gillespie in Strathglass and Corriemoney in the 1790s," said Jennie. "Strathglass is in Inverness County, to the northwest of Loch Ness. It seems Gillespie was a lowlander who took advantage of bankrupt lairds, bought their lands at bargain prices, then kicked out the tenants and moved vast flocks of sheep in."

"There!" I said triumphantly, "See?"

"What about Lake?" Patrick asked,

"No, nothing yet, Super," Jennie said.

"Randy?"

"No, sorry, boss. Still looking."

The officers spent ten more minutes searching while Patrick and I sat in silence. At length, Jennie and Randy stopped and looked up.

"Nobody by the name of Lake," Randy said.

"Same here," said Jennie.

We stared at one another for what seemed like an eternity. Then it struck me like a bolt of lightning.

"Patrick, if the Witherspoons changed their name to Withers, who's to say Leonard Lake's people didn't do likewise?"

"But from what?"

"What is the Scottish term for lake?"

"Loch!' Randy and Jennie shouted in unison.

"Exactly. Elementary my dear Watson," I said, then, to the others, "Can you find that, Randy, Jennie? This would be a man's name, not a geographical feature."

"Right."

For the first time I noticed the ticking of a clock on the wall. The sound seemed almost ominous.

Then Jennie spoke up. "Here it is. James Loch agent for Lord Stafford, the Duke of Sutherland. In the early 1800s he ruthlessly cleared hundreds, some say thousands, of people off his master's lands. Their houses were burned and many of them died of exposure. Some of those who took to small boats were drowned. Apparently, Mr, Loch made lots of money for himself, as well as for the Duke, because he ended up a huge landowner with large flocks of sheep."

"No wonder his family changed their name," I said, "The bastard."

Patrick looked thoughtful, then turned to me. "Okay Marc, I'm sold."

He dismissed the officers with his and my thanks. "On the phone, you said you knew not only what but who."

"Yes, I did. I think I know."

"Alright, who is our killer?"

"A crazed fanatic called Duncan Chisholm. He lives in Arisaig in Antigonish County. I was at his place only yesterday. Patrick, this character is a complete nutcase. He's steeped in all this Highland grievance stuff, has all the documents and memorabilia, and wears a kilt and a coat with silver buttons."

"Sounds like you may be right. But let's sleep on it. He doesn't know we're on to him, so he's going nowhere. I have to think about how to handle this. I haven't figured out yet how much manpower I'll need. Do you know if he's armed?"

"No I don't, but it wouldn't surprise me if he was. His father has hunting rifles in the house, and Duncan carries a *sqian-dubh* on him at all times."

"What the hell is that?"

"A knife. He wears it in his sock."

"Look, why don't you call Rosalie and tell her that you're staying with Ruth and me tonight. But tell her no details at this stage. I will have a quick word with my Chief Super and tomorrow we'll draw up a plan of action."

While Patrick went to speak with his superior, I called Rosalie on her cell. There was no answer, so I called the landline at home and, getting the answering machine, left a message explaining I was spending the night at the Kennedys. I guessed she was out with Rachel Bland somewhere, and would call her again in the morning.

Patrick returned soon, saying his Chief had been put in the picture and would make preliminary arrangements.

I followed Patrick to his house and parked the Bugatti alongside his car. For once, I felt as if something had been achieved, and that the day had definitely not been wasted.

Patrick shared my sense of satisfaction, especially when I showed him the bottle of Barolo I had taken for him from the late Victor Ransome's cellar.

33

Patrick and I left for his office early the next morning, intending to have breakfast, which he had instructed his staff to prepare, delivered and eaten in the situation room. His superior, Chief Superintendent Clarkson, would be there ahead of us.

I had met Clarkson before and had thought him a cold fish, uptight and punctilious, and was a little nervous as to how he would see my involvement in the case.

I was still frustrated that I had been unable to get Rosalie on her mobile, or on our land line at Grand Pre. If indeed she had been with Rachel Bland she might well have stayed the night at the Blands' house in Port Williams. I knew Rachel and Ray's numbers were unlisted, and I did not have them in my phone because I had only recently purchased it and had not yet programmed it.

I had no choice but to wait until Ray's car franchise in New Minas opened at nine, and call him there.

Clarkson frowned when he saw me accompanying Patrick into the situation room, and called me over to where he stood on a raised platform.

"Kennedy has told me all about your involvement in this case," he said sternly, "and that's fair enough. You can stay, but you must not speak unless you are asked a question. Do you understand?"

"Yes, Chief Superintendent."

"And whatever happens today, you are to stay well to the rear of any action. If I find you pushing yourself into a position which could compromise our work, I shall have you arrested. Clear?"

"Quite clear."

"Good." Clarkson dismissed me with a wave, and rapped on a desk to get everybody's attention. "Right. Listen up! You have all been briefed on the general situation, but I want to bring you up to date."

I glanced across at Patrick, who seemed uneasy at what his chief had

228

just said. I made a questioning face, to which he responded by shaking his head.

"Superintendent Kennedy put me fully in the picture yesterday," Clarkson continued, "and, based on his information, I ordered officers from our detachments in Antigonish, Port Hawkesbury and Guysborough to proceed to Arisaig and detain Duncan Chisholm."

Patrick gasped and cursed under his breath. He glared at Clarkson.

"The suspect was not at that address," Clarkson went on, "but his father said he had gone to his summer camp near Glencoe."

"Where's that?" a sergeant asked.

"In Cape Breton, roughly between Judique and Mabou. Two officers have remained at Arisaig to ensure that the suspect's father does not try to communicate with him. The others are on standby."

"Chief, when did the suspect leave Arisaig?" the Sergeant asked.

"Some time yesterday."

"What time yesterday?" Patrick asked, his voice betraying his annoyance.

"Chisholm senior didn't know. He said that after his guests had left he was out on the farm most of the day."

"What is the suspect driving?" a fat inspector asked.

"Mr. LeBlanc, perhaps you will enlighten us?"

"A black Mercedes," I said. "Which is consistent with the black car reported at the scene of all four murders."

"What?" Clarkson barked.

"Yes, Chief," Patrick said. "I've been to all four sites and at each one a large black car was reported as having been seen in the days preceding the murders." He said this in a matter-of-fact way, but then added with emphasis, "It's all in the file."

"Yes, yes." Clarkson was obviously irritated. "The officers not engaged in keeping Mr. Chisholm senior company have been ordered to wait at the Canso Causeway until our forces from Division arrive. They will include armed officers under Inspector Davidson." He inclined his head towards a huge man dressed in riot gear. Flanking him were four other officers similarly attired, and bristling with weapons.

"Is the suspect armed?'" Davidson asked.

"We believe so. Chisholm senior said several rifles were not in their cabinet and he supposed that the suspect had taken them. The object will be to surround this camp, move in when considered appropriate, and arrest the suspect. Russell, can you show us exactly where this place is, please?'

Another sergeant stepped forward and pinned a large map to the wall. Using a pointer, he indicated that Duncan's hideaway was on a dead-end track which ran north off the road between Upper Southwest Mabou and Glencoe.

Russell said that it appeared the camp was on the summit of a small mountain, surrounded by a forest of spruce.

During this lengthy exposition, I slipped out of the room to see if I could reach Rosalie on the phone. I called Ray at the car salesrooms, but he said my wife had not spent the night with them, and that they had not seen her the day before. I then called Louise and, stressing the need for speed, begged her to close the wine store for half an hour and go to Grand Pre. I gave her the code to get into the house and asked her to call me as soon as she was there.

When I eased myself back into the situation room, Davidson was laying down the law on the do's and don'ts in the event of an armed confrontation. I did not know if it was usual, but it seemed to me there was certain tension between the armed response officers and the rest, who were sneaking looks to each other which suggested that they considered their armed compatriots to be trigger-happy cowboys. In any event, I became bored with the technical details and went back out into the corridor. I was looking out of the window when Louise rang me back.

"Marc? I'm in the house."

"Is anyone there?"

"I don't think so. Rosalie wasn't on the ground floor. I'm climbing the stairs now."

"Maybe she's in bed?"

"No....as far as I can see, all the beds are made."

"All of them?"

"Yes."

"Okay. Check the cellar and the garage if you can."

"Right." I heard the sounds of the cellar door opening and Louise walking down. "Wow! Some lovely bottles here."

"You can have some if you find Rosalie."

"I'm going out to the garage now." The big doors made a grinding sound. "No. Nothing here."

"Damn! Okay just go back into the hallway and tell me what you see. She might have left a note."

"I'm here now. I can't see a note. There's mail on the floor."

"Just take a look at it."

"Telephone bill...junk...letter from wine merchant in London...electricity bill...hello, what's this?"

"What is it?"

"Looks like something from one of the churches."

"Read it to me," I said, my blood running cold.

Louise read:

> Jeremiah 8:12
> *Were they ashamed when they committed abomination?*
> *No, they were not at all ashamed;*
> *they did not know how to blush.*
> *Therefore they shall fall among the fallen;*
> *when I punish them, they shall be overthrown.*

"Christ!"

"What is it, Marc?"

"He's got Rosalie. That crazy son of a bitch has kidnapped her!"

"Oh, Marc!"

"Just lock up and go back to the store. I'm with the police now. Thanks, Louise."

I staggered back into the situation room and interrupted the proceedings.

Clarkson glared at me. "What is it?"

"He's got my wife. Duncan has snatched her. I haven't been able to reach her, and my business partner has found a biblical warning in my house...just like the ones the other victims received."

"But why?" Clarkson seemed annoyed. "Why would he kidnap your wife?"

"I can guess," said Patrick. "Jennie, are you here?"

"Yes, sir!"

"Marc, what is Rosalie's maiden name?"

"Fletcher."

"You told me recently that you saw her ancestor's gave in Scotland when you were there?"

"Yes."

"Who was he, and where did he come from?"

"He was Archibald Fletcher and his grave was at Orchie in Glen Caoineadh."

"Can you spell that, please?" Jennie called.

"C-A-O-I-N-E-A-D-H."

"Got all that, Jennie?"

"Yes, thanks."

"Kennedy, what is all this about?" Clarkson was edgy.

"Just a minute, sir, and you'll find out."

We waited, the only sounds coming from the sharp rustling of the armed response uniforms.

Finally Jenny jumped up. "Here it is. Archibald William Fletcher. Born Inverlochy 1796, died Orchie 1858. He was factor and main man of business for the Earl of Caoineadh. Although born a local man of humble origins, Fletcher rose in the laird's service until he was manager of all of his master's estates. He carried out the laird's plans to clear the lands of tenants to make way for flocks of Cheviot sheep. Over some nine years he was responsible for the forcible removal of 314 people, of whom an estimated 64 died of cold in the winter of 1846 because their houses had been pulled down."

"There's your motive," said Patrick. "Revenge. He's going for a fifth victim."

"Right," said Clarkson loudly. "We'll have a five-mile cordon covering all roads in and out. Davidson's men will penetrate the forest to an initial distance of no closer than 200 metres. MacIntyre...where's MacIntyre?"

"Here sir," said a small, but fit young officer at the back of the room.

"You will crawl through the undergrowth and spy out the lay of land, but on no account be seen."

"Yes, sir."

"Then come back and report to Davidson. When we know more we'll decide what to do next. No radios until well out of sound range."

"Chief Superintendent!" a sergeant called out.

"Yes?"

"We have a report of a black Mercedes passing through Low Point last evening, heading north."

"Did they see who was driving?"

"A young man. Also a passenger."

"Identity?"

"Couldn't make out, but quite possibly a woman."

"Alright everybody, let's get up there!"

~

Patrick came with me in the Bugatti because he knew we would get there ahead of the others, and he wanted to assert some control over a case which Clarkson had, somewhat high-handedly, pursued without consulting him.

"It was a bit shitty," I said, "but he is your senior officer. And what would you have done differently?"

"I wouldn't have gone barging into Arisaig without first finding out who was there and who wasn't. And I certainly wouldn't call in Davidson's rough riders. I'm a lot more worried about them now that Rosalie is involved."

"I know what you mean. I certainly would rather they didn't start shooting all over the place if she's inside."

"Precisely. Still, our crowd has lots of experience. We'll get her back safe and sound."

We reached the causeway, and Patrick gave instructions to the assembled officers. Then we proceeded in a cavalcade to just beyond the river at Upper Southwest Mabou, where we left half our contingent to set up a roadblock.

We all went on to a mile beyond Glencoe. There we stopped, the remaining cruisers sealing the road and awaiting instructions.

Before he got out, Patrick gave me a stern look. "Marc, this is as far as you go."

"But Patrick, Rosalie is up there."

"I know, but you couldn't help her even if I allowed you to get any closer. As it is, you will only get in the way of the professionals."

"Okay, but you'll keep in touch with me?"

"Of course, on a regular basis. I have your number."

He reached over and clapped me on the shoulder. "I must go now, Marc."

Patrick headed off towards the police vehicles. I watched him conferring with the officers for several minutes, then I listened to the radio for half an hour. I was desperately worried about Rosalie and extremely frustrated that I could do nothing but wait. Unless Duncan made a move, the operation could take hours.

I thought maybe I should take a drive to distract myself, so I pulled out the map to see where I was and where I might go.

Much to my surprise. I discovered that I was only about 30 kilometres from Sky Glen, where Lachie MacLeod's farm was. Lachie had been a great favourite of mine since the first whisky tasting and I felt badly about his plight. Consoling him might keep my mind off my own troubles, so I decided to take a run over and see him.

I drove slowly through Glencoe Mills, Brook Village, and the curiously named Nevada Valley. Soon the thick forest gave way to more open land where sheep and cattle could be seen grazing. Houses were dotted about the landscape.

Then I saw the mailbox on the right hand side of the road: MacLeod, so I slowed down and pulled onto a dirt road which was heading up the hill. Above the trees I could see a tall, white silo and the top of a red roof.

Then the phone buzzed. I slowed the car as I took the call. It was Patrick.

"Marc, bad news."

"What?" My heart was in my mouth.

"Davidson's team went in and nabbed Duncan."

"And? So?"

"Duncan was there shacked up with his boyfriend."

"What?"

"Yeah, some kid called Brian Grant."

"What about Rosalie?"

"No sign of Rosalie. It was a false alarm."

"Fuck!"

"Sorry, Marc. I guess it's back to the drawing board."

At that moment, the car gently rolled forward along the lane so that the front buildings of the farm became visible. I immediately stood on brakes and switched off the engine. There in front of the barn was parked a 2020 black Lincoln Continental.

"Lachie! Shit, it's Lachie!"

"Marc, what's up? What's happening?"

"Patrick. I'm in Sky Glen."

"Where the hell is that?"

"Only 30 minutes away. I just came to see Lachie MacLeod, but as soon as his yard came into sight, I saw a big, black Lincoln!"

"The big black car!"

"Yes. We had the story right. We just had the wrong suspect."

"Marc, if you can, gently back away out of sight. We'll be with you soon. Don't do anything."

"Right."

"Marc, do you hear me? Do not under any circumstances approach the suspect!"

"Yeah. I hear you," I said without conviction, then ended the call.

It was all very well for Patrick to tell me to wait, but in 30 minutes Rosalie could be dead.

I couldn't wait. If I subsequently found out that Rosalie had been killed while I was waiting for the police to arrive, I would not be able to live with myself. I knew Lachie would be armed, but there was nothing I could do about that. I just had to hope that my youth, strength and wits could match a deranged, old man.

I let the car silently roll back down the hill and swung it into a field entrance. I hopped over into a field, crept along behind a hedge, so as not to be seen from the house, and came up to the wall on the side which had no windows. I carefully sneaked around a corner and peered through a window.

Straight ahead of me was Lachie, seated in an armchair with a half-consumed bottle of malt on a table by his side. There was a twelve-bore shotgun lying on a footstool. Rosalie was nowhere to be seen.

Ducking down I slowly crawled along the wall to the door, which was open.

"Come you in, Marc LeBlanc," Lachie called, "I've been expecting you."

"Good day, Lachie," I said, entering the room. He made no effort to pick up the shotgun, but poured himself another drink.

"Will you take a dram, Marc? It's a 35-year-old Glenfarclass. And very good it is, too."

"No thank you, Lachie. Where's Rosalie?"

"Suffering the fate of those murdered by her forebear."

"So she's still alive?"

"Oh yes, I should think so. For the time being."

"This vendetta is crazy, Lachie, after all these years."

"Justice will finally be done!" His eyes lit up and he drained his glass.

"Justice! You call punishing someone for what their ancestors did justice?"

"I do."

"The why didn't you go after the descendants of the owners? The earls and dukes who ordered the clearances? They were the ones really responsible."

"I must respect the lairds. They may have been venal and made mistakes, but their positions were decreed by God. But those who betrayed their own kind, the common people, for money were despicable and should be shown no mercy!"

"What a twisted view of history! So illogical, it's—"

"Insane, were you going to say?"

"Look, Lachie, I know you are very ill, and I'm very sorry for it, but don't you see that it has affected your mind, warped your sense of perspective, of what is right and wrong?"

"It no longer matters," he said sadly, "Whatever happens, it is the end of Lachlan MacLeod."

Lachie just looked at me, his red-rimmed eyes dimming. He poured himself another glass, raised it, then downed it one.

Then he bent down, picked up the twelve bore and, before I could get to him, had put it to his mouth and blown the back of his head off. The wall behind him was an appalling mess of horror.

I stood there, gaping, spattered with his blood. After the initial shock, I realized that I had to find Rosalie.

I racked my brain, desperately trying to recollect the ways Lachie had killed his victims. It came back to me in a rush: Drowning, burning, exposure, and starvation were how Bill Withers, Struan Robertson, Alex Gillespie, and Leonard Lake had been dispatched. It seemed unlikely he would employ the same method.

I wandered aimlessly around the house, looking in each room, but Rosalie was nowhere to be found.

Then I remembered Jennie saying, *Over some nine years he was responsible for the forcible removal of 314 people, of whom an estimated 64 died of cold in the winter of 1846 because their houses had been pulled down.*

That must be it! Lachie would freeze her to death!

I rushed around, looking for a fridge, but a small one in the kitchen yielded nothing. Then I saw a door in the hallway which I guessed led to the cellar.

I descended the stairs as fast as I could take them and saw a massive freezer against the far wall. I raced to it and wrenched the door open.

Rosalie fell out like a sack of potatoes. Her face was white and her breathing was unsteady.

I took her in my arms and carried her upstairs. We came out into the hallway as Davidson's squad came crashing through the front door.

Patrick came behind them. As I staggered past I heard him calling for an ambulance.

As the ambulance pulled away, Patrick said that the paramedics had told him that Rosalie's condition was not serious because I had got to her just in time.

I sat on a wall, gazing out over the fields of Sky Glen, wondering what misconceptions of history and peculiarities of the human brain could have driven Lachie to slaughter innocent people in such bizarre ways.

"You should have waited for us to get here," said Patrick. "But I'm very glad you didn't."

So was I.

Jeremy Akerman

This book is dedicated to the memory of **John Prebble** (1915-2001).
While nobody could accuse him of being impartial, for all its manifest faults
his great body of work stands as remarkable testimony to
the multitudinous sufferings of the Highlanders
and to the unpitying brutality of their kings, lairds and masters.

Jeremy Akerman

About the author

Jeremy Akerman is an adoptive Nova Scotian who has lived in the province since 1964. In that time he has been an archaeologist, a radio announcer, a politician, a senior civil servant, a newspaper editor and a film actor.

He is painter of landscapes and portraits, a singer of Irish folk songs, a lover of wine, and a devotee of history, especially of the British Labour Party.